# DESPERATION

*By*

**Clifford J. Fazzolari**

Pittsburgh, PA

ISBN 1-56315-264-9

Paperback Fiction
© Copyright 2000 Clifford J. Fazzolari
All rights reserved
First Printing—2000
Library of Congress #99-65311

Request for information should be addressed to:

SterlingHouse Publisher Inc.
The Sterling Building
440 Friday Road
Pittsburgh, PA 15209
www.sterlinghousepublisher.com

Cover design: Michelle S. Vennare—SterlingHouse Publisher
Typesetting: Kathleen M. Gall

This is a work of fiction. Names, characters, incidents, and places, are the product of
the author's imagination or are used fictitiously.
Any resemblance to actual events or persons, living or dead,
is entirely coincidental.

Printed in Canada

# DEDICATION

*To Kathy, Matt and Jake.*
*You're the reason for everything I do.*
*I love you.*

10/14/00

To Nancy,

Keep writing — this is
a story of a man doing
the right thing.

Cliff Fazzolari

# ACKNOWLEDGEMENTS

*This story was inspired
by the thought that I was born into a terrific situation.
I'm fortunate to be blessed
with great friends and a loving family.*

*My life is made complete because of the
Fazzolari and Foutz families;
Grandma Schryver;
all of my friends—past, present, and future;
my beautiful nieces and nephews;
and the Lions softball team—we're champions every year!*

*I'd also like to thank
Jennifer Piemme of the Lee Shore Agency
and Cynthia Sterling, Annick Rouzier, Michelle Burton and
all the people at SterlingHouse Publisher—
it wouldn't be out there if it weren't for you.*

*To the Renaldo family—
the strength and love you offer is truly an inspiration.*

*Finally, to the memory of
Albert DeCarlo—
a man who helped me define personal success
by living a life of love.*

# PART ONE

*"Every Creation has a purpose."*

—Anonymous

# CHAPTER ONE

*August, 1991*

Twelve-year-old Jackie Gregory turned his eyes away from the bright midday sun. He looked to his mother who sat in the front seat with her eyes fixed on the open hood of the car.

"I'm going to see how Dad's doing," Jackie said. He waited for his mother to voice a protest, but his fourteen-year-old brother Alan spoke instead.

"I'm going, too."

"No, you both stay put," Jackie's mother said. "Dad's almost done. We'll get going soon."

"We aren't going anywhere in this piece of crap," Alan said.

Anna Gregory turned in the seat, and Jackie read worry in her eyes.

"Your father worked on this car for months. He wants to get to Boston just as much as you do. He'll be upset if he hears you saying these things."

"I don't know why we're going to Boston," Alan said. "My friends in Savannah are all out playing baseball right now."

"Who cares about baseball with your stupid friends?" Jackie said.

"Shut up, mister sad eyes," Alan said.

"That's enough," Anna said.

"We don't have anything to eat," Jackie said to his brother. "Doesn't that bother you more than playing baseball?"

Once again, Jackie read pain in his mother's eyes.

"We'll get going in a few minutes," Anna said. "You'll see, everything's going to be fine."

Jackie turned and faced the back window. His mother's words echoed in his ears, but he knew they probably weren't true.

"He's not going to fix it," Alan whispered. Jackie wished he could block it from his mind.

Half an hour passed before Jackie saw his father emerge from the front of the car. Nelson wiped his hands on his jeans and swiped at his brow. Jackie was praying silently when his father winked at him.

"Let's give it a try," Nelson said, slipping in behind the wheel. Jackie leaned forward and shot a look of anticipation back at Alan.

"It'll never work," Alan mouthed.

"Come on, baby," Nelson said. He turned the key, and the car shuddered and struggled for life.

"It'll start," Jackie said, hopefully.

The engine caught and then died.

"I told you, we'll be stuck in Connecticut for the rest of our lives."

Anna spun around and scolded Alan with her eyes.

"Come on, Dad," Jackie said.

Nelson turned the key, and the engine didn't make so much as a sound. Jackie breathed deep, realizing it was over.

"She's dead," Nelson said. He slumped back against the front seat. "We'll be all right guys."

In a couple of minutes that seemed like an eternity, Jackie understood that things probably wouldn't be all right.

"What we need, is a game plan." Nelson turned in the seat to face them. Jackie nodded and smiled, and Alan groaned.

"We'll get our stuff together and go to the hotel. It's only a couple of miles." Nelson faced Anna who nodded. "We'll have dinner and get a room. You guys can rest, and I'll walk back and get the car going. By tomorrow night, we'll be in Boston."

"Do we have money for this?" Anna asked.

"We have enough money," Nelson said.

Jackie opened the door and stepped out onto the shoulder of the road. He stretched his arms high above his head and looked up at the sun.

*Here we go again*, he thought as he walked to the back of the car.

"Hey, buddy," Nelson called. "I don't think it's anything major." Nelson placed his hands on Jackie's shoulders. "We'll be fine."

"I know," Jackie said. "You always come through, Dad." Nelson tousled Jackie's hair, and Jackie instinctively looked to the ground.

"Alan's still pretty sore at me," Nelson said. "He wanted to stay in Savannah, and I know it's tough. He had a lot of friends."

Nelson turned the key, opening the trunk of the beat-up Ford.

"I know," Jackie said, as he kicked away the stones near his feet.

"My friend in Boston is a good man," Nelson said. "He's been a friend since I was your age. He promised he'd find us a place to stay. We'll have a better house than the one in Savannah."

"I know."

"He promised me a job, too. I'll work every day, for a long time."

"We have to go," Jackie said.

"That's right," Nelson said. He turned from the open trunk and looked directly into his son's eyes. "I need you guys to know this'll be a lot better. We'll have our own rooms, and you won't have to go outside to use the bathroom. It won't be too cold in the winter or too hot in the summer."

Jackie looked away from his father's eyes. He'd heard the words so many times, but he desperately wanted to believe the dream. Instead, he looked to the ground.

"You're always so worried," Nelson said. "My little boss." Nelson lifted a cardboard box filled with clothes from the trunk. "Try to cheer up, huh?"

"I will," Jackie said.

"All right, let's get some clothes for tonight." Nelson ran his hand through Jackie's hair once more.

"Is Mom talking to Alan about it?"

"She's trying to help him not miss his friends so much," Nelson said. "We'll make a lot of friends in Boston. You'll see."

The back door of the car swung open, and Alan stepped out. Anna followed him to the trunk.

"We have nine boxes of stuff," Nelson said. "Thirty-eight years and I have nine boxes of stuff." Nelson shook his head, running his hand over his sweaty face. "We need clothes for tonight and the morning. We can leave the rest, I guess."

"I'll carry a box," Anna said as she joined them. She clapped her hands and smiled, and Jackie was drawn to her emerald green eyes. Jackie was sure he had the prettiest mother in the world.

"How you doing?" Nelson asked.

"I'm great," Alan said. He held his arms out, and Nelson handed him a box.

"All right, Jackie, step up for loading."

They struggled down the road one step at a time. Jackie tried not to think about how hot it was or how much he was sweating. He thought only of putting one foot in front of the other, and he walked the shoulder of the road, watching his feet through a small opening above the box.

"How you guys making it?" Nelson asked from behind. "Anybody need a breather?"

"I'll make it," Jackie said, and, once again, it was almost as though he believed what he was saying.

After a few minutes, Alan stumbled forward. The box slipped from his grasp and tumbled to the ground.

"Whoa, hold up," Nelson called out.

The sweat burned Jackie's eyes. He slowed to a halt, setting the box down long enough to wipe the sweat away.

"How far is it?" Alan asked. Jackie looked to the horizon barely seeing the hotel sign in the distance.

"Another half-mile," Nelson said.

Jackie stretched his arms above his head and sighed before bending to pick up the box again.

"God, this sucks," Alan said.

Jackie didn't want to hear it anymore. He wished they were already starting over in Boston.

"Dad, why'd they fire you at the warehouse?" Alan asked. "Couldn't you have waited until they needed someone again?"

"There were too many people and too few jobs," Nelson explained. "But when we get to Boston, I'll have a job as long as I want one." Jackie sensed his father's smile without even turning around.

# CHAPTER TWO

Jackie set the box beside a red sofa in the front lobby. He watched the other travelers moving through the front room knowing his family was different from the others. It was always the way. Even in school, Jackie knew his clothes were different from the other children's clothes. He sat down on the sofa, realizing that the furniture in the hotel lobby was worth more money than their house in Savannah.

"So, Boss, what do you think?" Alan asked. "It's all screwed up again, ain't it?"

"It wasn't that long a walk."

"It sucked," Alan said. "Look around. These people know how pitiful we are."

Jackie didn't want to be having this conversation. Alan shook his head in mock pity, and Jackie was keenly aware of their differences. Not only did Alan inherit his mother's emerald green eyes and light blonde hair, while Jackie had his father's dark features, they had also developed completely different outlooks on life.

"We'll be all right," Jackie muttered.

"Yeah, right!" Alan said, laughing. "You know that story that Dad's always telling us?"

"Which one?" Jackie asked.

"That stupid one about when he's thirteen and walking home from his factory job." Jackie gave his brother a blank look.

"You know, the one where he sees the guy drowning down at Taylor's pond."

"I remember," Jackie said.

"He jumped in the water and tried to save the guy."

"I remember it," Jackie said, annoyed.

"You remember the point of it?" Alan asked. "You remember that Dad saw the guy go down for the last time from ten feet away?"

"Yes, I remember it all," Jackie said.

"That's the story of our lives. We're ten feet short of saving ourselves. Dad would've had a great job if he'd finished high school."

"I don't want to hear it," Jackie said.

"Mom would've been a wonderful dancer if she hadn't hurt her knee." Alan held his right knee and made whimpering noises. "Sure, we would've had a new house if someone would of lent us some money."

"Shut up!" Jackie said. "Why do you say those things?"

"Only because it's true, Boss. We're always starving. Dad's got a great job in Boston and here we sit in Connecticut. They'll probably tell us there ain't no rooms at the inn."

Jackie shivered at his brother's laughter. He walked away from the sofa toward his mother and father with the sweat and tears still stinging his eyes.

"Think about it," Alan said. "You're the big thinker."

"Leave me alone," Jackie said, turning to lock eyes with his brother.

"Remember how Dad said he'd never forget the eyes of that drowning man?"

"Yeah, so?"

"So, that's the look in his eyes," Alan said. "He looks like he's ready to go under the last time."

Jackie walked away as the tears made their way to the surface. He didn't want Alan to know he was crying, and he didn't want to hear any more about failure.

They carried the boxes to a room on the third floor. Jackie followed close behind his parents. He didn't want to talk to Alan, and the bright walls of the third floor offered him a sense of strength and security.

"I saw a restaurant next door," Nelson said, "You guys get a burger, and I'll be back with the car in a little while. There'll be a television set in here, too, and it'll work." Nelson laughed nervously. "You don't have to worry about the water, either. You can stay in the shower as long as you want. We'll get a good night's sleep, and we'll be ready to roll."

"If you can fix the car," Alan said.

Nelson ignored the comment and slipped the key into room three-two-three. He opened the door and turned around smiling.

"Look at this place," he said.

Jackie's eyes widened at the simple room. There were two full-sized beds, a dresser with a television set, a desk, and a small reading table. The shades were open, and the full window looked out to Interstate 95.

"I think we got adjoining rooms," Nelson said. "They gave us two rooms for the price of one." Nelson moved through the room quickly, placing the key in the lock at the far end of the room. Jackie stood at his father's side as he opened the door, revealing another room set up exactly alike.

"This is your room," Nelson said. "Alan, come on, take a look."

They walked around the two rooms, amazed at their sudden good fortune. It was all more than Jackie could comprehend.

"Why can't we just stay here?" Alan asked. "This place is way better than our house in Savannah."

Nelson laughed. "This is the kind of place we'll live in when we get to Boston," Nelson said. "I'll get the car, and we'll watch some television when I get back."

Nelson put his arm around Anna, pulling her close.

"When I get the car fixed," he said, "I'll stop by the liquor store and get a bottle of wine to celebrate." Nelson kissed Anna, and Jackie turned from their embrace. His father didn't look like a drowning man, he looked like a guy who could win.

\*     \*     \*

Jackie pulled the covers up around his neck. He tried to block out the sounds of traffic as the cars passed by on the interstate. For some reason, each car that passed seemed to trigger fear inside his mind.

"You know," Alan said from the bed beside him, "it'd be really cool to be normal someday." Jackie didn't respond.

"I know you aren't sleeping," Alan said.

"I'm trying to," Jackie answered.

"Listen to me for a minute," Alan said. "Wouldn't it be cool to have an extra pair of pants or a pair of sneakers that everyone didn't laugh at?"

"It doesn't matter," Jackie said. He looked at the ceiling in the quiet darkness of the hotel room.

"Think about it," Alan said. "We've spent all our lives hoping Dad would get another job."

"I don't want to talk about it," Jackie said.

"You're right," Alan said. "We shouldn't talk about it. We're too young to be worried about all this shit."

Jackie tried covering his ears with the pillow. He wanted to cry again, but he fought it off.

"You got to admit, it feels good to sleep in a real bed," Alan said. "I don't think I've ever slept alone in a real bed. Imagine sleeping alone in a real bed every night with a full belly. It could happen, too, if Dad wasn't so stupid."

Jackie yanked the covers back.

"Shut up! Leave me alone!"

"I'm right, and you know it," Alan said.

"You aren't right," Jackie said. "And I'm not talking to you anymore."

Jackie moved to the door that connected the two rooms.

"You're the stupid one," Jackie said. He opened the door and stepped through into Nelson and Anna's room, slamming the door behind him.

"Hey, Boss," Anna said. She sat cross-legged on the bed. She flicked the off button on the remote control.

"I can't sleep," Jackie said.

"I can't either," Anna said. She moved to the far corner of the bed and patted the spot next to her. "Come on up here with me." Jackie sat on the edge of the bed. He felt like a baby, but he needed to be next to his mother.

"Alan's driving you crazy, isn't he?"

"It's sure taking Dad a long time, isn't it?"

"He'll be back soon," Anna said. "We have rotten luck, but your dad never stops trying." Anna kissed Jackie on the forehead, he felt even more like a baby, but he stayed right beside her.

"Don't let Alan get to you. He's sore about leaving his friends. It'll be awhile before he's back to normal."

"He keeps talking about having a normal life. Will we ever have a normal life?" Jackie asked.

Anna's eyes filled with tears, and Jackie wished he could take the words back. The last thing in the world Jackie wanted was to see his mother cry.

*     *     *

Billy Barth held an empty can of beer in his lap. He tried to keep his eyes focused on the road as it stretched out before him, but three separate problems diminished his ability to do so. Billy was extremely tired. He worked all day in the hot sun doing physical labor as part of a road gang. The setting sun was creating havoc with his eyes, and he was having a hard time fighting it off. He was very drunk.

Billy searched the roadside for a place to pull off to take a piss. He rolled down the side window and tossed the beer can out, and, when he looked back to the road, he saw Nelson Gregory's car. Billy slowed and turned to look inside the vehicle. The car was empty, but Nelson's motionless body was a few feet in front of the vehicle. Billy pulled to the shoulder of the road and slammed on his brakes, stopping just a few feet short of the fallen man.

Billy stood over Nelson, trying to figure out what to make of the dead man on the side of the road. He put his right foot against Nelson's rib cage, kicking him over on his stomach. Billy did this as though kicking a dog into a ditch. He bent down on one knee and picked the wallet out of Nelson's back pocket. Billy leafed through the wallet, stopping long enough to admire the photo of Anna and the boys.

"That's a shame," Billy said. "A goddamn, crying shame."

Billy took another look at Anna's picture before stuffing the wallet into the front pocket of his jeans. At the next exit he'd call the police and report it. It was the least he could do. After all, it really was a shame.

*       *       *

Jackie opened his eyes. It took him a full minute to realize where he was, and he sat up in the bed and focused on his mother. Anna sat beside the full window, looking out at the passing cars. A bright, neon sign flashed vacancy every few seconds, and Jackie concentrated on its rhythmic blinking.

"Dad isn't back yet?"

"Not yet," Anna said without turning around. "Honey, go in your room and get some sleep."

"He's been gone a long time," Jackie said.

"Come on, Boss, get some sleep. Dad'll be mad if you aren't ready to go in the morning."

Jackie got off the bed and shuffled toward the door to his room. He was glad his mother hadn't turned around, because he knew she was crying.

# CHAPTER THREE

Jackie sat upright in bed, already knowing that something was happening that would change his life for a long time to come. He got out of bed and walked through the darkness to the door that connected the rooms. He opened the door and saw his mother still sitting by the side window. Her head was bowed to the floor, and a great sense of dread filled Jackie's heart. Just as he moved into the room, Anna stood bolt upright, and her hands went to her mouth. She let out a short cry and turned to face Jackie.

"Go in the other room," she said.

"What's wrong?" Jackie asked.

"Please, God," Anna said.

Jackie saw the flashing blue light reflected in the window. He held the doorknob, and his mind was caught between confusion and prayer. He stepped through the door and held his breath as he waited to hear the knock on the outside door.

"What're you doing?" Alan asked. "Get back in bed."

"Be quiet," Jackie whispered. His voice gave out before he could finish.

"Are you crying?" Alan asked.

Jackie heard the knock on the outside door.

"The police are here," Jackie said.

Alan was at his side. They heard their mother greet whomever was on the other side of the door.

"Let's go," Alan said.

Jackie opened the door to see two police officers standing on either side of his mother. They guided her to the desk chair as if she were frozen. The older police officer locked eyes with Jackie and quickly looked away.

"Come here, boys," Anna said, weakly.

"Missus Gregory, I don't think it's a good idea."

"We're a family," Anna said.

The older officer didn't seem to know what to say. He shuffled in his spot on the floor beside Anna and tried not to look at the boys. He looked like he wanted to be somewhere else.

Jackie held his mother's hand. Her voice sounded strange, and a single tear rolled down her right cheek.

"I'm afraid I have some bad news," the officer said.

Jackie looked to the younger officer. The man's head was bowed to the ground, and Jackie knew what was coming next.

"He's dead, isn't he?" Anna asked.

Her words hung in the air. The color drained from the young officer's face, and the older officer took Anna's hand.

"We think he had a heart attack," the older officer said. "We did all we could."

Anna hugged the boys close to her. The room was spinning out of control, and Jackie felt dizzy and sick to his stomach. He wanted to just fall to the floor.

"We got a call from someone who saw him on the side of the road. The paramedics were there in minutes, but they couldn't do anything. I'm sorry. We found the hotel receipt in his pocket."

Anna let go of the boys. She buried her head in her hands, and Jackie stumbled away and leaned against the wall. Jackie caught Alan's eyes for a moment and saw his brother's tears. Anna continued to sob, and Jackie slipped down into a sitting position with his back firmly up against the wall. He covered his ears with his hands, and the tears rolled down his cheeks.

Only a few minutes passed before Jackie reopened his eyes, but it seemed as if weeks had gone by. The young officer sitting directly in front of Jackie held out his hand.

"How old are you?" the man asked. "I figure you're about twelve."

Jackie managed a nod.

"I'm Tony Miller," the officer said, extending his hand. Jackie couldn't take the man's hand. He felt separate from everything happening around him.

"I have to see him," Anna said. Jackie faced her, wishing he could stop the crying.

"We'll take you as soon as you're ready," the older officer said.

"I knew something would happen," Alan said. "This is always how it is."

"Shut up," Jackie said. "Just shut up, Alan."

Anna got to her feet. She looked as if she might fall, but she motioned for Jackie to come to her. Jackie was crying harder than he had ever cried in his life. He struggled to his feet and met his mother in a tight embrace. Jackie buried his face in his mother's shirt.

"I need a few minutes," Anna whispered. "Come on, Alan."

The door to the hotel room opened and closed again. Jackie held onto his mother for all he was worth.

"Listen to me," Anna said. Her voice cracked, and she hesitated before going on. "We have a lot of work to do now," she said.

"What can we do?" Alan cried. "How can we do anything without Dad?"

"I don't know," Anna said. "Sweet Jesus Christ, I don't know, but we have to do it together. You guys need to help me."

Jackie felt a hard aching in the center of his chest. He knew the ache would always be there.

"We need a game plan," Anna said. "I have to go with the policemen, but we need a plan to get through this."

Anna held the boys in her arms and slowly rocked them. Her sobs shook their bodies. "Boys, we have to get through tonight. We have to go one day at a time."

# CHAPTER FOUR

A swift breeze from the south did a dance across the back of Jackie's bowed head. He shivered slightly, knowing his mother would go crazy with worry if she woke and found him gone. Yet, Jackie couldn't lift his head from the ground as he walked through the parking lot toward the highway. He had to get away from that room. He needed to distance himself from it.

Jackie wasn't sure how long it'd been since the police knocked on the door. In fact, it really didn't matter what time of day it was. He couldn't go to sleep when his whole life had been torn away. He'd spend a million days without a big bed to sleep in if it meant having his father back.

The night was brisk and deathly quiet. Although it was still dark, Jackie was more afraid of the room than he was of being alone. He looked up at the hotel sign and kicked at the stones. How long would they stay here? Would they be sent back to Savannah? Did any of it matter?

"What are we going to do?" Jackie asked the dawn. "What's the game plan now? I don't know if you can hear me, Dad, but I'm scared."

Jackie felt the tears coming back, but he fought them off.

"You always hated me crying," Jackie said.

He took a few more steps and stopped as a lone car passed on the highway in front of him.

"Alan's mad at you for dying," Jackie said. "He says everything's your fault. And, Dad, Mom won't stop crying. She fell asleep, but I don't know what I can do to make her not cry."

Jackie put one foot in front of the other. He was a few yards away from the shoulder of the highway. He wished he could go back in time to when they had walked the road toward the hotel. He wiped his eyes, wrapping his arms tightly around himself.

"The police told us about you dying. They kept saying it was going to be all right. Everyone always promises me that," Jackie said. He couldn't hold it back any longer, and the tears rolled down his face.

"The old cop said we could stay at the hotel for awhile, and they'd pay for it."

Two cars passed by at a high rate of speed, and Jackie watched their taillights fade in the distance.

"I don't blame you," Jackie said. "I just wish we knew you were sick. I'm going to really miss you, Dad."

Jackie couldn't walk anymore. His mind was cloudy, and he felt a pain in the center of his forehead. He dropped down to his knees and wiped at the falling tears.

"I'm sorry for crying, Dad, but I don't know what to do. I can't sleep in that big bed and think it'll all be fine. You always said I worried too much for a little boy, but how will I ever stop worrying, now?"

Jackie picked a handful of pebbles into his hand and bounced them in the air. He followed their descent to the ground and wiped at the tears once more.

"You always took care of us," Jackie said, looking to the star-filled sky. "You always watched us, and now you're gone."

He picked up another handful of stones and mindlessly tossed them toward the road.

"Promise me, Dad, you'll keep watching."

Jackie struggled to his feet. The stars shined brightly, almost as if they were mocking him.

"We can't live in a hotel. We can't make it to Boston or back home. Just watch us, Dad, please."

# CHAPTER FIVE

Jackie fell asleep a little after seven o'clock. He slept soundly for exactly twenty minutes and then opened his eyes suddenly. He sat up quickly, wiping the tears and perspiration from his face. He looked over at Alan, who was still asleep.

Jackie took a deep breath and choked back a sob. He wiped his face with his hands once more. He couldn't remember ever feeling so tired. He knew it was only a matter of hours since his father's death, but he felt as if he hadn't slept in a month.

From the other room, Jackie heard the sound of a ringing telephone. The phone rang three times, and Jackie heard his mother rustling around. Jackie threw back the covers and stepped into the room. He had to be strong for her sake.

"Yes, I'm Anna Gregory."

Anna was sitting up in the bed, and Jackie couldn't remember ever seeing her pretty face look so drawn. Jackie sat down on the edge of the bed. Anna held the phone to her ear, but she wasn't talking.

"I'm sorry," she said. "I'm not thinking clearly." Anna motioned for Jackie to sit beside her, but Jackie didn't go to her. They'd have to do something more than cry now.

"It doesn't seem possible," Anna said, as a sob escaped her. "Thank you, I need some positive words now." She wiped her eyes again.

Jackie stood up and paced the floor in front of the bed. He listened to his mother's hurried words of despair. He stopped pacing only when his mother had returned the telephone to its cradle.

"That was Officer Bennington," she said. "He was the older man, I think. He'll be here in an hour. He wants to talk to us about everything."

Jackie hugged his mother to his chest, silently promising that he'd take care of her himself.

\*     \*     \*

Billy Barth moved across the cluttered floor of his one-room apartment. He had trouble adjusting to the light of the new day as the sun blasted its way through the only window in the place. He turned back toward the fold-out couch that he used for a bed. He saw the outline of the woman who'd accompanied him home from the night at the bar. He tried to recapture the events of the night, but alcohol had wiped his memory clean.

Who was the woman lying naked on top of the sheets? Had he fucked her?

Billy shook his head violently from side to side. He stumbled to the sink and lifted a filthy glass from the counter. He turned to look at the woman's body as he ran water into the glass. She didn't look the least bit familiar. Billy took the water to the side of the bed and looked down at her with disgust gnawing at his brain.

She had a tattoo of an eagle on the inside of her right thigh. Her legs were spread wide, and Billy was repulsed by the rolls of fat on her body. He turned away, lifting the glass to his lips. He wasn't able to swallow the water. A persistent cough gave way to violent spasms. He dropped the glass, and his body tried to rid itself of last night's whiskey. Sweat dripped through his hair, and he begged for the strength to hold what was left inside his stomach. He continued to retch until his entire body trembled. He felt an ache from his toes to the top of his head.

In a matter of minutes, Billy gained control. When he could focus again, the woman was sitting up on the bed smoking a cigarette. She didn't make an attempt to hide her nakedness, and her smug smile sent flashes of anger through Billy's mind.

"What the fuck is so funny?" Billy screamed.

Her smile grew, and Billy felt his fist clench in rage. His next action was as involuntary as the spasms that shook his body. He punched her hard across the mouth, sending the cigarette to the corner of the room. She emitted a loud, piercing scream, and Billy felt the blood on his body as he moved on top of her. He forced himself into her, feeling she truly deserved all the pain he could give her.

\*　　\*　　\*

Jackie sat at the foot of his mother's bed. Anna walked back and forth in front of the window in quiet anticipation of her meeting with the officers. As much as he hated to admit it, Jackie knew his mother was as confused as his father had been when their car quit on the highway. She had that look of defeat in her eyes, and Jackie was sure she'd soon be telling him how it'd all work out.

"Okay, boys, this is what we're up against," she said softly. She sat at the desk facing them. "We'll meet with the officers and find out what they can do, because we're pretty much at the mercy of the world."

"If we go back to Savannah we can get friends to help us," Alan said, hopefully.

Anna looked away as if she were trying to answer the question without having to tell them that they'd failed again. Jackie looked for the right words to say to help his mother, but his head was jumbled with thoughts.

"When I went down to see your Dad," Anna's voice cracked. "When the cops took me down there, the officer explained he'd have to tow the car away. They couldn't let it sit there. The officer said that someone called to report Dad's death and that whoever called took your Dad's wallet." Anna was shaking, and the tears came all at once. Jackie looked to Alan, who turned away.

"So, we don't have a penny?" Alan asked.

"That's right," Anna said. "We're penniless, and we couldn't leave if we wanted to." The tears were rolling down Anna's cheeks. "And your father deserves at least a funeral," she said, sobbing the final three words. "The police have to help, or I don't know what'll happen to us."

A knock at the door mercifully stopped the discussion. Jackie got to his feet and went toward the door.

"Wait a minute," Anna said. She wiped her eyes with a tissue. "I'm not hiding any of it from you," she said. "I need you guys, you know?"

Jackie nodded. Slowly, he opened the door and stepped to one side as the same two officers entered the room. The younger officer was carrying a bag from McDonald's. He set the bags on the desk in front them.

"I wasn't sure if you ate," he said.

"Thank you," Anna managed.

"How're you doing?" the older officer asked.

"We're hanging in there," Anna said.

Jackie looked to his feet again. Out of the corner of his eye, he saw that Alan's head was also bowed to the ground.

"My name's William Bennington," the older man said. "This guy here is Tony Miller, and we're going to help you get through this."

The young officer nodded.

"This is the hardest thing you'll ever go through," Bennington said.

Jackie felt instantly mesmerized by the gentle tone of Bennington's voice.

"Tomorrow you'll go into that memorial service believing that you'll never be able to walk out."

The overweight officer ran his fingers through his thinning, gray hair.

"But you will come out of there, and every day it'll get a little easier to get out of bed. The pain you feel will lessen a bit each day. You'll never forget a minute of last night, but, somehow, it'll get better. Believe me, it will."

Bennington scanned the room, and his eyes settled upon Alan's still bowed head.

"We can't stay here," Alan said, his voice nearly a whisper.

"For a little while you'll be able to," Bennington said. "I talked with the manager and our captain, and we'll be able to help you for a little while."

"What about a memorial service?" Anna asked. "You said something about a memorial service. I can't pay for anything like that."

"The state of Connecticut will pay for that," Bennington said.

"It'll be a nice service," Tony said.

Bennington forced a smile and shot a nervous look at his partner as if to say he'd handle the discussion.

"What about Nelson's wallet?" Anna asked.

The two officers exchanged a knowing glance.

"Did you find it?" Anna asked hopefully.

"No, ma'am," Bennington said.

"Was it stolen?" Anna asked.

"The man who reported your husband's death may have taken it. It was an anonymous call, and he probably took the wallet."

"What kind of guy would steal from a dead man?" Jackie asked.

"The lowest form of existence possible," Bennington answered.

*       *       *

At that precise moment, Billy Barth rolled off the body of the tattooed woman. He picked Nelson's wallet off the table and pulled on a dirty pair of jeans. He walked out the front door of his broken-down apartment into the bright sunshine of the new day. As he slammed the door, Billy dropped Nelson's wallet to the driveway. He bent down to pick up the billfold and noticed Anna's picture staring back at him. His heart seemed to skip a beat, and he held the picture close. He'd have to do a lot of acting, but he could get the woman looking back at him. She was the most beautiful woman Billy had ever seen, and, if his thinking was right, she was in a state of complete confusion.

# CHAPTER SIX

A driving rain pelted the windows of the hotel room. Jackie crumpled the foil hamburger wrapping and tossed it in the direction of the garbage can. The paper hit the side of the can and bounced into the corner. Jackie gained his feet and placed the wrapper in the can. His eyes wandered to the window where Anna sat watching the rain.

"We don't have any money," she said softly. "Not a single nickel." She cried softly, and Jackie forced himself to look away.

Bennington reached to his back pocket, and extracted his wallet. He pulled out two twenty-dollar bills, placing them in Anna's hand. Tony followed suit, lifting thirty dollars from his own wallet and handing it to Anna. She held tight to the money and a torn tissue.

"It's not much," Bennington said. "Hopefully we'll find a way to sort this out."

"Thank you, for everything," Anna said.

\*     \*     \*

Billy stood before the full-length, rest room mirror. His long, greasy hair hung just below the shoulders, and he ran his hand through it. He smoothed out his beard, smiling at his reflection. It would take an incredible amount of work to capture the attention of Anna Gregory.

Billy held the picture close to his face. He crossed to the rest room door and turned the lock, not once taking his eyes away from Anna's face. She was the most beautiful woman in the world, and this was his chance to get close to her. Billy brought the picture to his lips, closing his eyes to the world around him. He kissed the photo, imagining Anna's lips on his own. He could almost feel her tongue inside his mouth. Passion raged inside of him, and he reached inside his pants. He began groping inside his jeans, smiling at the picture, pronouncing his love over and over.

Just as quickly, Billy snapped his head back away from the picture. He caught sight of himself in the mirror, and the evil smile returned.

"You will be mine," Billy whispered. He let the picture fall to the tile floor of the dirty bathroom. "You will be all mine."

Billy imagined the days of love ahead of him as he began to shave away his hair.

*    *    *

Jackie studied the expressions on the faces of the seven people who gathered to say good-bye to his father. Yet, more than anything else, Jackie concentrated on the words of the elderly priest who'd introduced himself as Father Peter.

"It's important for us to remember that life, as we know it, has changed not ended. For Gregory Nelson, eternity will be spent in the arms of the Lord."

"The old bastard can't even get his name right," Alan whispered. "He's burying him, he should at least know his name."

Jackie knew that it was the way his father's life would draw to a close. Nelson Gregory had lived his whole life to have his name uttered backwards at his funeral. Adding to the shame, Jackie looked to the front of the church where the hired pallbearers waited impatiently to take Nelson to the grave.

"We are left to ask the Lord to take care of this family. Lord, we beseech you to watch over this family."

"Amen to that," Alan whispered.

Jackie looked to the ceiling of the church. He mindlessly wondered about how they painted the Bible scenes in such explicit detail. He took in the sunlight through the stained glass windows, and his eyes settled upon the crucifix of Christ.

"Jesus, you must have a heck of a plan for me," he whispered as if in prayer, and, for some reason, he turned toward the back of the church and locked eyes with an odd-looking man. A quick shiver of fear made its way down Jackie's spine.

*    *    *

Billy was having a hard time trying to decipher the hurried words of the old priest. He just wanted to get out of the hot church. He mentally sorted through his plan of action. Slowly, he removed the small mirror from his inside jacket pocket and slicked back his hair with his right palm. Why wouldn't the old windbag just shut up and bury the husband? Why was church always so dramatic?

Billy hadn't counted on the cops attending the funeral. Didn't they have anything better to do? To make matters worse, he knew the cops from a drunken escapade just months ago. Would they recognize him?

Billy shrugged his shoulders. He was certain he didn't look much like the man they'd dragged in that night. Suddenly, Billy felt the eyes of the younger boy on him.

He tried to look away, but something about the child's intense stare locked in each of Billy's senses. As the boy finally turned away, the old priest finished his sermon.

"Thank God," Billy said. "On with the show."

He looked down at Anna's picture and smiled.

"This time my love will be perfect," he whispered.

Bennington led the procession down the center aisle of the church. He hung on Anna's arm, and Jackie stepped in pace between Tony and Alan.

"We'll go to the cemetery," Tony said. "The priest will say a few more prayers, and that'll be it."

"Back home, they have a lunch or something," Alan said. "They do that so the family isn't alone, but I'll guess we're going to be alone."

"We won't leave you alone," Tony said.

"You can't stay with us forever," Jackie said.

They walked out the door of the church, and, as Jackie turned to look back inside, he again caught the eyes of the strange man.

*     *     *

Billy's mind did a quick flip. He was missing his chance. The feelings of desire were stripping him of his opportunity to carry out the plan. His eyes remained riveted on the spot where Anna had passed before him, and he felt a little like an actor on opening night. Everything seemed to be in order, but, as the curtain was drawn, he froze in the lights. He couldn't shake her from his mind. She was simply the most beautiful woman in the world, and, even as she wallowed in grief, she provided Billy with feelings of immense desire. Billy longed to feel her body underneath his own. He thought of cradling her in his arms and touching every inch of her skin. The feeling passed over him like a wave, and he thought he'd pass out right there in the back of the church.

Almost too late, Billy returned to reality. He made it to the door of the church as Bennington approached the driver's side of the car. Billy drew in a deep breath. His mind worked to calm the feeling of lust, and he shouted for Bennington to stop. The officer spun around, shut the door of the cruiser, and walked toward Billy.

Billy felt a wave of nausea as Bennington's hand dropped near his side holster. Not only would Billy have to convince the woman of his love, he was also going to have to sway the goddamn cop.

"Can I help you with something?" Bennington asked.

Billy judged the man's tone of voice to be more curious than aggravated. Yet, Billy couldn't draw the words from his mouth. Almost as if his non-response were a crime, the second officer emerged from the car.

"I'll handle this," Bennington said. The younger officer ducked back into the car.

Billy used the slight pause to gain his composure. He stifled his animal instincts and put on his most compassionate look.

"Sir, I have something the family may desperately need."

Bennington stopped a few feet short. His hand moved from his holster and Billy drew another gulp of air.

"What is it?" Bennington asked. Billy cleared his throat.

"I found the man's wallet."

Billy extended the wallet and Bennington reached for it. The officer held it as if it might bite him.

"I was out walking with my girl," Billy said.

He paused for a moment for any indication that Bennington believed him.

"I found it out on Interstate 95."

Bennington's eyes took on a look of suspicion. He opened the billfold and thumbed through the cash.

"Every penny's there. I saw the death notice in the paper."

"Not everyone would turn this money in," Bennington said. "We all like to think we're honest until we have a handful of another person's money." Bennington slapped the inside of his palm with the wallet. "Thank you. The family will appreciate it. You're an honest man, the last of a dying breed."

Billy stifled a grin as he realized the cop bought the act.

"They really seem to be in a bind," Billy said.

"They sure are." Bennington turned to walk away.

"Excuse me, sir?"

"What is it?" Bennington asked.

"If it isn't too much of a bother, may I personally return the wallet?" Billy was having trouble hiding his desire. "I'd like to extend my sympathies."

"Of course," Bennington said. He handed the wallet to Billy.

Billy leaned into the car. He looked directly into Anna's sparkling eyes. Although she looked somber, she was even more beautiful up close. He extended the wallet, feeling a slight tremor in his heart as they brushed hands. He closed his eyes and bowed his head.

"Please accept my condolences."

"Thank you for returning this," Anna said. She offered a slight smile, and Billy's knees went weak.

"It's my pleasure," Billy said, backing away from the car. He was having a hard time catching his breath. He walked away without looking back.

# CHAPTER SEVEN

Jackie sat in front of the television. The sound was turned down low, and he hardly paid attention to the action on the screen. Instead, he listened closely to his mother's uneven breathing as she slept. She'd been sleeping for two hours, and Alan had also slipped off over an hour ago. Did they just think they could sleep through it all?

Jackie peered out the window to the parking lot. They had buried his father today, and the words of the priest were still ringing his ears. The old man said that their lives had changed and not ended, but Jackie knew he'd never again hear his father's booming laugh. He'd have to learn to live without the sparkle in his father's eyes as they discussed the game plan.

"His life didn't mean anything to anyone outside this room," Jackie whispered. He thought of his father scolding him for being too serious.

"Hey," Anna said, softly. She sat up in the bed, and Jackie was surprised to realize that he had been crying.

"Oh, Mom," he said. "This isn't fair."

Jackie ran to her.

\*   \*   \*

Billy had loved Gina. In some ways, he loved Gina even more than he loved Anna. After all, Gina had been his first love. He just hadn't been able to make her understand.

He had first spotted her about one year ago. Gina was on her lunch break, sitting with her back to him on the center bench in the park that long-time residents referred to as the Green. Gina wore a tight, black dress. Billy couldn't take his eyes from her.

He watched her eat an apple while paging through *Redbook*. Every movement she made was etched upon his mind, and yet Billy hadn't been able to approach her that first day.

Over the next three weeks, Billy became a changed man. He dressed flawlessly and sorted through the ways to make his plan work. He would make Gina love him. Somehow, some way, she would feel like he did.

On the last day of July, Billy forced Gina into his car. Three witnesses said they thought it was a domestic argument. Inside the car, Billy expressed his feelings of love. Gina answered with a tearful plea for her life.

"You don't know how much I love you," Billy explained. Gina offered her jewelry and money.

Billy drove to a secluded trailer park. He opened his pants and shook his head violently to get rid of the sweat in his eyes.

"Please, God, please don't let this happen," Gina cried.

\* \* \*

Three hours later, he sat on the edge of the bed. Gina was tied to the posts, and she squirmed under the touch of his hand.

"I love you," Billy said.

"Please don't kill me," Gina cried. "I have a baby girl at home."

"Kill you?" Billy asked. "I don't want to hurt you. I just want to love you."

Gina cried out again.

"This isn't right," Billy said. "I tell you how I feel, and you turn from me. How do you think that makes me feel?"

Billy paced the floor. He lit a cigarette, and Gina closed her eyes.

"What can I do about you, now? It's obvious you don't feel like I do."

"I do," Gina said, softly. "I love you, too."

Billy's heart was racing. Her eyes were closed, but she wasn't squirming anymore. Maybe it was true. Billy move to the edge of the bed. He moved his hands between Gina's legs once more. Gina struggled to be free of his touch.

"You don't love me," Billy said. "You say you do, but you don't."

Billy cupped her left breast and ran his hand over the nipple. Gina couldn't choke back a sob.

"You're beautiful, but you're fighting it," Billy whispered. "You couldn't relax and enjoy it, could you?"

He was back on his feet. He opened a drawer on the bedside bureau.

"You'll call the police and tell them you never loved me."

"I won't," Gina said. "I'd never do that."

"I love you with all my heart," Billy said, as he raised the gun. "And I always will."

Gina never had the chance to scream. The bullet made a neat hole in the center of her forehead.

"I always will," Billy said.

He loaded the body in the trunk of his car and drove toward New York. He stopped only long enough to bury the body behind a rest station near Stamford. He abandoned the car just beyond the George Washington Bridge. Although he got away with the deed, Billy knew he'd made too many mistakes.

Love had passed him by with Gina, but Billy had taken the lesson to heart. Now, love was before him again. Billy placed the photograph in his lap. Love had come to him once more in the form of Anna Gregory.

\*      \*      \*

Anna sat cross-legged on the bed. She held the telephone receiver to her left cheek, and the buzz of the disconnected line sounded across the room to Jackie's ear.

"That was about the hardest call I ever had to make," Anna said. A stray tear worked its way down her cheek.

"Your father grew up with David Waters," she said. "Dad would've had a great job in Boston. I know we would've made it."

Jackie tried to shake the thought from his mind. He could almost hear Alan telling him they would always fall just short of making it.

"What did he say?" Alan asked. "Will Dad's friend still help us?"

"I didn't ask him for help," Anna said. "How could I ask him to worry about us? He's not our guardian. David has his own family to worry about."

"That's great," Alan said.

"He said he'd send money until we get back on our feet."

"Wonderful," Alan said. "We can count it until we run out."

A long silence took hold, and Jackie knew his brother was right. Yet, there had to be an answer, somewhere.

There was a soft knock on the outside door. Anna opened it slowly, and William Bennington stepped inside. He grabbed Anna's hand and motioned all of them outside, and into the police car.

"We have to take it a step at a time," Bennington said. "This is the first step."

Bennington looked into the back seat where Jackie and Alan sat with their hands folded on their laps.

"You have to learn how to start all over again," Bennington said. "One of my favorite places in New Haven, is along the waterfront." He pulled the cruiser into a parking lot bordering the edge of the Long Island Sound. He led them down along a paved walk just yards away from the water.

"On most every summer night, you can walk this stretch for miles, and practically the whole city will be out for a stroll. Everyone walks or jogs around here, looking to the water for peace."

"It sounds thrilling," Alan said.

"Think of it as therapy," Bennington said. "The salt, the fresh air, and the water have a calming effect."

"It's beautiful," Anna said.

"Three years ago, I beat a real path along this strip. I would come down here when my shift was over, and I'd walk all night. I walked up and down until my feet begged me to stop."

Jackie followed the big policeman's eyes as he scanned the waterfront. The blue of the late afternoon sky was overshadowed by the people milling about.

"I needed therapy something awful back then," Bennington said.

"Is it legal to fish here?" Alan asked.

"Mister Bennington's talking," Anna scolded.

"It's all right," Bennington said. He pointed to the water. "There's a great fishing spot a couple of miles from the pier. Maybe I'll take you there sometime."

"Can I walk on the pier?" Alan asked.

"Sure," Bennington said. "You can head out there, too, Jackie."

"I'd rather walk," Jackie said.

"Jackie's the boss. He has to know everything you say to me," Anna said.

"That's good," Bennington said. "That's the way it should be. But I have to tell you, I can't walk as far as I used to. I let myself get out of shape a bit." Bennington ran his hand over his belly.

"That's fine," Anna said. She watched Alan make his way down to the pier. "It really is calming out here." She pointed toward Alan. "Of course, he doesn't need as much therapy as we do."

"That's okay, too," Bennington said. "Everyone handles things in their own way."

"Why were you walking?" Jackie asked. "What happened to make you start walking out here?"

"You don't miss a trick, do you?" Bennington asked. "With questions like that you'd make a real good cop."

"I just figure something bad happened," Jackie said.

"You're right. About three years ago, I got ready to take an early retirement from the force." He gazed to the water, and his breathing became labored.

"My wife, Deb, and I planned on finding a little retirement house in the country. There's a town called Clinton about twenty miles from here. We were going to settle there." Bennington paused as if he lost his train of thought. "We bought a piece of land and hired a contractor to build the house we always dreamed about. It was going to be fun setting it up exactly like we wanted." Bennington motioned toward a park bench. "Let's sit for a while," he said as he wiped the sweat from his brow.

"On the day we were set to move in, I left Deb alone because of a big case. I never should have spent so much time at work. Anyway, I took Deb and a truckload of things up to the house. She was so excited about putting everything in the right place."

Bennington focused on Alan moving out across the pier. He didn't speak for a long time, and Jackie sensed the heartbreak of the rest of the story.

"She was so good at decorating. She always wanted to make me comfortable. I thanked God every day for the chance to be with her."

Bennington wiped his eyes.

"I helped her carry everything inside and kissed her good-bye. At least I kissed her good-bye." Bennington's voice trailed off again. He struggled to his feet, and Jackie wasn't sure if he could handle the sight of the big officer crying.

"I would've called, but the telephone wasn't hooked up yet." Bennington paced the area in front of the bench.

"As I drove toward the house, I thought of all the years we'd spend out there."

"I'm so sorry," Anna said.

"She had a blood clot on the brain. One moment she was completely alive, and the next moment she just wasn't. Deb was only sixty. She'd never been sick a day in her life. The doctor said we never could've known."

Jackie looked to his mother. He knew she wanted to cry again, and he wanted to wrap his arms around her.

"When I opened the front door, she was there at my feet. I'll never get that image out of my mind. That's why I've been spending time with you. I know how it feels to have your dreams taken away. You want to make it all right, and you just can't."

Bennington sat down on the bench. Out on the pier, Alan skipped rocks into the water. The anonymous people moved from place to place, and Jackie wondered how many of them were trying to forget something. He shifted in his seat and kicked at the stones at his feet.

"I spent a lot of time wondering why it happened," Bennington said. "I cried every night and thought it was my job to drink all the bourbon in the world. I couldn't chase away the idea that God owed me a little time with Deb in that house."

"How'd you get through it?" Anna asked.

Bennington winked at Jackie.

"It takes time. I needed a lot of time and a lot of friends. I sold the house and moved to an apartment near the precinct. I traded in everything we owned and started over. I didn't retire, of course. Instead, I found a few people who still loved me, and I stayed away from everything that reminded me of the two of us. After a little while, it got better. Now I can think of everything we had, and, even though I miss her a lot, I found a way to make myself comfortable."

Bennington tousled Jackie's hair like his father used to do.

"That's why I think you should spend some time here," Bennington said. "You might not want to stay forever, but spend some time. Get your mind straight."

Alan was making his way back. Jackie focused on his brother's approach and tried hard to figure out exactly what Bennington was telling them.

"I walked this strip a million times," Bennington said. "I got over the pain and finally figured out that the secret was knowing when to remember to forget."

The tears stung Jackie's eyes. He turned away, knowing Alan would laugh at him for crying.

"At least for the first week, try and think normal thoughts again. I'll worry about the other stuff." Bennington patted Anna's hand. "Right now, you can't worry about money and moving. Take the time to get over the shock, and get ready to keep fighting."

Bennington was up and moving toward Alan.

"There's a fish in there as big as me," Alan said. "I watched him swim for five minutes."

"One of these days I'll take you out there to catch him," Bennington said.

Jackie couldn't help but wonder if it were all just another dream.

*　　*　　*

On the following evening, Billy Barth sat in his car in the hotel parking lot. The radio was broadcasting the news of the day. Billy scanned the parking area. He was beginning to think he might have missed Anna and the boys as they made their way across the lot to the restaurant. He focused on the front door of the hotel, and, just as his sense of panic grew, they stepped into view.

The younger boy crossed in front of the car, and Billy slipped down beneath the wheel, leaving himself just enough room to watch Anna's approach. Her head was to the ground, but Billy imagined the half-smile that always seemed to cover her face. He longed to see her bright eyes, and he prayed she would lift her head.

Billy clicked off the radio and moved forward in the seat until he was inches from the windshield. A sharp wave of desire surged through his mind and body. Billy felt it behind his eyes and in his chest. The sense of longing made his temples ache, and he closed his eyes tightly to keep from blacking out.

Billy brushed the sweat from his forehead. He gripped the wheel with his left hand and dropped his right hand below his belt. His mind centered on how he'd react to her touch. Billy laughed then, just as quickly, cried out, almost in a single sound. He opened his eyes and saw her passing. He was sure it would be perfect forever, but she kept her head riveted to the ground.

Billy caressed himself, believing they were Anna's hands. He could almost smell the perfume of her skin and feel the softness of her lips. Slowly, he dropped back against the seat, closing his eyes again.

"I have to stop, it's getting out of control again."

When Billy opened his eyes, he looked directly into the eyes of the younger boy. The child's eyes burned a hole right through him.

Frantically, Billy groped for the front of his jeans. His hands shook as he tried to hurry his movements. Finally, he turned the key just to get away from the staring eyes.

"Jesus Christ," Billy screamed. He slammed the car into reverse, and the tires let out a squeal. "Your eyes could freeze water, kid."

As Billy drove down Interstate 95, his mind cleared. He groped beside him for a cigarette and lifted one from the pack. He let his foot off the gas and drove mindlessly. He was nearing the city of Bridgeport. Billy realized he'd been blacked out for nearly twenty miles of the trip.

Billy looked to the front of his jeans. Somewhere along the way, his excitement had peaked. He ignored the mess and pulled the soiled jeans up around him. His heart was racing and sweat worked its way down his back. The love and desire he felt for Anna was the most powerful feeling he'd ever had.

"I love you more than life itself," Billy cried out.

Billy tossed the cigarette out the window. He searched the ashtray for the joint he'd saved for the occasion. He lit the marijuana, knowing his love would be perfect this time. Billy took a heavy drag and formulated his plan.

# CHAPTER EIGHT

The waitress stood before them with her hand on her hip. She held the pad to her chest as she peered down at Alan with a look of disgust on her face. Jackie waited for his brother to react, but Alan acted as if she weren't there.

"Shall I come back?"

"He'll be ready in a second," Anna said.

Alan shrugged his shoulders and smiled. The waitress sighed heavily.

"Bring him a cheeseburger," Jackie said, and the waitress didn't hang around long enough for Alan to argue.

"I might as well have a stupid cheeseburger," Alan said. "I got cheeseburgers coming out of my ears." Alan was daring their mother to reprimand him.

"I live in a hotel and eat cheeseburgers," Alan said. "That's the way it'll be until I die, which, at this rate, won't be long."

"Shut up," Jackie said.

"At the end of the week, they'll toss us out into the street," Alan said. He crossed his arms in front. "By the end of the week we'll have about fifty bucks left. We'll live two more weeks before we starve to death."

Alan pushed the menu to the floor, daring Anna with his eyes.

"I'm doing what I can," Anna said.

Jackie knew that his mother's heart was breaking. She pushed the chair back away from the table.

"Oh, good, now we'll cry some more," Alan said.

Anna looked down at Alan. Her eyes were shrouded by tears. She simply left the diner.

"Why would you say those things?" Jackie asked when his mother was out of sight.

"Because it's true," Alan said. "It's been two days since that fat cop told you the sob story about his wife and we're still sitting in this restaurant like we're on vacation. You think anybody cares about us?"

Jackie threw his hands up in resignation.

"Mom's calling everyone to get help. She got money from Dad's friend. She talked with the welfare lady for a long time this morning. She's trying to get us help if we need it."

"If we need it?" Alan asked, laughing. "We don't have anywhere to live. We don't have a dime. I think we need it." Alan laughed as if it were the funniest thing he'd ever heard. "I can guess what Mom told the welfare lady, too. She gave the lady the same crap Dad used to say about wanting to earn his own way."

Jackie picked at the napkin in front of him.

"It ain't going to happen," Alan said.

"It will happen," Jackie whispered.

"No," Alan said. "We'll sit here and cry that it ain't fair. The fat cop won't save the day, either." Alan paused, waiting for Jackie to answer. Jackie couldn't find the words to argue.

"Do you think the cop will take us to paradise?"

"I don't know, but it's not Mom's fault," Jackie muttered.

"It's her fault, and it was Dad's fault. We're losers, and that's it."

Jackie wanted to throw the ketchup bottle at Alan's grinning face. Tears stung his eyes, but he fought them.

"I'm not going to die like a dog," Jackie said. "You can talk about dying, but me and Mom will be fine."

Jackie moved from the table amidst sounds of Alan's laughter. Jackie was crying as he pushed through the door and stepped out into the warm night air. They'd have to do something fast.

*     *     *

Billy pulled into the trailer lot as his mind drifted back to the day when he had professed his love for Gina in the third trailer from the road. He looked at the trailer, and a smile creased his lips. Billy pulled next to the fourth trailer. He patted the front pocket of his jeans. The dope was safe and sound, and it was time to trade it all for a place to live. Billy jumped from the car in one mad hop. The front door of the trailer opened slowly.

"Hey, Billy boy," Perry said through the screen door. "You're right on time."

Billy eyed his friend cautiously to see if the skinny, black man were sober. Perry seemed to be moving all right.

"How you been?" Billy asked. He took the two steps to the door, and Perry pushed the screen door open for Billy to enter.

"Good, come on in. You got it?"

Billy slapped his pocket as Perry ushered him in.

"Jesus Christ," Billy said, as the smell of the room reached his nose.

"Sorry about the place, man," Perry said. "The old lady left for good and the maid doesn't come in but twice a month," Perry laughed.

"You *could* take the fucking garbage out," Billy said.

"Fuck it," Perry said. He led the way to the kitchen table, pushing a pizza box and three beer bottles away.

"Is it safe for you to live here again?" Perry asked.

"Why wouldn't it be?" Billy asked.

"You killed that bitch here, man. You're returning to the scene of the crime."

"I'm all right," Billy said. He lifted a sandwich bag of cocaine from his pocket, setting it down between them. He lit a cigarette, watching the desire grow in Perry's eyes. Perry lifted the bag, and the smile was replaced by a frown.

"It's awful fucking powdery."

"It's the best stuff you'll get around here. Get the blade."

Perry shook him off.

"I thought you'd have a couple of rocks. I wanted to sell some."

"Sell it like this," Billy said. "Or should I leave?" He blew a ring of smoke into Perry's face.

"I didn't say that," Perry smiled. He picked a razor blade off the counter.

"Let me try it."

"No problem," Billy said. He lifted the blade and set lines on the table. The smoke of his dangling cigarette made him squint his right eye as he bent over the task. "Now, about our real estate deal," Billy said.

"Two and three are open," Perry said. He leaned to the refrigerator and plucked two beers from the shelf. He slid one to Billy.

"I get free rent for the first month, right?" Billy asked.

"I can't do it for two units," Perry said.

Billy set the blade on the table. He opened the bag without taking his eyes from Perry.

"I can't afford a free month on two," Perry pleaded. Billy ran his hand across his chin. He stared Perry down.

"Man, I got to eat."

Billy lifted the bag of dope and bounced it in his hand. He took a swig of beer, never taking his eyes from Perry's face.

"We have a problem," Billy said. "I already spent the first month's rent."

"Do us both a favor, get the money from the bitch," Perry said.

Billy leapt from his chair as if shot from a cannon. He caught Perry's throat in his hands and sent the chair onto the floor. Billy held tight. He felt his own eyes bulging as he squeezed Perry's throat. Perry fought to break free of the stranglehold and was finally able to buck his legs enough to release Billy's grip. Both men scrambled off the floor. Perry coughed in an attempt to get air into his lungs. Billy punched Perry flush in the mouth.

"If you ever say anything about her again, I'll kill you," Billy said. He grabbed the beer from the table. His breathing was heavy, but it didn't compare to the sounds Perry was making as he tried to cough and choke his way to normal breathing.

Billy fought the urge to leave. He sat down knowing he couldn't walk out without the trailers. Anna needed a place to live. He couldn't let it fall apart.

"I'm sorry," he said. "I been a little crazy lately."

Perry held his throat as if someone were going to steal it, but he nodded slowly.

"I can't let it go out the fucking window," Billy said. "I love her so much it's killing me." Perry nodded again.

Billy picked the blade from the table. "Come on, let's try a little."

Perry's eyes finally showed signs of life.

Billy stretched out four lines. He worked with the precision of a surgeon. He rolled a dollar bill and waved it in front of the man he'd nearly killed.

"You do the first one," Perry said.

Billy shrugged and smiled. He held the bill to his nose and sniffed. He did the second line without a break, dropped the bill to the table, and threw his head back. The rush was enough to make his eyes water and his mind race. He leaned back to allow Perry the room to have a taste.

Six hours later, the two men were still at it. Billy's mind did a dance from ecstasy and power to the love he felt for Anna. Somewhere along the way, he signed the lease agreement on two units. He sealed the deal with a promise of one more bag of dope. Billy wasn't worried about the cocaine, anyway. His road to power existed just beyond his front door. Within two days, the woman he loved would be living right beside him.

*   *   *

Jackie sat on the edge of the bed. A rerun of *Gilligan's Island* played, and, while he had a hard time concentrating, at least it was offering companionship. Alan had gone looking for a basketball court over an hour ago, and Anna was in the other room, asleep again. Jackie had heard her cry herself to sleep over the senseless rambling of Gilligan.

What would they do to stay alive? Where was the cop? Alan had been right about that much, the cop wasn't going to save them. Yet, without Bennington, there was little reason to even hope.

The front door banged open, and Jackie spun around. Alan stepped through the door with the younger policeman at his heels.

"Look who I found," Alan said.

Jackie felt a smile cross his lips.

"*Gilligan's Island*, huh?" Tony Miller asked.

"Where's Mister Bennington?" Jackie asked.

"At the station, he sent me down with the good news. Where's your mom?"

Jackie saw the envelope in Tony's hand, but for some reason he focused only on the gun at Tony's side.

"She's in the other room, crying again," Alan answered.

"She's sleeping," Jackie said.

At that moment, the door to the adjoining room opened, and Anna stepped through.

"Evening, ma'am," Tony said. "I'm sorry for waking you. William asked me to bring this letter from your friend in Boston."

Tony extended the envelope, and Anna took it from him, avoiding his eyes the entire time.

"Also, William may be able to help you land a job."

Anna looked up suddenly. She turned the envelope over in her hand.

"A job?" Alan asked. "What can she do?"

Anna faced Alan with the tears already glistening in her eyes. "Alan, I'm telling you once, keep your mouth shut or leave the room."

She dropped the envelope on the dresser. She ran her hand through her hair. "Please, sit down," Anna said. She extended her hand toward the desk chair.

"I'm fine, ma'am, thank you."

Tony shifted his weight from one foot to another. Again, Jackie's eyes went to the gun.

"Peter Hanratty is the most productive businessman in town," Tony said. "He owns a number of businesses and has a lot of property along the waterfront. Actually, he has more clout in the city than the mayor." Tony laughed slightly and shook his head. "He owns a construction company and a warehouse. He has five hundred employees and is always looking to gain more ground. He's also one of the most miserable, arrogant people in town. That's probably why he's successful."

Anna nodded, her face showing a hope that Jackie recognized all too well.

"Regardless, Peter is a friend of the police, and he's done us a favor or two."

"You don't care for him, do you?" Anna asked.

"No, I don't," Tony said. "I think he has ulterior motives, but William's a friend. He absolutely swears by him."

They were all patiently awaiting the bad news.

"I just want to be up front with you," Tony said. He took off his hat and twirled it in his hands.

"Please, do," Anna said.

"Peter helped William through his wife's death. He helps the police force by giving jobs at our request. Personally, I think there are two sides to the man."

Once again, Tony shifted nervously in place. Jackie ran the words through his mind, trying to get the message.

"I talk too much," Tony said. "The truth is you need a job, and Peter has one. Love him or hate him, he can help. He'll go a long way to help you out."

Tony backed toward the door.

"We paid for the room through the weekend. We'll try to help you find a place. Maybe you can look around a little."

"I will," Anna said. "Thank you for everything. This hasn't been real easy."

"No, ma'am."

Tony gripped the doorknob. "We'll get the boys into school, too," he said. "One thing at a time." Tony stepped into the bright sunshine of the summer afternoon. "Little by little, it'll get better."

# CHAPTER NINE

Billy inspected his handiwork. The sweat poured out from underneath his baseball cap, and his hair felt dirty and greasy. He lifted the cap and scratched his temples. He wiped the sweat with the back of his hand.

Unlike himself, the trailer apartment was immaculate. He spent six hours scrubbing the floors and repairing the furniture. To his tired eyes, it looked ready.

The place would be cramped. There wasn't anything he could do about that. His eyes centered on the couch, which took up over half the living room. It was a beat-up piece of furniture, but the slip cover hid most of the damage. Billy placed a small black and white television on milk cartons in front of the couch. The set had come from Billy's place.

"It really ain't bad," Billy said to Anna's picture.

Billy faced the kitchen. Like the living room, it was barely big enough for human comfort. The sink was badly stained, and, although he had scrubbed it for an hour, he couldn't quite clean it.

The stove had also seen better days, but he'd got three of the four burners working.

"It'll do," Billy said. He turned to the tiny refrigerator tucked away in the back corner of the room. He cupped the picture of Anna in his right hand as he opened the door.

"How about this?" he asked as he ducked his head inside. He held the picture to his eyes, and the familiar desires burned inside. Before he had the chance to close the door on the coldness, panic took control of his mind.

Billy ran toward the small room tucked off in the back corner of the trailer. There was just one bed. Actually, it was just a battered mattress tossed into the back corner of the room.

"Where will we make love with the goddamn kids sleeping in here?"

Billy's mind turned over, and he felt dangerously close to a blackout. He thought about the old couch. They could make love on the couch if they had to. Billy clapped his hands, and suddenly the sense of panic was swept away as quickly as it came.

"We have my apartment." He laughed loudly. The beads of sweat raced down his face. Billy slapped his forehead with an open palm, and the laugh continued to grow inside of him.

Billy knelt down on the mattress and brought the picture to his lips. Before he even realized what was happening, the laughter inside of him shifted to tears of joy.

"This time, it'll be perfect."

\*　　\*　　\*

Jackie watched his mother clean the hotel room as if it were their house back in Savannah.

"You don't have to clean," Alan said. "There's maids who do that."

Anna tossed one of Jackie's shirts into a box.

"We have to take our clothes," Anna said smiling.

"You're dusting," Alan said. "They'll dust after we leave."

"I know," Anna said. She sat on the bed beside Jackie. "I clean when I'm nervous. They were nice enough to let us stay here. I'm trying to help."

Anna put her arm around Jackie's shoulder.

"It'll be all right, I promise."

When Jackie looked into her bright eyes, he couldn't help but smile.

"We'll find an apartment. David sent enough money for a while, and I'll start working. We'll make it fine."

"I know, Mom," Jackie said.

"Let's get ready," Anna said. She got off the bed and dusted the dresser. "If we aren't out of here by noon they'll have to pay for another day."

\*　　\*　　\*

Billy stood in the center of the hotel lobby. In his right hand, he held a large arrangement of flowers. His three-piece suit was pressed to perfection, and his hair was clean and neatly combed. He felt more like a senator than a common thug. He nervously glanced to his watch. If it all went according to plan Anna and the boys would be with him inside an hour.

"Anna Gregory's room, please," Billy said. He smiled at the skinny, gap-toothed, Chinese man behind the counter.

"I'm not allowed to give out that information."

Billy silently cursed himself for not remembering the room number.

"I understand," Billy said. "I'm their cousin. They're waiting for me. You heard about her husband's death, right?"

"Oh, yeah, she's got two little boys. It's awful."

"It sure is," Billy said, shaking his head as if consumed by grief. "She's ready to check out. I want to make sure they have somewhere to turn."

"I see," the man said. He studied the lines of Billy's face.

"It's very traumatic for all of us."

"I understand. They're in three-two-three."

"Why, of course," Billy said. "I guess, in the commotion, I forgot. Thank you."

"It's the third door on the right," the clerk said.

"Thanks, I'll find it," Billy said. He smiled brightly and walked to the door.

"Sir?"

Billy felt a hot wave of panic.

"You forgot your flowers."

Billy slapped his forehead with an open palm.

"I swear, sometimes it's like I've lost my mind."

Billy laughed nervously, but sweat was already soaking his shirt.

*     *     *

Alan peered at the newspaper's classified advertisements. Jackie entered the room, closing the door on Anna's frenetic cleaning.

"I wish I knew where these places are," Alan said. "Like here." He circled an ad with his pencil. "There's a place on Sycamore for four hundred a month. There's two bedrooms and a bath."

Jackie sat beside Alan, looking at the ad.

"How much will they pay Mom?"

"I don't know," Jackie said shrugging.

"Dad got five bucks an hour," Alan said. He looked to the ceiling as if there were an answer printed there. "She'll probably get three bucks an hour. They usually work forty hours a week."

"A hundred and twenty dollars," Jackie said.

"I know," Alan said. "I'm trying to figure out how much that'd be for a month."

"Four-hundred-eighty."

"That's not enough," Alan said, grimacing. He threw the pen down. "We'll have to get a place with one bedroom and sleep on the floor again."

"They might pay Mom more than that," Jackie said. "There's minimum wage."

"That's right," Alan said, with a gleam of hope in his eyes. "How much?"

"I'm not sure," Jackie said, "but it's more than three bucks."

"Can you imagine if Dad kept that job?" Alan asked. "We'd have two hundred bucks a week."

"Eight hundred a month," Jackie finished.

"We would've been able to live anywhere. I'm so mad at Dad for dying," Alan said. "I know it wasn't his fault, but I get so mad."

"I know," Jackie said. "I get mad and pretty sad too."

The knock on the outside door brought their conversation to a close.

\* \* \*

Jackie opened the door to the adjoining room just as Anna reached the outside door.

"Who's there?" Alan called over Jackie's shoulder.

"I don't know," Anna said. "I didn't open the door yet."

"It's probably William and Tony," Jackie said, as Anna turned the knob.

The strange man who had attended the funeral stood in the doorway. He extended flowers to Anna.

"Who is he?" Alan whispered.

Anna stepped back, and the look of surprise on her face scared Jackie more than anything else.

"He's the guy at the funeral," Jackie said. "He had Dad's wallet."

"He's a creep," Alan said.

"Only, now, he's a creep in a suit and tie," Jackie said.

They stepped into the room to hear what the man had to say.

\* \* \*

"I wanted to extend my sympathies," Billy said. His voice crackled, and he cleared his throat.

"I imagine what a terrible time this must be for you. I can't help but feel a tremendous heartache for your family."

Billy feigned a smile of respect. Inside, his heart ached with desire. Up close, Anna was even more beautiful than he had imagined. She held a look of beauty that tore at his insides.

"Thank you," Anna said. She accepted the flowers and moved away from the door, allowing Billy into the room.

"I'm sure this is rough," Billy said. "I would like to help if I can."

Billy smiled at the boys standing near the side door; the goddamn kids seemed to be looking right through him.

"I was thinking that what you probably need more than anything is a place to live. Am I right?"

Anna nodded as if his words had somehow hypnotized her. She turned to the desk and placed the flowers beside their tattered and torn belongings.

"I looked through the paper," Anna said. "Most every place wants a deposit, and I don't have much." Her voice trailed off as if she had already said too much.

"That's what I figured," Billy said. He wiped at the sweat on his forehead.

"I've lived in New Haven all my life," Billy said. "Since you were on my mind, I checked for you."

The voice in his head called to him. *Stay away from the eyes. Her eyes will kill you. It has to be better this time.*

Billy moved to the window. He looked out on Interstate 95 as the cars rushed by. His breathing grew increasingly heavy.

*I'm blowing this. I'm fucking it up.*

"Are you okay?" Anna asked.

Billy turned to face her. He felt tears in the corners of his eyes.

"I've always been sensitive," he said. "I'm a very Christian person, and it pains me so to see suffering." Billy wiped at a tear.

"We'll get back on our feet," Anna said. She looked at the boys.

"I know you will," Billy said.

Billy tried to gauge Anna's expression, but she kept turning away. Why was she worried about the kids?

"I have some good news," Billy said. He didn't wait for her response. "I found an apartment. Actually, it's a trailer. It'll be nice for you and the boys."

"You didn't have to do that," Anna said.

"We need a place to live," one of the boys said. For the first time, Billy felt he might pull it off.

"That's right," Billy said. He moved toward the boys, but they backpedaled away just as Anna had done.

*This time it will be perfect.*

"It's a nice place," Billy said. "It isn't the presidential suite, but it'll do. A friend of mine owns the place, and he's agreed to a free month's rent."

"I don't know," Anna said. She moved around the room timidly.

"He's a good friend of mine. I did some work for him, and he owes me money. I thought of you and decided to call in the favor."

Anna looked at the boys nervously.

"You have to trust someone, right?" Billy asked. "I've lived here all my life. I'm a good guy to trust."

"We need a place to stay," Anna agreed.

Billy pounced on the opening.

"It can't hurt to look," Billy said. "I'll drop you by there."

Anna glanced at the flowers and the boys as Billy followed her eyes.

"The address is written on this card." He extended the card to Anna, and her hand softly brushed his during the exchange.

"I'm headed that way," Billy said. He flicked sweat out of his eyes. "I live in the same lot. I'll drop you at the door."

"This is unbelievable. We're about to check out."

Billy's heart did a flip. It was working as planned.

"The boys will love it. There's a lot of room to play, and it's close to the bus stop."

"Okay," Anna softly said.

He felt the excitement surge through his body. He had to get away before he lost control.

"I'll wait in the lobby."

"Thank you," Anna said. Billy escaped to the hallway. His breathing was too heavy. He had to get away.

When he left the room, Anna turned to the boys. "What do you think?"

Jackie was at her side. He picked up a pair of his pants and placed them in the box.

"It's not a good idea," Jackie said.

The familiar look of pain crossed her eyes and was quickly replaced by a frown.

"It'll be all right," Alan said. "It's better than not having anywhere to go."

"Five minutes ago you said he was a creep," Jackie said.

"Five minutes ago we didn't have a apartment," Alan said.

Anna lifted the box from the desk and placed it in front of the door.

"We have to be out in eleven minutes," she said. "We have enough money for a little while, and I got the job. We need a place to live. Right?"

"Yes," Jackie said, reluctantly.

"It isn't like we're living with him," Anna said. "He has a place. We need a place, and we don't have to stay more than a month."

"I guess," Jackie said. He sat on the edge of the bed. "What if we waited for Tony and William?"

"We have ten minutes," Anna said. She looked to Alan. "Are you okay with this?"

"It's a great idea," Alan said.

"Help me get this stuff together," Anna said. "Jackie, it's the only idea we have right now."

Jackie couldn't believe they had to go out into the world today. He bent down and picked up a box.

"He's the guy who was at the funeral, right?" Jackie asked.

"Yes, he gave me the wallet back."

"There aren't many guys who'd do that," Alan said.

"It seems like he wants something, though," Jackie said.

Anna's face dropped. She replaced her worried look with a smile, but Jackie saw the moment of fear in her expression.

"He's got weird eyes," Jackie said.

# CHAPTER TEN

Billy's hands were wrapped tight on the steering wheel. He was having a hard time focusing on the road as he fought the desire to look at Anna. The silence of his passengers was too hard to handle. After all the fantasizing about how perfect it would be, fighting his feelings of desire was making it seem painfully dire.

*It's turning into Gina all over again. If she keeps thinking about the kids, we'll never fall in love.*

Billy glanced in the rear-view mirror where he caught the intense stare of the younger boy. The kid was looking at him as if he'd come over the seat to help his mother.

"How old are you guys?" Billy choked out. Neither boy answered.

"Alan's fourteen, Jackie's twelve," Anna said.

Billy shook his head in an effort to show sympathy.

"It has to be so tough," Billy whispered. He locked eyes with her, and her beauty piqued his desire. He quickly looked away.

*Stay away from the goddamn eyes.*

"Things'll work out," Billy said.

*They'll all learn to love you. You'll be the husband and the father. You'll make love to her every night. It will be perfect.*

"Your new home is just a few miles away," Billy said.

Billy turned right onto Chapel Street. The road was a bustle of activity as students of Yale University hustled from building to building. The students were all dreaming of fancy homes, big cars, and trips to the Gulf of Mexico. They were the rich people of tomorrow, and Billy silently cursed them. Billy was sure Anna's dreams of a great life were gone, but he would do all he could to make things special again.

"My buddy and I set things up," Billy said. "You can change whatever you want."

Anna nodded, but her head remained riveted on the world of the college students. Why wouldn't she look at him? Didn't she know he'd be the one to give her life again?

They traveled east down Chapel Street, and, slowly, the world outside the window changed. The homes were progressively more run down, and men who hadn't worked in months sat on their porches. Billy eyed the men suspiciously as if they'd steal the very car he was driving.

Billy was struck by the fact that Anna would be alarmed by the condition of the neighborhood. He looked at the side of her pretty face as she gazed out the window.

The streets were covered with garbage and discards of human life. The air reeked of decay and human defeat. Billy got the urge to reach across the seat and take Anna into his arms. He wanted to tell her it would be different when they were together.

Billy made a left turn into the trailer lot. Perry's car was parked across the way, and Billy slowed to allow an old lady with a mangy dog to pass. He waved, and the lady waved back.

"This is it," Billy said. He pulled up to the second trailer and killed the engine. *We're home at last.*

The familiar ache began in his loins.

*   *   *

The next morning, Jackie opened his eyes to his new surroundings. The birds seemed to be serenading them in their new home. Above their singing, Jackie heard Alan's even breathing. They were sharing the mattress in the back corner of the trailer, and, even though they had found shelter, Jackie shivered with a strange type of fear.

Jackie rolled onto his back, looking. His mind's eye focused on the image of Billy, and his sense of fear grew stronger. There was something wrong with Billy, and everyone was looking beyond the craziness in his eyes.

*This could be bad.*

Jackie closed his eyes, and the image of his father rushed to the foreground of his mind.

"What's happening Dad? Who's this guy, and how can I keep him away? Is there anyway you can help us? I know you're gone, but I need to hear from you. Is there something wrong with this guy, or am I worrying too much?"

Jackie opened his eyes, and a stray tear worked its way down his face. He thought of Bennington and Tony and wondered why his mother hadn't waited. Couldn't they find a place?

*I don't know why we didn't call 'em.* He ran a hand through his hair. *We've got to call them today.*

He closed his eyes again and drifted toward sleep, but a knock on the front door caused him to sit straight up.

Jackie waited for the second knock, hoping it wouldn't come. Billy was the only person they knew, and Jackie didn't want him around. The second knock came louder than the first, and the sense of fear that started in the pit of his stomach made its way to his throat. The third knock brought Jackie to his feet. He had to stop his mother from letting Billy in.

Jackie rubbed his eyes and stepped into the front room. He felt very tired and wondered if he would ever feel normal again. It was almost as if his father's death had robbed him of his strength.

Jackie watched as his mother peered through the ragged curtains on the screen door. He sensed she was feeling the same sense of dread.

"It's William," Anna said with a sigh of relief. She turned the lock and swung the door open.

William entered quickly. His face was a picture of anger, and Jackie took a step back.

"Welcome to our home," Anna said.

William took in the surroundings. All at once, he turned and faced them.

"Why would you go anywhere without telling me?

He didn't wait for an answer. "Trusting the wrong people will get you killed."

Anna held out her palms as if to ask what she was supposed to do.

"We needed shelter."

William paced the floor. He went to the kitchen sink and ran the water as if to check if it were safe for human consumption.

"I'm trying to help," William said.

Anna sat on the couch, which made a tired sound under her.

"I went crazy last night, wondering what happened. I spent the night trying to figure it out. I got a description from the hotel clerk on who you left with, and it occurred to me that you might be here. Do you know who Billy Barth is?"

"I'm sorry," Anna said, ignoring the question. "I didn't know what to do. I still don't. I couldn't leave the hotel with nowhere to go. We're not your responsibility. When he mentioned the place, I figured what did we have to lose?"

"Your lives! I know Billy Barth." William caught Jackie's eye and stopped speaking.

"What did he do?" Anna asked. William waved his hand, and Jackie knew it was because of his presence in the room. William sat beside Anna.

"We have to do what we can to survive," Anna said. "I didn't know what else to do."

Jackie wanted to shout at William to leave her alone.

"You have to rely on something, but I'm not sure this is the best place."

47

"We don't fit in anywhere. What's wrong with Billy?"

"He's been in trouble before," William said. He looked nervously at Jackie.

"And?"

"And you should've called," William said.

"What'd he do?" Jackie asked.

William took in the entire scene, then chuckled slightly.

"I'm a part of this," Jackie said. "What'd he do?"

William lifted his cap off and ran his hand across his head. "Are you sure you're only twelve?" He paused, but Jackie knew that, this time, he'd tell them.

"Barth's been arrested a dozen times for a lot of reasons. He works for Peter Hanratty so we can keep an eye on him."

"I'm not going to be working with him?" Anna asked, horrified.

"No, he's on a construction site, and you'll work in the office. I wouldn't put you in that position, but here you are, living next door to him."

"I didn't know. If he's such a criminal why isn't he in jail?"

"I'm just telling you this to scare you. He's not the kind of guy who's going to break in, but he's not the best guy in the world, either."

"So what do we do?" Anna actually shivered.

"I talked with Hanratty. He owns a lot of property and the job's set. But he doesn't have an open apartment right now. School starts in a week. We'll enroll the boys, and I guess you can stay put until a place frees up."

"That's what I was thinking," Anna said. She was wringing her hands as though she were the criminal.

"I'll get you out of here. Barth isn't helping you out of the goodness of his heart."

"I know," Anna said, "but who should I trust? What about Hanratty? Why is he helping me?"

"Out of the goodness of his heart," William said.

"So, now we just wait?" Anna asked.

William scratched his head. He reached into his jacket and withdrew a small handgun. Anna looked at him in confusion, and Jackie took a step closer.

"The boys need to know this is available, and you need protection."

"I don't want a gun," Anna said, "Nelson never had a gun."

William looked over his shoulder at Jackie. He held the gun out for Anna's inspection.

"You've seen the men standing on the corners. You've heard the sirens. You need this." William extended the gun toward Anna. Her hands were wrapped around one another, and her eyes found the floor.

"It's a Colt .45. It's a popular gun on the streets, because it was mass-produced for the war. It's cheap and easy to get your hands on. Yet, it's very safety-orientated. I took that into mind when I got it for you."

Anna turned a lighter shade of pale. Jackie took another step toward the gun.

"The boys won't ever have the chance to use this," William said. "It's for your peace of mind." Again, William moved the gun to Anna. "It's not loaded."

Anna moved her hand forward, and William placed the gun in her palm. Anna gripped the brown handle and ran her hand across the black, long-nosed barrel. Her hand was shaking, and Jackie wondered if his mother was going to drop the gun.

"Can I hold it?" Jackie asked.

Anna lifted her head with a look of determination showing on her face. She held the gun out to Jackie.

Jackie took the gun from his mother's hand. It was heavier than he imagined, but he aimed it to the floor, imagining what it might feel like to pull the trigger.

"He's right," Jackie said. "We might need it to stay alive." Jackie handed the gun back to William. He looked to his mother's crying eyes and nodded.

"It's a simple gun," William said. "The Colt .45 is capable of firing eight shots. It holds seven cartridges in the magazine and one in the chamber." William withdrew the magazine and held it up for inspection. Jackie watched every motion. Slowly, William re-inserted the magazine.

"Okay, there it is." William leaned back against the couch. He wiped his left hand across his brow. "Now, I can show you how to fire the weapon. It's going to sound more complicated than it really is. Do you want to call the other boy?"

"No," Anna said. "Alan's different. I don't know why, but just Jackie knowing seems like enough."

"All right," William said. "Now, with the right hand wrapped around the receiver and with the trigger untouched," William wiggled his finger to emphasize his actions. "The left hand will pull back on the slide." He pulled it back a couple of times to illustrate his point.

"Doing this will expose the barrel and the first cartridge, which is right here under the slide opening."

Anna nodded, but Jackie didn't know how much of the demonstration she'd actually understood. Jackie stared at William's hands. He was certain he could mimic the movements.

"The slide will automatically snap forward, thus pushing the cartridge off the top of the magazine and into the chamber." William demonstrated the action. "As you see, with the slide locked open, the first cartridge is clearly visible. Now, with the slide released to push a live cartridge into the chamber, the hammer is pushed back into the full-cock position, and the gun is ready to be shot. Remember, holding the trigger down produces one shot and not a series of shots."

William removed his cap and wiped at his brow. "Basically, without shooting the gun, that's how it works."

William settled on Anna's suspecting eyes. He removed the magazine and handed the components to her.

"Try it," William said.

Anna shook him off.

"It might save your life," William said.

Anna took the gun. Jackie was afraid his mother might cry and ruin it all, but Anna took the gun and awkwardly worked through the motions. Her hands were shaking badly, and when Anna had the gun assembled and ready to fire, she pushed it back toward William.

"I don't know," she said. Her voice trembled slightly.

"It's only for protection."

Anna glanced at Jackie, and he nodded to her.

"What about the safety features?" Anna asked. "I don't want to leave it around here loaded."

William turned the gun over in his hand.

"If you want to keep it empty, you can. However, you can also keep it loaded and carry it in the full-cock position, and it won't fire unless you disengage the thumb safety," William pointed to the v-shaped notch at the end of the slide. "Also, the hammer is a constant reminder of the condition of the gun. If the hammer is down the gun can't be fired. If the hammer's back, the gun can only be fired if the thumb safety is disengaged."

"Okay," Anna said.

"Number two is something I should've told you before. The gun can't be fired with trigger pressure alone. You have to have your hand wrapped around the grip, and you also have to squeeze the grip safety," William removed the magazine, showing them what he was explaining.

"This will reduce your chances of an accidental discharge. There's one other safety feature, but I doubt you'll need it."

"What's that?" Anna asked.

"When the gun is empty the magazine will slide off automatically, showing you that you must reload. I don't think you'll have to reload," William smiled, but Anna lowered her eyes.

"I'm so scared of all this," Anna said.

"I'll be here to help you," William said. "This is just in case I can't be."

William patted Anna's hand and looked to Jackie.

"It'll be all right, Boss," William said.

Jackie hoped that, this time, the words were true.

# CHAPTER ELEVEN

Billy sat with his back pressed against the concrete wall. He dropped his hard hat to the floor of the parking garage. Although he was supposed to be working, Billy felt in need of a break. He lit a joint, ran his fingers through his hair, and took a hit of the marijuana. As the smoke filled his lungs, Billy centered his mind on Anna. He hated being away from her.

*Someday it'll all pay off. When she's living with me and we're together as a family, this fucking job will have been worth it.*

Billy scanned the area around the parking garage for a glimpse of his foreman. Even though there were over fifty men in the area, Billy was aware there was a chance he'd be missed. He took another hit of the joint and ducked behind a scaffold. He couldn't afford to be thrown off the job, now, not with rent to pay.

*Everyone's fucking chasing money. We get a little money, and we chase more.*

Billy noticed the shadow of a man approaching quickly. He dropped the joint to the ground and picked up his hard hat.

"Hey, Barth, what are you doing?" the foreman, Al Jackson, asked.

"Trying to cool off," Billy said as he put the hat on his head.

"Didn't I tell you to clean up the area near the carpenters?" Al asked.

"I was doing it. I got hot."

"You know," Al said, "if it were up to me, I'd run your sorry ass off this job."

Billy turned and walked toward the job site.

"It ain't up to you," Billy said.

"They want you in the office."

Billy stopped walking and spun to face his foreman.

"Oh, do they now? You don't seem to understand, I'm a big man around here." Billy offered a full smile.

"Get the hell out of here," Al said.

Billy couldn't help but smile at his good fortune. If his instincts were right, Hanratty's call would bring a handsome payoff and a chance to do some real work. The procedure was always simple and was usually the same. Hanratty would give Billy his assignment, and the payoff would be delivered in cold hard cash.

Billy clapped his hands together as he reached the front step of the office building. He'd use the money to make dinner for Anna and the boys. Whether it was selling drugs or roughing up a customer, Billy would be able to do it with the thought of Anna in the back of his mind. His life was becoming more perfect by the hour.

Billy swung the door open and sauntered inside, full of new found confidence. He stepped into the reception area and smiled at Justine, the beautiful, young blonde behind the desk. She turned away.

"Been dreaming about me?" Billy asked.

Justine rolled her eyes.

"Come on," Billy said, "I see that hungry look in your eyes."

"That's a look of disgust," Justine said. She pointed to Hanratty's door. "He's waiting for you. Please, go in so I can't see you."

"Aw, don't be like that," Billy said. He moved closer, bowing down so his face was just inches from her. "Deep down, we both know you want me. Let's stop fooling ourselves."

"Get the fuck away from me," Justine whispered, batting her long eyelashes for effect. "You're a disgusting, sorry excuse of a human being, and if you come on to me again, I'll poke your eye out with this pencil." She twirled the pencil around and offered a bright smile.

"That's right," Billy said, stepping back and slapping his forehead in mock surprise. "It's Sonia that wants me so bad. Where is she?"

Justine clicked the intercom alive, calling for Hanratty. Billy stood at attention as Justine announced his presence.

"Send him in," Hanratty growled.

"Let Sonia know I stopped," Billy said.

"Get lost, scumbag," Justine said.

Billy walked away with all of his confidence intact. It didn't matter what Justine thought. Soon enough, Billy would have Anna on his arm.

Hanratty's door was open a crack, and Billy stepped through. He was fishing inside his jacket for a cigarette when he locked eyes with Hanratty for the first time.

"Don't smoke in here," Peter said. "I've told you that before."

Billy returned the cigarette to his front pocket and smiled brightly. "I'm sorry," he said. "I was just trying to figure out what I could get away with."

"Don't test me," Peter said. He lifted his huge frame from the chair. Billy couldn't help but wonder how a man could get so fat.

"I've brought you in for a special job." He motioned for Billy to sit in the chair directly in front of the desk then stood just inches away from Billy.

"If you screw this up, you're on your own."

"Of course," Billy said.

"This is more risky than your usual task," Peter said.

"I'll handle it," Billy said. He thought about asking for his fee but knew that Hanratty would set the agenda. Absent-mindedly Billy reached for the cigarette. He actually brought it to his lips before he caught Hanratty's eyes.

"Put it down," Peter said. "I'm telling you, Barth, if you fuck with me, I'll kill you."

Billy felt the color drain from his face. He took the cigarette away from his mouth. His confidence was beginning to fade.

"Geez, man, I forgot. It was a reflex action. I'm sorry."

Hanratty stared Billy down. The anger showed in Hanratty's bright red cheeks, and Billy looked to the floor.

"It's a tough job, but one you'll enjoy."

Billy nodded, aware that one more screw-up could cost him the job.

"William Bennington's been a life-long friend. Recently, however, he's been teamed up with a new partner."

"Tony Miller," Billy said. "He's a young guy, right?"

"Right," Hanratty said. "I'm glad you know him."

"What's the problem?" Billy asked.

"He's full of piss and vinegar," Peter said. "He spends a lot of time talking about investigating me. It's beginning to get on my nerves."

"Do you want me to kill him?"

Peter shook his head, laughing heartily as he did so.

"Of course I don't want you to kill him," Peter said. "He's a cop for Christ's sake." Hanratty wiped his mouth as laughter shook the rolls of fat on his body.

"I want you to rough him up. I want him to know to keep his mouth shut."

"I can do it," Billy said. "He's a pain in the ass."

Peter paced in front of the desk.

"There are a couple of things to remember. Bennington and I are close, and he knows who you are."

"Right," Billy said.

"He also knows you're a scumbag, and I agreed to find a place for you to keep you off the streets."

"They asked you to hire me?" Billy asked.

"Yes," Peter said, "and they know who you work for, understand?"

"I understand."

"And you, also, understand that if you're caught, I'll make a goddamn example out of you."

"I understand that, too," Billy said.

Hanratty unfolded two one hundred dollar bills and placed them on the desk.

"There may be more, depending upon how well you pull this off."

Billy reached for the money, and Peter placed his chubby hand over the top of the bills.

"I want you to do it tonight," Peter said. "If you mention this to anyone, I'll have your tongue removed."

"It's under control," Billy said. "Geez, you aren't much for pleasantries today, are you?"

"This isn't pleasant. It's business."

Billy pushed out of the chair, and Peter stepped in the path to the door.

"By the way," Peter said as he wrapped his arm around Billy's shoulder, "when you walk out of here, I don't want you saying one fucking word to the girls. They don't care for you."

Billy nodded in a moment of intense fear as Peter's hand reached for the center of Billy's chest. Peter plucked the pack of cigarettes from Billy's front pocket. He squeezed tightly, mangling the pack between his chubby fingers.

"You shouldn't smoke, it's bad for you."

Billy reached for the doorknob, wishing he were on the other side of the door.

"Don't fuck this up, or I'll fuck you up."

"Understood," Billy said as he strained for a breath of air.

\*       \*       \*

The air hung heavy as the threat of a powerful thunderstorm lingered in the early evening sky. The wind had grown steadily more powerful as the day progressed, and the weatherman was calling for buckets of rain.

Jackie sat on the front step between Alan and his mother and soft-tossed pebbles at imaginary targets. He couldn't get his mind off the fact that there was a gun in the trailer and that Billy Barth was the enemy William was talking about.

"It's going to rain," Alan said. "It sure rains a lot here."

"We'd better get inside," Anna said, feigning a smile.

"Hey, look who's coming," Alan said, pointing out Billy.

"Let's get inside," Anna said.

The rain pelted the dirt road. Jackie got to his feet and stared after Billy. Anna followed Alan inside the door as Billy's car pulled up.

"Get in here," Anna said to Jackie. "Come on, don't worry about him."

Jackie wished that Barth would look at him.

"I'm not afraid of him," Jackie whispered. He ducked inside the front door, out of the rain.

\*     \*     \*

Billy sat in the entranceway of the Graybar apartment complex. The rain danced on the sidewalk beyond the overhang. He smoked his third cigarette in less than a half an hour and cursed the fact that Miller hadn't appeared.

Billy took another long drag on the Marlboro and began humming. He thought of his love for Anna. Lately, he always had a song in his heart. His love would carry him through.

*I'll be home soon, honey. I have to work late, but I'll be near you soon.*

Billy laughed softly, but all at once his mind shifted to the look of confrontation in the eyes of the youngest boy.

*It's going to be a lot of work to make you love me, but I'll do it.*

No sooner had the thought slipped from his mind when Billy noticed the approach of Tony's car. Billy clapped his hands excitedly.

He shielded himself behind a row of bushes. The intensity of the rain increased, and Billy knew everything was in his favor now. The attack would be quick, and the rain would block out Tony's cries.

Billy pulled the ski mask over his face and snapped on dark, leather gloves. Adrenaline surged through his body. He wrapped the chain tight in his hands, thinking about what a good time he was having. He almost felt bad about taking Peter's money.

Tony looked at the keys in his hand. Billy was close enough to hear the cop whistle a tune. Billy positioned the chain and jumped out, catching the officer tight around the neck.

\*     \*     \*

Billy was on the run. His heart thumped and the feeling of excitement coursed through his veins. He had done the job very well. The sight of the officer's blood had turned Billy's mind into a frenzy as he thought of yanking on the chain.

*Who gives a fuck if I killed him?*

Hannratty's directions streamed back to his brain. He was only supposed to rough him up.

*They can't pin it on me. I was perfect.*

The street lights seemed a bit too bright. Billy slowed to a fast walk, tucking the mask and gloves into his back pocket.

*I'll be home soon to make love, my sweet Anna.*

*       *       *

Billy sauntered into the lot as if returning home from an evening at the coffee shop. His hands were stuffed deep into his pockets, and he was whistling the tune that Tony was whistling just before the attack. It felt good to be whistling again and to know that life was nearly perfect.

Billy walked past his own trailer without breaking stride. He strolled to Anna's door as if he had the God-given right to do so. He knocked softly on the door, whistling the tune once more as he waited for Anna to respond. He knew she'd answer the door. After all, deep inside, Anna was as much in love as he was.

"Who's there?" Anna called. Her voice wavered, and Billy wanted to take the fear away.

"It's Billy. Is everything all right?"

"We're fine."

"Is there anything I can do for you before I turn in?" Billy asked. He moved his hand down to the crotch of his pants. He felt a warm sweat on his forehead, and the light rain did little to cool him off.

"No, thank you, everything is fine."

"Okay," Billy sang out.

"Good night," Anna said.

The two words froze Billy in his tracks. She was opening up. Tonight she wished him good night. It would all roll from there.

Billy whistled the now, familiar tune. It had been a real good day.

# CHAPTER TWELVE

As Jackie awoke, the unmistakable smell of bacon and eggs immediately filled his mind, and he faced Alan, who was just a few feet away.

"Alan, Mom's making breakfast."

Alan turned over.

"What time does the bus come?" Alan asked.

"Seven-thirty, but Mom wants us to take the city bus at seven."

"Yeah, we'd better go with her," Alan said.

"It's going to be tough," Jackie said. "School's easier than work."

"This sucks for everyone," Alan said. He got off the mattress. "The kids'll look at us like we're a couple of morons. Who knows what this place is going to be like."

"Boys, breakfast is on the table."

"She sounds like she's in a good mood," Alan said.

"We got to sink or swim," Jackie said. "What else is there?"

Jackie turned the covers back.

"She's got to be nervous," Jackie said. "Let's pretend we're excited about going to school."

"It's a thrill a minute," Alan said.

\*     \*     \*

Billy swung his hard hat as he stepped through the construction gate. Although he hated everything about work, he was actually in good spirits. He had roughed up the cop and had gotten a good night's sleep, and it was wonderful to be in love. Anna had whispered good night. It would be better each and every day. Her love for him was all he'd ever need.

Billy strolled into the scaffolding work area, whistling as he walked. He moved through the debris-littered ground with the grace of a figure skater.

"It is a beautiful morning, isn't it?" Billy asked a worker. From a distance, Billy saw Al Jackson's rapid approach.

"Don't even put the fucking hat on your head," Al said.

Billy froze in place. "What's up?" The happy thoughts were gone.

"You're out of here," Al said. He shot his thumb over his right shoulder. "Get the hell out before the man sees you."

Al was a few feet away.

"What the fuck are you talking about?" Billy asked, spreading his arms in bewilderment.

"Just go," Al said. "Make it easy. Get the hell out."

"Enough's enough," Billy said. "What the fuck's going on?"

"I got instructions to let you go," Al said.

"You better do more explaining than that, you rat fuck bastard."

Al slammed his hard hat to the ground. He was inches from Billy's face. "I spent an hour getting my ass chewed, because you fucked up your after-hours duty." Al's words were followed by a steady stream of spittle which settled on Billy's face. Al strained for his next breath, and his eyes dared Billy to answer. "You almost killed him. What the hell were you thinking?"

Billy held his hand up to stifle the questions. He looked around nervously. "Shut up! We'll all be making license plates."

"Then leave," Al said. "Get out, and don't look back. It ain't worth it." Al bent to pick up his hat. "Some day this is all going to blow up."

Billy stood in place with his hands on his hips. He could walk through the construction gate, or he could face Hanratty. "Fuck it! I ain't afraid of the fat man."

Billy walked toward the office.

\*     \*     \*

Jackie entered the classroom cautiously. He felt the other children's eyes on him, and he hesitated at the front of the room before deciding on a seat in the back. The kids stared at him, and Jackie knew what Alan had been talking about earlier that morning. They were the outsiders, and it would be a long time before they felt comfortable again.

Jackie sat down slowly and immediately looked to the floor. The chatter going on around him seemed almost senseless to him. It was as if the children were speaking another language. The sounds of laughter seemed to be a million miles from his realm of understanding. Jackie was still looking down at the floor when he heard his teacher's voice.

"All right, everyone, let's settle down."

Jackie brought his head up. The teacher smiled slightly as the chatter subsided.

"I see a lot of familiar faces. I remember seeing you in the halls last year, but you're the sixth graders this year. I'm expecting big things from you."

The teacher moved back and forth in front of her desk. She locked eyes with each student. Jackie looked to the floor when her eyes settled on him.

"My name is Miss Ramsey. I'll be seeing your smiling faces every day from now until June. I have a pretty good idea about your reputations as students, but I'll judge all of you equally until you give me reason not to."

Miss Ramsey moved down the aisle and stopped to look at the student directly beside Jackie.

"How's that sound to you, Jeffrey?" Miss Ramsey asked, and there was a wide chorus of laughter.

"What? I didn't do anything yet," Jeffrey said in mock horror.

"Let's keep it that way. By the way, while I know most of you and most of you know one another, we have one brand-new student this year."

Again, Jackie felt every eye in the room on him. He wished he could crawl under the desk.

"Why don't you stand up and introduce yourself?" Miss Ramsey asked.

Jackie didn't make even the slightest of moves, and Miss Ramsey crossed in front of him to her desk. She peered down into a notebook.

"Your name is Gregory, right? No, I'm sorry, it's Jackie Gregory, right?"

Jackie thought of the priest mispronouncing his father's name at the funeral. He shifted nervously in his seat.

"Do you talk?" Miss Ramsey asked.

The students laughed.

"I can talk," Jackie said.

"Okay, why don't you tell us about yourself?"

"No, thank you," Jackie said.

Again, the students laughed uproariously.

"I'm kind of making you," Miss Ramsey said, her smile still intact.

"I'd rather not," Jackie said. His eyes found the far corner of the room. The laughter was enough to send his mind into a frenzy, and he thought he might cry.

"Jackie, come with me," Miss Ramsey said.

She moved to the door, and Jackie struggled to his feet. He wished he could fly away.

"Everyone, please, sit quietly," Miss Ramsey said. "We'll be just outside the door, so you'd better behave, Jeffrey."

The sound of the laughing voices was almost too much for Jackie to take, and he felt so dizzy he wasn't sure he'd make it to the door. He felt Miss Ramsey's arm around his shoulder as she led him from the room.

*     *     *

As Billy walked in the direction of the main office, the anger of losing his job was tempered by the thought of being with Anna. Yet the anger worked its way through his mind and finally rose to the surface.

"They fucking told me to rough him up, and now I'm getting blamed. How did he expect me to do my job if I had to worry about not killing the guy? Hanratty knows the risks."

"They're all a bunch of fucking assholes," Billy said. He dug through his pockets quickly.

"God, I wish I brought a joint," he said, slapping his hand to his forehead without breaking stride.

Billy was oblivious to the traffic passing by him. He was a few hundred feet from the office when Hanratty's Mercedes screeched to a halt in front of him. The back window of the car opened, and Peter stuck his head out.

"Barth! Get in the fucking car!"

Billy took a step toward the vehicle, and the back door flew open. Peter leaned out of the car, and the bright redness of his face froze Billy in his tracks.

"I said, get in this fucking car," Peter screamed.

"I'm getting in," Billy shouted back.

*     *     *

Miss Ramsey was looking at Jackie with eyes filled with pity. Jackie was sure it was a look he'd see for the rest of his life.

"I know how hard it has to be," Miss Ramsey said. "When I was little, I had to move to a new school. My father got a job in Buffalo, and I didn't want to go. But in the end I was glad I did. I made some good friends in Buffalo."

Jackie dropped his eyes away. He wanted to explain everything, but he was afraid he'd cry. That was the last thing he wanted.

"If you try it'll be a lot easier," Miss Ramsey said. "The other kids'll help you get settled. I'll make sure they treat you just fine."

Jackie spun away and looked down the long, empty corridor. He heard the other children talking inside the classroom, and his mind was filled with their jumbled voices.

"It's not the other kids," Jackie said. "I was never worried about making friends with anybody."

Miss Ramsey looked at him quizzically.

"It's my mom and my brother I'm worried about." Jackie looked to the tiled floor. "I'm worried someone's going to take them from me."

Jackie was crying, and he turned away and walked down the long corridor. He wanted to just walk through the big doors and keep on walking. He felt Miss Ramsey's hand on his shoulder.

"I can't even imagine how hard this is, but, I promise, no one will take your mother or your brother away."

Jackie looked into her pretty face. Her eyes were stained with tears and Jackie looked away.

"I've heard so many promises. I don't believe them anymore."

\*       \*       \*

"I'm only going to say this once," Peter folded his chubby hands and placed them into his lap. "Listen carefully, and when I'm through you'll have a chance to speak."

The driver pulled away from the curb, putting up the back window as he moved into traffic.

"If we discuss this rationally, we can reach an understanding."

This was all going wrong. Billy wanted to get into the car with both guns blazing, but the sight of Peter's bright red face stopped him in his tracks. The idea of driving through New Haven in a black Mercedes was making him uncomfortable.

"Last night, William Bennington called me," Peter said. "The man was crying, because his partner was in the hospital with a severe head injury and a trachea that was nearly crushed."

"You told me to rough him up," Billy said.

Peter held his right index finger in front of his nose to silence Billy.

"William's wife died a few years ago. I was the man who took William in, and over the years we've built a healthy, working relationship. Can you even begin to understand what having the police on my side has done for me and my business?"

Billy shrugged, opening his palms wide. Sitting in the back seat of the moving car left him feeling powerless against Peter's soft words.

"I like William I honestly do. I don't want to see my friend upset, and it wasn't my intention to have William hurt by this attack."

Peter poked his finger in the center of Billy's chest.

"I told you it was a special assignment. I don't like sending messages to people, least of all policemen, but Tony was too big for his britches."

"I didn't mean to hurt him like that."

"I said shut the fuck up when I'm talking," Peter said, his voice never rising above a whisper.

"The thing is, Billy, what I've built in the last twenty years is an empire. I have three houses, a dozen expensive cars, and eight prospering businesses. I have mayors and governors bowing to me. I control more people than you can count, and I get off on making people react to me."

Peter's breathing grew heavy, and he sat back and closed his eyes. Billy couldn't help but think he was having a heart attack, but he thought better than to ask.

"Everything I touch turns to gold," Peter said. "And there's a reason for it. I calculate every step I make. That's why I hand out the assignments. I rarely make a mistake, but, when I do, I make amends."

Billy couldn't help but think that getting into the car may have been a fatal mistake.

"Right now, we're on the way to pick up a new friend whom William asked me to help. She's starting a new life for herself, and I'm giving this woman her air to breathe."

Billy's mind was working overtime as he tried to find a way out of the car.

"I have the power to give life and to take it away," Peter said.

Billy actually thought about jumping from the moving car.

"If you listen to me and do as you're told, I won't kill you. Do you understand?"

"Yes," Billy said.

"You can believe that, too. I never go back on my word."

"Yes, sir," Billy mumbled.

"We're pulling up to a bus stop on Church Street. I'm going to get out and lead a scared and lonely woman into this car and take her back to my office. As I've said, she's a friend of William's, and she deserves the finest treatment. On the way to the office, I'll talk with her, calm her fears, and help her make a smooth transition. You're not to say one word. Do you understand?"

"Yes."

The car eased into a spot directly behind the city bus.

"When we return to the office, we'll make a deal that'll benefit both of us regarding this unfortunate incident involving Officer Miller. Is that understood?"

"Yes, sir," Billy said. He looked at the passengers exiting the bus. His mind was a whirlwind of confusion. He avoided looking directly at Hanratty.

"If you say a word on this trip, I'll kill you Billy I promise you, I'll do it."

Billy nodded. Hanratty meant every word, and Billy would do as directed.

"That's good, Billy," Hanratty said. The window separating them from the driver was lowered slowly.

"Mister Hanratty," the driver said, "I believe your passenger is the lovely woman in the light blue blouse."

"So she is," Peter said.

Billy caught Anna's approach just as Peter opened the back door.

"Oh, Jesus Christ," Billy said. He inched forward in the seat and dropped his head. He wondered how he'd keep from blacking out.

# CHAPTER THIRTEEN

Panic swept through Billy's body as Peter led Anna into the car by offering a chubby hand. Billy looked to the spot where their hands met, and sweat broke out on his forehead. His eyes bulged with rage, and he faced the side window.

"William said you were beautiful," Peter said, "but he, honestly, didn't do you justice."

Peter moved closer to Billy and turned in the seat so he could face Anna. Billy saw the shocked look of recognition on Anna's face.

"This is my construction labor foreman, Billy Barth. Say hello, Billy."

"Hello," Billy said. Anna looked away.

"William's told me all about you," Peter said. "The easiest way for you to make the transition into your new role is for me to meet you and show you around."

Billy watched the road pass by outside the window. He was certain that he couldn't face Anna.

"The first day on any job is the toughest," Peter said. "When William sends someone to me under strained circumstances, I go out of my way a little to make that person feel comfortable."

"I appreciate it," Anna said.

The sound of her voice made Billy's heart ache.

"Have you ever ridden in a Mercedes before?"

"No, sir."

"I have one rule I'm going to hold you to. You're to call me Peter."

Billy stole a quick glimpse of Anna. Her emerald green eyes were shining, and she was giving Hanratty every ounce of her attention.

"I heard about your husband and I'm truly sorry. He was probably a very fine man."

Anna nodded. She offered a slight smile and looked to her lap. Billy wished he could jump over the top of Hanratty and hug her to him.

"Thank you, for the job," Anna said.

"It's the least I can do," Peter said. He placed his fat hand on Anna's shoulder, and Billy fought an urge to punch Peter in the back of the head.

"It's William you have to thank," Peter said.

Billy turned back to the view from the side window as the driver pulled the Mercedes onto Interstate 95. The feeling of hate grew in his mind, and he knew he'd have to say something to get Anna's attention away from Hanratty's goodwill speech. He remembered Hanratty's threat of death and looked away once more.

"The job'll be a challenge for you. I have an extremely busy office, and you'll be working with two girls who've been with me for a long time. Justine and Sonia are extremely personable and very competent, but lately they've been all over me to get some help."

"I don't know much about much," Anna said, "but I'll try."

"You'll do fine," Peter said.

Peter's hand was still resting on Anna's shoulder.

"This first week will be spent learning. I have a huge operation, and you'll need to find a place where you can help. Life is about fitting in and doing the job correctly."

Billy felt Hanratty's eyes on him.

"Isn't that right, Billy?" Peter asked. "The meeting Billy and I were having this morning was all about that, wasn't it?"

"Yes," Billy said.

Billy couldn't wait for it to end. Anna was seeing him bow to the fat man, and it was humiliating.

"Justine and Sonia will show you what to do. I'll let you set your own schedule. I know you have to watch after your boys, but I expect a good day's work from all my employees, I'm sure you won't disappoint."

"I'll do my best."

Peter let out a booming laugh that rang in Billy's ears.

"You're so scared. I don't know what William told you, but I don't bite. Billy, I don't bite, do I?"

"You're always fair," Billy said.

The car pulled into the office lot. The only thought in Billy's mind was that someday he'd kill Peter. The embarrassment of having to sit quietly like an obedient child was too much to handle. Someday, Anna would know that Billy bowed to no one.

*　　*　　*

Jackie followed the children to the playground. Their shouts of celebration sounded in his ears, and, again, Jackie felt alone. He walked onto the soccer field, wishing he could, somehow, become invisible to everyone.

The children chose up sides and Miss Ramsey refereed the procedure, making sure each child was chosen. She handed out light green T-shirts to distinguish the two sides. Jackie heard his name mentioned, and he was motioned over to the far side of the field by a short, fat kid. Mindlessly, Jackie crossed to the child's side.

"I'm Brian, you're on my team."

"I'm not very good," Jackie said.

"You'll be all right," Brian said. "Stay out of the way."

Jackie moved toward the sideline. He wanted to grab Brian by the face and tell him that none of this was important. He wanted to run from the playground with his hands in the air to let everyone know he was giving up. He heard his name being called above the chatter, but he kept walking away.

"Jackie, you're on the green team," Miss Ramsey called.

"I'm not playing," Jackie called back.

He wasn't sure where he'd go. He heard Miss Ramsey tell the other children to start the game. Jackie knew she was following him across the huge playing field, but he continued to walk away. He sat on the front steps of the school and avoided looking at the playing field. In a matter of minutes, Miss Ramsey sat beside him.

"You have to play with the others."

Jackie could smell her perfume. He looked up at her, but the words wouldn't come. He didn't know how he could explain that none of it mattered.

"What's wrong?" Miss Ramsey asked.

"I want to stay out of the way," Jackie said, finally. He crossed his arms in defiance.

"Is someone bugging you?" Miss Ramsey asked. Jackie shook his head.

"I can stop people from picking on you."

Jackie looked to the field. The children ran, kicking the ball back and forth, and screaming as if the game were the most important thing in the world.

"We didn't have anywhere to stay," Jackie said. "My dad died, and we didn't have anywhere to go."

Jackie looked into Miss Ramsey's eyes. He paused, not sure if he wanted to continue.

"This guy came and met us at the hotel and asked us to go with him. He said he had a place for us, and he took us there."

"People will help you," Miss Ramsey said. "There are a lot of good people in the world."

"But he's not good, " Jackie said. "The cops arrested him before for a lot of things, and I'm scared. That's why playing soccer doesn't matter. I'm worried about what he'll do to us."

Miss Ramsey looked at him thoughtfully. She pinched her lower lip with her left hand, and Jackie could tell she was searching for the right words.

"The way I see it," Miss Ramsey said, "is that your mom probably realized this guy isn't the best guy in the world, either. Everything's going to be all right, you'll see. The police officer will help."

"But we have to help ourselves."

"That's true, but you're a little boy. You can't let this bother you so much."

"I know," Jackie said. He watched the children running up and down the field. "I want to be like the other kids, but I'm not. Dad said I worried too much, but I can't help it."

Miss Ramsey had tears in her eyes. She put her hand on Jackie's shoulder.

"When I was a little girl I used to worry, too. I used to think I'd never be as pretty as the other girls. I was real skinny when I was your age, and I was worried I'd never be like the other kids."

"You're plenty pretty enough," Jackie said.

Miss Ramsey laughed nervously.

"Thank you, but being worried didn't get me anywhere. You know the best way to do things is to face them head-on. If you're afraid of this guy, remember that, and then just live with it, you know? You don't have to like the guy, but you need a place to stay so you should make the best of it."

"I know," Jackie said. "We got to go on."

"Why don't you come out and play ball with the other kids? When things settle down, you'll really like living here. Pretty soon, you'll wonder why you worried about anything."

"It's really hard," Jackie said.

"I know." Miss Ramsey smiled brightly. "When I was real skinny and real ugly, I never thought it'd go away. You have to be tough."

"I'm tough," Jackie mumbled.

"You want to play with the green team?"

"Yeah, I'll play," Jackie said.

Miss Ramsey walked beside him as he moved toward the field. He was tough enough to play, and he would face it. As he ran onto the field, Jackie's mind shifted away from the thought of Billy. The ball quickly came to him, and he kicked it up the field and ran after it.

*　　*　　*

Peter ushered Anna through the office. Billy walked behind them so as not to miss a word. Sonia and Justine moved about the office, and the sound of a ringing telephone diverted their attention away from Peter and Anna's entrance.

"As you can see," Peter said as he waved a hand around, "what we have here is an organized mess. Sonia and Justine have worked long and hard to create this mess, and now the three of you will uncreate it."

Anna nodded and smiled, and the brightness of her smile tore at Billy's insides. Anna looked as nervous as a mouse in a maze, but Billy couldn't take his eyes away.

"As you can see, some of the filing has gotten the better of us. We work using purchase order forms, requisitions, and proofs of sale. We have a very diversified bookkeeping procedure but one that works, when you do everything right. When William called me to offer your services, I immediately thought of adding you to this office. It's important to run a professional operation, and it's getting out of hand."

Peter turned away and motioned Billy to a chair outside his office door.

"Mister Barth," Peter said, "give me a moment to introduce Anna, and I'll be right with you."

Billy moved to the chair. He'd wait all day if it meant having the chance to watch Anna.

"Girls, come here a minute," Hanratty said. "I want you to meet Anna."

Justine finished her telephone conversation and joined Sonia.

"Sonia Harrison, this is Anna Gregory," Peter played master of ceremonies.

"Hi," Anna offered weakly. The sound of her voice sent a shiver down Billy's spine.

"It's nice to meet you," Sonia said. "I hope you can help us. Just answering the telephone will free us up a little."

"Sonia's worried about getting out earlier," Peter said. "She just got married, and she likes to be home a little more."

"He works us like dogs," Sonia said, her light brown eyes flickering with a hint of happiness.

Billy watched the introductions with little enthusiasm. He was thinking about how he could slip out of work for the day and have dinner waiting for Anna when she returned home.

*I'll get steaks and a bottle of wine. When she comes home with the kids, I'll have it all setup. It'll be just our family.*

"Don't worry about Peter," Justine said. "His bark is worse than his bite. We do the real work around here."

"All I know," Peter said, ignoring Justine's playful look, "is that you'd better treat Anna right, and you better get the paperwork system flowing again."

Peter took Anna's right hand between his two fat hands.

"Take your time. Have a cup of coffee, and take a look around. The girls are top-notch. They'll explain everything to you, and my office is always open."

"Thank you," Anna managed. She scanned the office, and Peter allowed her hand to slide free.

"Now, if you'll excuse me for a moment, I have some business to attend to."

Peter walked toward Billy. For a brief moment, Billy caught Anna's eye. She looked to the floor, and rage burned inside Billy's mind. Peter was making her act differently.

"Barth, get in my office," Peter said.

Billy followed Peter into the office. He turned and looked back in Anna's direction. He smiled out to her, but she wasn't looking at him.

*       *       *

Peter's office was a picture of organization. Management books lined the bookcase along the back wall. The desk held a calendar, one loose-leaf notebook, and two pictures; one of a young Frank Sinatra and the other of a snarling German shepherd. Peter said they reflected his gentle and aggressive sides.

Peter entered the room and shuffled slowly behind the big desk. He waited for Billy to close the door before sweeping the desk clean with one angry push.

"What the fuck were you thinking?"

Billy took a step backwards. He wished he could've crawled under the door. Peter's face was bright red, and the veins in his neck were standing out at attention. Billy was sure the fat man was about to have a heart attack and collapse face-first on the desk.

*It'd solve a lot of problems.*

"Where the fuck is your brain?"

Billy shrugged as the feeling of resolve surged through him once more, and the thought of Anna took control. Billy stepped by Peter, moving to the seat behind the desk. He hadn't thought Peter's face could grow any redder, but his ass in the big man's chair had done the trick.

"My brain's here, don't worry about that, and it's telling me you have more to lose than I do." Billy set his feet on the desk and reached into his shirt pocket for a smoke. "Unless you plan on killing me, I suggest we talk."

"Get your feet off my desk," Peter said. He slapped at the bottom of Billy's shoes.

"The way I see it, I can go straight to the cops."

"You did it," Peter said.

"You hired me to do it," Billy said. "If I go to them with that, you'll be watched carefully."

Billy was pushing Hanratty about as far as the man could be pushed. He slid out of Hanratty's chair and directed Peter to it with a smile.

"We'll get through this," Billy said. "I figure all we got to do is outsmart Bennington." He lit the cigarette. "It shouldn't be that difficult."

Peter sat behind the desk. He bent to retrieve the picture of the snarling dog.

"I want you to stay away from this," Peter said. "I'll take care of it now. If that cop dies, I swear to God, this isn't going to be a laughing matter."

"Oh, I plan on staying away from it, but I want more money. I handled my end of it." Billy blew a smoke ring into the air.

The intercom buzzed, and Sonia's voice filled the room.

"Mister Hanratty, William Bennington is on line three."

Billy smiled brightly. He thought about winking but decided not to press his luck.

"Have him hang on for a minute," Peter said.

Peter stood up slowly. Absolute disgust covered his fat face. It wasn't often that Peter was up against the wall.

"I'm going to put William on the speaker phone. I suggest you pay attention to what he says, because your future is hanging by a thread right now." Peter leaned to the intercom. "Sonia, put William through."

Billy couldn't believe his ears. He had stood up to Hanratty, and, still, the man was making threats. Billy entertained the thought of screaming out what happened so Bennington could come down and slap the cuffs on Hanratty's thick wrists. Of course, the thought left his brain as quickly as it came.

"William, how's Tony doing?" Peter asked. "Is there anything I can do to help?"

"I have to find out who did this," William said. His voice through the intercom was strong and clear.

"You know, I'll do whatever I can," Peter said. His eyes didn't leave Billy's face. For a moment, Billy thought he read anxiety in Peter's stare.

"He's in rough shape," William said. "Like I told you last night, I thought he was dead."

"How could something like this happen?" Peter softly asked.

"I don't know," William said. "I need you to help. Have you heard anything since we talked?"

"Not a word," Peter said. "But I'm going to make sure I *do* hear something. I know a lot of people. I'll figure it out."

Peter slammed his fist on the desk, and, if Billy weren't a part of it all, he would've sworn that the facts of Tony's beating simply infuriated Hanratty. Billy smiled smugly, shaking his head.

"It was a real sloppy beating," William said. "Part of me wants to think it was some low-life thug, but I just don't know."

"I'll help figure it out," Peter said. "Sons of bitches, this shit's got to stop."

"I have to know who did this," William said softly.

"You will," Peter answered. "We'll find the bastard."

The look on Peter's face sent a shiver of fear up Billy's spine.

# CHAPTER FOURTEEN

"So how do we get around this?" Peter asked as he clicked off the telephone line.

"I think I should still work for you," Billy said. "It'd look kind of funny if you fire me the day after it happens."

Peter contemplated the statement, twirling a pencil around in his fat fingers.

"All right," Peter said, finally. "Go back to work. What else?"

Billy felt a little as if he had Peter on the run.

"I want the rest of the money for the job. You gave me two hundred and said there'd be more if I did the job right. I did the job."

Peter's face reddened before Billy's eyes. It looked as if he'd been slapped. Peter leaned back in the chair. He dug his hand into his front pants pocket and extracted a wad of bills. He took a couple off the top and placed them on the desk.

"You realize I can kill you without even moving from this seat."

Billy nodded, knowing it was true.

"I could call your foreman right now and arrange an accident. I could have you gutted like a deer, or I could pick you off in the middle of the night."

"I got the idea," Billy said.

"If I even hear so much as a rumor that you've stepped out of line, I'll do it." Peter paused, leaning closer to Billy's worried face.

"I learned a long time ago that for every action there's a stronger reaction." Peter looked as if he were straining for his next breath. He casually moved the money across the desk. "There's a price to pay for everything. Sometimes we pay the price with anger in our hearts, but, occasionally, we get to pay the price with a smile on our lips. If you betray me, I'll pay you back with a huge, shit-eating grin."

Peter grinned, and Billy darted his eyes toward the floor, away from the smile.

"Is there anything else?" Peter asked.

Billy sized up the situation in his mind. In the span of a couple of minutes, Hanratty had offered him money, threatened his life, and smiled at him like a cheerleader as he promised eternal revenge.

"Well, now that you mention it," Billy said, "I'd like to have the rest of the day off. I got a hot date tonight. I'm in love, you know."

Peter laughed uproariously. He tossed his head back and howled in exaggerated delight.

"Do what you have to do, Barth," Peter said between guffaws. "But keep your fucking mouth shut, or you'll pay the price."

Billy reached for the money on the desk and Hanratty slapped a fat hand down on top of Billy's.

"That's a fucking promise."

"I got it, boss."

Hanratty allowed Billy to slide his hand free. Billy put the money in his front shirt pocket and nodded at Hanratty before turning away toward the door. Billy couldn't help but think that it had gone according to plan.

*     *     *

As Billy re-entered the front lobby from Hanratty's office, his eyes settled on Anna's bowed head. Anna sat at Justine's desk, mindlessly nodding as Sonia rattled on about purchase orders and the rest of Hanratty's happy bullshit. Anna looked like a scared child on the first day of school, and Billy fought the urge to go to her and take her into his arms. How he hated that he had to leave her here.

"You keep the original here for Peter's signature and then make a copy and file it in sequential order and log it into this book."

Sonia was running through the instructions as if she were reciting the alphabet, and Anna continued nodding. All at once, Sonia shot a look of annoyance in Billy's direction. A strange cry of fear worked through Billy's mind.

"What?" Sonia asked. "What do you want?"

"I wanted to wish Anna luck," Billy said as he took a step closer to the desk.

"Get out," Sonia said. "She's got enough on her mind without you bothering her."

Billy looked directly into Anna's scared eyes.

*She's so fucking beautiful.* His mind was clear of all thoughts of Tony Miller and Peter Hanratty. *She's the only one that's important, the only one. She's my life and my love, and everything else is bullshit.*

Billy tried to will the words into Anna's mind.

"Good luck, ma'am," Billy said. He turned and walked to the door. As he swung the door open, bright sunshine fell across his face.

*     *     *

No one would ever be able to say that Billy Barth didn't know how to treat his women. Billy returned to his trailer and began his plan of seduction with a long, hot shower. He shaved his face and dressed in a suit. His actions were slow and deliberate, each seeming as if it were being performed in a dizzy, smoke-filled haze.

Billy went from store to store, picking the tools of his pursuit. Visions of the coming night exploded into his brain, and he hardly remembered the trip. He stopped at the grocery store for four porterhouse steaks, a half-dozen ears of corn, and prepared macaroni salad. At the bakery he chose a two-layer, chocolate cake.

"My two boys are going to love this," he told the girl at the bakery.

Billy also stopped by the liquor store for a bottle of white wine. A stop at the florist provided a dozen long-stemmed roses.

Finally, Billy searched the town for a small barbecue grill, a red-and-white tablecloth, and the necessary charcoal and lighter fluid. Over and over in his mind, Billy knew it would be a night to remember forever. On their anniversaries together, Anna would laugh at him for the trouble he went through to set up their first date. From this day forward, everyone would know that she was his. She would realize that her life could go on without Nelson.

*It's truly the first night of the rest of our lives.*

\*     \*     \*

At a little before four o'clock, Billy made a grand spectacle of himself in the trailer lot on Church Street. He paused for a moment to take in the scene that he'd worked so hard to put together.

The picnic table in the center of the lot was perfectly decorated. There were four places set with roses as the centerpiece. The steaks were ready for the fire and the sun was smiling down on the dinner plans.

*Pure destiny. This love is pure destiny. Anna's name is written on the wind. Tonight I'll make her mine.*

Billy wiped his hands on his apron. He took a heavy gulp of air, feeling as though he'd pass out from the joy in his heart.

\*     \*     \*

Jackie sat, alone, on the front step of the school building. The sun shone in his eyes and he wiped the sweat on his forehead. He squinted his eyes and looked to the place where the cross-town bus would be pulling up. He wondered where Alan was and how his day had gone. He hoped it hadn't been as weird for Alan as it had for him, and he traced the ache in his heart to worry over his mother and how they'd handle it every day.

Jackie shook his head to rid himself of the urge to cry. He knew Miss Ramsey was right, and they'd have to face their challenges. If Billy was going to be the problem, they'd have to meet him face-to-face and solve it. A surge of energy swelled inside of him, and he wiped the sweat away again and gained his feet. He saw his brother coming toward him with two other children. They were all laughing as if life were a picnic.

The bus pulled to a stop, and Jackie descended the front steps and made his way across the school yard. He saw his mother come down the steps, and Jackie struggled to stifle the urge to run to her.

*　　*　　*

Billy flipped the steaks as the bus came to a stop in front of the trailer lot. Billy's heart jumped in his chest as the older boy bounded down the steps. His heart was firmly in his mouth when Anna made her way into his line of vision. She held hands with the younger boy and stopped dead in her tracks when she noticed Billy.

*Please, God, please let 'em keep walking.* Billy's mind drifted to utter panic. He held the barbecue fork in his right hand and tried to fix a smile upon his face. When Anna and the boys began walking again, Billy knew it was time to take control.

"It's a beautiful day for a barbecue," he sang out. He opened his arms wide and gazed toward the sky.

"Yes, it is," Anna said, but Billy heard apprehension in her voice.

*Don't worry, baby, I'll make it all right.*

"I hope you don't mind, but I thought it'd be neighborly of me to make dinner. I know the first day of work is stressful."

They were right in front of him, and Billy felt the weight of each eye looking back at him. He saw a strange look of confusion crossing Anna's face, and, all at once, she looked down at the ground away from Billy's eyes. Rage burned across Billy's mind, and he swallowed hard to regain his perspective. He caught the eye of the older boy who seemed to be looking beyond him at the steaks.

"What do you say?" Billy asked. "You want a steak?" The older boy nodded as the voice inside Billy's head pleaded with God for Anna's approval.

"Let's do it," the younger boy said suddenly, and Billy turned his head in a whiplike motion to look into the kid's demanding eyes.

"We've got to live next to him. Let's be friends."

"I don't know," Anna said.

Billy's heart was racing. He was so close, and he hoped the kid with the wide, staring eyes didn't cave in.

"We have to get to know him, or we'll never be able to live next door to him."

When Anna shook her head, Billy noticed a single tear racing down her left cheek. He wished he could kiss her tears away. Instead, Billy remained silent, hoping she would see it his way.

"I really want a steak," the older boy said, and Billy knew he'd win.

Anna pulled her sons close to her bosom. For the first time, she allowed her eyes to meet Billy's.

"Okay," she said. "We'll have dinner with you."

*     *     *

Jackie kept a close watch on Billy's movements. He couldn't stop thinking about the gun, and over and over in his mind he replayed his conversation with Miss Ramsey. They had to solve this problem, even though he knew that there was something desperately wrong with Billy.

Jackie heard only snippets of his mother's conversation with Alan about the first day of school. Instead, Jackie concentrated on Billy's movements in taking the steaks from the grill.

"I got two medium rare and two well done," Billy announced. He put the meat on the platter and Anna cleared a spot on the table. The heat rose from the steaks, and, for a moment, Jackie followed its ascent skyward.

"What are you waiting for?" Billy asked. "Dig in."

Billy smiled directly at Anna, and Jackie saw the strange look behind Billy's crazed eyes. Alan moved across Jackie's line of vision, reaching across his mother to grab one of the steaks. Mindlessly, Jackie followed his brother's lead and plopped the meat down on his plate. He would have to go along with it.

*     *     *

Billy concentrated on cutting the steak into small pieces. Realizing his actions were almost maniacal, he took a piece of the steak on the end of the fork and slowly and deliberately brought it to his mouth. He smiled at Anna as he began to chew the steak, and, for a fleeting moment, it looked as if she were about to smile back.

"How is it?" Billy asked.

"It's great," the older boy said. The kid's words were muddled, as he had answered in mid-chew.

"Alan," Anna said, "don't talk with a full mouth."

"This is a picnic. Anything goes," Billy said.

Alan looked smugly back at his mother, and Billy realized that he may have found an ally.

"How's your steak?" Billy asked Anna. His brain was clouded with nervousness as he awaited her answer.

"It's real good, thank you," Anna said. Her face was flush, and Billy found her embarrassment to be nothing short of a complete turn-on. He masked the excitement with a quick look toward the younger boy.

"How about you, Jackie?" Billy asked. The kid just glared back at him.

"What's the matter? No good?" Billy asked, trying to appear jovial. He followed Anna's eyes as she peered at Jackie.

"He don't like his," Billy said nervously. Alan shrugged in response. "Maybe you'll have to finish it for him." Again, Billy tried to make it appear that he wasn't dying inside.

*That kid's going to fuck it all up.*

"When this dinner's over, you're going to leave us alone," Jackie whispered.

"What's that?" Billy asked. He wiped at the sweat he imagined on his brow.

"No more dinners," Jackie said. The kid raised his head in defiance, and a shudder of fear raced through Billy's heart. The kid's stare was enough to bore a hole right through Billy's forehead.

Billy looked at his plate. He tried a silent prayer to control his rage.

\*     \*     \*

Jackie needed Alan's help. The television played static, but the sound of it put Anna to sleep. After a couple of moments, Jackie caught his brother's eye. He motioned for Alan to join him in the back room.

"What?" Alan asked in full voice. Jackie held his index finger to his lips, and, once inside the back room, he pulled the gun from under his shirt. Alan's eyes looked as if they were about to bug out of his head.

"Where'd you get that?"

"Bennington brought it," Jackie said. He turned the gun over to allow Alan to get a good look. "He said we need it for protection."

"Put it away," Alan said.

"We need it," Jackie said. "Billy's going to try and come back, and we'll need it to scare him away."

Alan was still looking at the gun as if it might come to life and attack them.

"I know how to load it," Jackie said. "We should get it ready just in case."

Alan considered the thought for a moment.

"If he comes in, it has to be ready," Jackie said.

Alan finally nodded in approval.

"Okay," Alan said. "Load it, but, when we go to bed tonight, I get to hold it. I'm older."

Jackie thought better of protesting, figuring that it really didn't matter who held the gun. Billy would see it and run off and that was all that mattered. Slowly and deftly, Jackie loaded a single bullet into the gun.

*　　*　　*

Billy sat alone in the trailer. He worked overtime to control his anger and frustration. He was on the verge of insanity, and, if this was going to be the night he would remember for the rest of his life, he needed to gain control.

*She does love me. It's just that insane fucking kid. That kid has hate in his eyes. That kid doesn't understand I could be the daddy he needs. That kid's going to have to be out of the way if I'm going to make it with Anna. That kid just might have to be choked to death.*

Billy's words started as thoughts, but, halfway through his mental dissertation, they were screams of anguish. He jumped from his spot on the couch, pounding his fist into his palm.

*Stop it! It has to be different this time. No death this time. Calm! Stay fucking calm.*

Billy slapped himself across the face and laughed. His stinging face turned his laugh into a sob.

*I'm fucking losing it again!*

He sat at the kitchen table, digging into the cocaine left over from his encounter with Perry.

*Just two lines, and I'll get myself together and go see her. I'll apologize to the kid. I'll win him over. Tonight, we'll make love.*

Billy laid a line out on the table, and his sob turned to laughter.

*A couple of lines and it'll be fine.*

The buzz circled his mind. A surge of energy enveloped him, and Billy jumped to his feet and clapped for nearly a full minute.

*Tonight's the night.* He plucked his keys from the table and clenched his fist tightly.

*I'm coming to see you, my love.*

He felt as if he were floating to her door.

# CHAPTER FIFTEEN

The door opened slowly, and Anna stood before him. She wore a green nightgown, and there was sleep in her eyes.

"Hi," Billy whispered. He read a look of resignation in her face. She tried to decide what to do as he stood there admiring her.

"Can I come in?"

Anna didn't respond, and the question hung over them like a threatening cloud. All at once, she stepped back to let him in.

"We need to talk about Jackie," Anna said. "Coffee?"

"Sure," Billy said. He did not want to wake the boys.

Anna held the kettle under the tap, looking down into the sink as she did so.

*She's absolute poetry in motion.*

The cocaine took control, and he battled his lust.

"I'm sorry if I scared Jackie. I was trying to be friendly."

Billy sat at the table, looking to the room where the boys were sleeping. He didn't hear any movement.

"It's not your fault," Anna said. "None of us are ourselves yet."

"That's understandable," Billy whispered. "I was trying to figure out a way to help."

Anna placed the kettle on the stove. She moved to the table, and Billy sensed apprehension in her approach.

"What Jackie suggested is probably for the best," Anna said. "We need time to be a family. We have to start over together."

"I understand," Billy said. "I've had to start over a couple of times."

The kettle began hissing, and Billy's eyes were drawn to the steam. Anna sat in the seat across the table. She offered a half-smile, and Billy knew it was time to take the stage.

"I had a girlfriend." He held his hands together, looking to his thumbs. "We were getting married. Then, one minute she was here, and then she was gone."

The tea kettle made its first attempt at a whistle, and Anna moved to it quickly. Billy gained his feet and followed her to the stove.

"She was murdered on the streets," Billy said to Anna's back, and she snapped her head around quickly.

"Someone picked her up out of the park. Whoever did it was a real monster. He took her up to New York, raped her, and killed her. They found her body behind a rest stop picnic table in Stamford."

Billy bowed his head, placed his hands over his face, and sighed deeply. "They never found the guy."

He raised his head slowly, wiping at tears in the corners of his eyes. They were tears that he didn't even have to fake as in his reeling mind, he honestly believed his love had been taken away.

"I wanted to die right at the moment I heard," Billy said, his voice crackling with emotion.

Anna didn't look at him. She poured the water, and Billy noticed her right hand which was shaking ever so slightly.

"They asked me to identify the body," Billy said. "I barely recognized her, but I'll never shake the image of her naked, black-and-blue body."

Billy returned to the table and sat down. Anna slid a cup of coffee to him and sat across from him.

"Gina wanted to be a dancer," Billy said. "We were going to go to California so she could dance in the movies." The tears were flowing freely from his eyes, and Billy had to breathe deep to gain control. "Someone took it all way from us."

"I'm sorry," Anna said.

"You have your own problems. It was a long time ago."

"I don't know what to say," Anna said.

Billy smiled through his tears.

"I drank a lot when it first happened. I lost my job and couldn't stay in my trailer, but God gave me the strength to go on."

Billy sipped the coffee. He actually wondered how far he could take the story. It was coming so easy, and Anna was showing true compassion.

"It was weird. One night, I was drifting in and out of sleep, and I swear I heard God's voice."

Anna leaned across the table to hear him. She held the coffee cup tightly with both hands, and Billy looked away from her eyes, hoping he could continue to find the words.

"I actually heard Him and started to weep. Right there in that bed, I begged Him to give me the strength to go on. I wept like a baby. God's voice told me to make her memory special. He told me He wanted to work His will through me. That was over a year ago, and it still feels like last night."

The excitement surged through Billy's body. Anna's mouth was open, and she seemed to be hanging on his every word. Billy sipped the coffee in an attempt to further calm himself.

"I met Peter after that, and he gave me my job. He got me back on my feet again."

"I owe Peter a great debt," Anna said.

"He's a good man," Billy said. He brought the cup to his lips. He looked into Anna's eyes for a long moment. He saw a certain light flickering in those eyes. The feeling down below his belt was beginning to crest, and Billy knew he had to take the charade even a step further.

"I go to church every week. I pray to God for acceptance with Gina's passing. I've learned to believe that she's in a better world. She's doing better things now, and she's waiting for me." Billy forced a tear. "I know she's still waiting for me."

Anna patted his hand softly and smiled.

Billy groped at her hand. Anna didn't fight him, and for a moment their hands met. By the time Anna moved her hand back toward her coffee cup, Billy knew he couldn't hold back any longer.

He quickly got to his feet. He took a long gulp of the coffee and started toward the stove.

"The water's still hot, isn't it?" His voice sounded hurried to his own ears, and he picked up the kettle, fearing his mind would go black. "Would you like more?" He tried to calm his voice. He held the kettle in the air as the voice in his head screamed.

"No, thank you," Anna answered, and Billy couldn't tell whether or not her voice had wavered.

Billy nodded and placed the kettle back on the stove. He took a teaspoon of coffee and swirled it around in the hot water. His back was still to her, and Billy was aware he'd have to get it under control before he turned to face her. Billy bit into the left side of his cheek, and the short blast of pain provided an instant moment of clarity. He tasted the blood in his mouth and swallowed hard.

"How have you been able make it through your husband's death?" Billy asked.

"I haven't made it through anything," Anna said. Her voice was now definitely shaking, and Billy had to regain control. He faced her, and the look of fear on her pretty face actually made Billy quiver.

Billy made his way back to the table. He shook his head in an exaggerated show of pity.

"But you really have." Billy smiled. "The children are back in school, and there's a roof over their heads. You've got a job, and those are major accomplishments."

Billy tried hard to forget what it had felt like to touch her hand.

"I'm walking in my sleep," Anna said. "I've had a lot of help, and that's the only reason we have a chance. Peter gave me the job, and Nelson's friend sent money. Officer Bennington has been real sweet, and you were sweet for getting me this place."

Anna smiled, and Billy couldn't fight the screaming in his head.

Slowly, Billy got up. He paced the floor of the trailer behind Anna's chair, and her body seemed to tense right before his eyes. She did not turn to face him, and Billy dropped his hand onto her shoulder.

"You never have to thank me," Billy said. Anna squirmed underneath his grasp, but Billy held her to the chair.

"Love is a beautiful thing," Billy said. "Love can come out of nowhere."

Anna tried to turn around. Billy held tight, caressing her shoulder through the thin nightgown.

"I love you," Billy said.

Anna pushed back in the chair, and it violently scraped across the wooden floor. Billy let go of her shoulder. He moved quickly to the front door. The picture in his head started to go blank, and he heard Anna's voice as if it were coming at him across a field a mile away.

"No, Billy!"

Billy turned back the lock on the trailer door. He didn't have so much as a fleeting thought of the children.

*　　*　　*

Jackie's eyes opened with the sound of the moving chair. He heard his mother's stern command asking Billy to stop.

"Alan," Jackie called in a loud whisper. "He's here."

Alan sat straight up on the old mattress. He moved across to the far side and fished underneath the mattress for the gun.

"Are you sure you want to do it?" Jackie asked.

Alan looked down at the gun for a moment. A blank look of confusion flashed across his face, and Jackie nearly took the gun from his brother's hand.

"I got it," Alan said. "Let's go."

*　　*　　*

Billy grabbed Anna by the shoulders.

"Just a kiss," he said as he pulled her up against him. Anna was fighting him, but Billy was so close that he could feel her breath. He lowered his mouth down onto hers, and a flash of light rolled through his mind. He felt her push hard at the center of his chest. Before he knew what was happening the kiss had been broken, and Anna was moving away from him.

"Please, Billy, just go," Anna said. She backpedaled away from his grasp, and Billy groped the air, reaching for her.

Anna backed up against the couch, and Billy knew she couldn't go any further. He reached for her, and she tried to step back. Anna slipped into a sitting position on the couch.

"I love you. I need you so bad." Billy groped at the button on the front of his jeans. He barely heard her whimpers, but as he pulled his zipper down, he heard a distinct sob escape her body.

"It doesn't have to be this way," Billy whispered. He covered her mouth with his hand. He felt her body underneath him. "Don't wake the boys," he said. Sweat raced down his face, and he blinked his eyes to clear his vision. He reached inside his pants with his left hand.

"Just touch me," he said, looking into Anna's wide, petrified eyes. "Touch me. Love me like I love you."

He pulled her hand to him.

"Look at what you do to me," Billy said. Anna kicked her legs in an effort to break free, but Billy had her under wraps.

"Touch me," Billy whispered. "Imagine it inside of you."

His eyes felt as if they would jump from his head. She pushed him away, but he thrust his body out to her.

"Isn't it nice? It's yours forever," Billy said, relaxing the grip over her mouth as he ripped at the nightgown. Anna kicked furiously, but Billy pressed down to keep her under him. A button flew across the room, and in one swift movement Billy ripped the nightgown free from her body.

"Look how beautiful," Billy said. He placed his hand between her legs, and Anna bucked hard beneath him. Billy fell back off the couch, and Anna jumped up, evading his sweeping arm.

"You're fucking it up!" Billy screamed.

Anna was on her hands and knees crawling toward the bedroom door. Billy got to his feet and stood looking at the older boy, who was shaking the gun out at him.

"No!" Anna screamed.

Billy heard Anna's scream from a world far away. She stood up, and Billy heard the gun blast. Anna stumbled backwards, crashing to the floor. Billy's world went completely blank.

* * *

Billy's ear-piercing scream blasted through the trailer. Jackie felt as if he were frozen to the spot on the floor where he had seen the bullet enter his mother's left eye. The tears came to him. The room spun dizzily out of focus.

"Stay away from her," Jackie said as Billy's second primal scream filled the trailer.

"You killed her you little bastard! She's dead!"

Billy was on top of Anna's body, holding her bloody head in his hands. Jackie stumbled back to the kitchen.

"I killed Mom," Alan cried from a world a million miles away. Alan dropped the gun to the floor, and Jackie realized that they'd put only one bullet in the gun. Quickly, his mind closed in on Bennington's instructions.

*The Colt .45 is capable of firing eight shots.*

Billy kissed Anna's face. The tears and sweat mixed with her blood, and Alan was directly in front of Billy staring down into the horror.

"Look at what you did!" Billy screamed. "Look at her!"

Alan was crying and shaking. Jackie held the bullets in his hand, feeling as if the scene in front of him weren't really happening.

"I didn't want death," Billy cried. "I didn't want death, but now it's here."

Jackie's hands trembled, and the bullets fell to the floor of the trailer. When he regained his feet with the bullets in his hand, he saw Billy's lunge for Alan's throat.

"No!" Jackie screamed. Billy was on top of Alan, choking the life from his body.

"Stand up," Jackie said. He held the gun out in front of him. *Eight shots.* His hand was steady on the trigger. His eyes were on his target, and Billy was crying hard.

"Please," Billy said as he struggled to his knees, extending his hands out before him. "Please don't."

Jackie fired, and the bullet struck Billy in the crotch. Billy didn't fall over backward like Jackie thought he would. Instead, he looked surprised. He stared at the spot where the bullet had entered him.

Jackie brought the gun back up. He aimed for Billy's head. Billy uttered an unintelligible sound. Jackie fired the gun, and Billy screamed out. The bullet hit Billy in the center of the forehead, and he toppled backward, just inches from Alan's dead body.

Jackie stood over the top of Billy. Billy's eyes were open, but the second shot had cut a neat hole in the center of his forehead. Jackie fired again, tearing off Billy's top lip.

*Five more shots.*

He began crying. He aimed for Billy's left ear, and the shot tore the ear clean away from Billy's head. Jackie held the gun steady, six inches away from Billy's skull. He quickly fired twice more. Jackie heard the slam of a car door outside the trailer, but he held his concentration.

*Two more shots.*

Jackie dropped to his knees. There was little left of Billy's head.

"I'm all alone," Jackie said. He shot Billy in the throat. "I'm all alone," he cried as he sent the final bullet into Billy's crotch.

"They're all dead," Jackie said. He buried the barrel of the gun in the opening of Billy's skull.

"I'll never be anything but alone."

Jackie was shaking violently.

# CHAPTER SIXTEEN

Moments later, Jackie heard Bennington's voice. He felt the officer's hand on his shoulder and turned his face toward the man who had tried to help them through his father's death.

"Will I go to jail?" Jackie asked.

"No," William said, simply. "You just have to tell us what happened."

"I won't," Jackie said. "I won't talk to anybody anymore."

Jackie didn't talk to anyone as his mother and brother were laid to rest. He did not utter a single word as the city of New Haven, led by Peter Hanratty, wrapped him in an emotional outpouring of love and sympathy.

It would be a number of years later before Jackie would learn that William Bennington had been terminated from his position as a police officer for handing the gun over to them.

His permanent file would be forever stamped with the words of his state counselor.

*Jackie Gregory—Mental imbalance due to severe psychological damage. Chances of full recovery are nearly non-existent. Jackie's life will forever be one of desperation and pain.*

# PART TWO

"One has to pay dearly for immortality;
one has to die several times while one is still alive.

—Nietzsche

# CHAPTER ONE

*September, 1998*

Counselor Mary Ellen Rossetti moved slowly to the front of the room. She stood behind the lectern and carefully arranged her note cards. Jackie watched her every move with a feeling of utter disdain. In just a few moments time, Rossetti would begin assassinating his character. She would spend the next hour telling everyone that Jackie was mentally unfit to rejoin society. Jackie fully expected Rossetti's dissertation to attack his character; it was the presence of William Bennington and his mother's former boss, Peter Hanratty, that he hadn't imagined.

William and Peter sat side-by-side in the front row. Jackie ran his hand over his unshaven face. Jackie didn't know Hanratty, but he was willing to bet that the man weighed over three hundred pounds. Bennington looked as if he had died all those years ago when they stripped him of his police uniform.

Bennington and Hanratty's presence didn't mean much to Jackie. The way he figured it, that part of his life was over the moment Billy Barth hit the floor. There wasn't any reason to relive it.

Jackie centered in on Rossetti once more. Her head remained bowed as she leafed through her note cards. Jackie had spent countless hours with Rossetti, and he regarded her with little more than indifference. She brought her head up to face her gathering. She nervously flicked her long, black hair back over her right shoulder.

"In the five years I've worked with Jackie Gregory, I have not known him to have a single friend or confidant. He speaks on occasion, but it is usually only out of absolute necessity."

Mary Ellen locked eyes with Jackie and then glanced back to her notes.

"Jackie's lack of communication skills have done little to hinder him as a student. His school work has always been completed to the satisfaction of his teachers. He's quite able to present his ideas in an efficient manner, showing great skills in reading, writing, and math. However, the work very often fails to hold his interest. Also, due to his lack of complete social interaction, he often received lower grades than what he deserved. Jackie's ideas aren't normal, and, from day one, he's existed in his own educational world."

William shot a hurried hand into the air and Rossetti nodded.

"Do you have an example?"

Rossetti carefully paged through a spiral notebook. To Jackie, she seemed slightly annoyed by the interruption but determined to prove her point.

"This is Jackie's journal entry from February third. His assignment was to write about how it felt to win or lose. The object of the lesson was to capture emotions in either regard."

Mary Ellen smiled nervously at William before continuing.

"Not surprisingly, Jackie chose what it felt like for him to lose. Let me further preface this by saying that most of the students talked of winning or losing a ballgame. Jackie's was by far the strangest of all the works, and I'd like to read it to you in its completed form. It is entitled *Losing at Life and Death.*

*"I have surrounded myself with grief. Doing this has allowed me the opportunity to extend a tremendous amount of hatred towards myself. While I have had a few, fleeting pleasant moments, and though I'm a young man, I often dream back in time to the days when I had a chance to survive. Up to this point in my life, in order to mask my feelings of inadequacy, I have lived a life of certain solitude. It's an inevitable fact that can't be changed by time. Often times, I torture myself into believing I am a demon, one that is constantly scorned by beastly images.*

*"Love is a completely separate entity that deserves a proper identity. It honestly deserves a different perspective, perhaps, from someone with a more fortunate background. I've been hurting myself by attempting to disregard the gnawing feelings within my heart. When you talk about loss, I guess it is safe to say that I have lost my soul.*

*"Death is the only certainty in that no one has ever survived it. Even if I were to live to tell of my experience of death, I would fail miserably in that I was never, truly, alive to experience life. Therefore, I feel I am losing again, as I can not continue with this assignment."*

Mary Ellen sent her dark eyes out across the silent room. Jackie smiled slightly at the thought and shrugged his shoulders at Rossetti as if to show it meant little.

"A lot of people write bleak stories," Hanratty said.

"Do they believe them?" Mary Ellen asked. "Do they live them?"

Jackie moved forward in his chair. Mary Ellen was looking at him, waiting for him to defend himself but Jackie simply smiled.

"Jackie was disciplined on a number of occasions. At the age of thirteen, his counselor withheld dinner privileges for a day, because Jackie defaced his bedside lamp shade. In magic marker, Jackie had written the words, *Desperate people must live in pain.*

"Jackie's counselor administered the punishment, because, frankly, he was a little confused as to why such a thought would come from a boy's mind. The punishment, of course, did not faze Jackie."

Mary Ellen paced the floor in front of the lectern. To Jackie it looked as if she were gaining confidence in her attempt to prove him incompetent to enter the outside world.

"Jackie was also punished by his eighth-grade teacher for exhibiting behavior detrimental to the welfare of the student body. It is not certain, exactly, what Jackie had done, but, when pressed for an answer, the teacher who handed out the penalty said that Jackie was a 'walking time bomb.'"

"You never even found out what was bothering him?" Peter asked. He looked back at Jackie, but Mary Ellen cut off any possible exchange.

"We attempt guidance and rehabilitation for children like Jackie. We attempt to guide with temperance and good values. We apply different techniques to each child and attempt to alleviate the distressing behavior by looking at the cause of the behavior. In Jackie's case, we knew right where to start. We tried to elicit feelings left over from his family situation, and he wouldn't answer our questions. We toyed with the idea of drugs or hypnosis, but he was such an uncooperative patient that we just had to hope he could overcome some of these things through time."

"Time?" Peter asked. "You thought time might miraculously take these things away? He watched his mother and brother die, for Christ's sake. You know how much time he'd need to get through that?"

"Evidently more time than he's had here, and that's my point."

Jackie shifted in his chair again. It was becoming too much to handle. He ran his right hand through his hair and sighed.

"Would you like to say something?" Mary Ellen asked. "Because, believe me, Jackie, we've been waiting for you to say something for a long time."

"I don't have anything," Jackie said. "I'm rather enjoying listening to this, though. Please continue."

Mary Ellen shook her head condescendingly. She looked down at her notes in what seemed like an effort to drive her point home.

"The most alarming aspect of Jackie's life is his stubborn belief that if society is to flourish, it will have to be changed through radical action. It's our belief that Jackie harbors thoughts of a thorough revolution, and, given his intellectual abilities and his obvious disregard for social interaction, we feel he may be quite dangerous outside the confines of an institution."

Jackie felt like laughing, and he leaned in as if enraptured by Mary Ellen's theory.

"We believe Jackie will also be of harm to himself. He thinks of himself as a poor man who'll never be able to escape the chains of poverty. Jackie has used those very words on numerous occasions. Simply put, we feel that he'll try to organize a violent fight for the poor and underprivileged in this country."

"That's ridiculous!" Peter shouted. "This kid's never had a chance. I can't believe we're talking about a cock-and-bull story about the plight of the poor. How can you stand up there and condemn Jackie because he has a self-defeatist attitude? He never committed a crime. He's a victim of a crime, and he's been locked away for years. I don't know about you, but I can understand why he's not full of honey and spice. Goddammit!"

Peter's face was bright red. He banged his fist on the table just in case he hadn't grabbed everyone's attention.

"So he writes a story on what it's like to be poor. Why wouldn't a thoughtful man question the premium placed on money and success when he comes from a world where his father was never allowed to think of himself as a success? Wasn't his father a success? Didn't he try to get up every morning and go to work? I don't even think you know what success is, counselor. If someone questions why they feel poor, you seem to want to institutionalize them forever." Hanratty paused to wipe the spittle from his chin.

"I was allowed the opportunity to succeed, and Jackie will have the same chance. If you ask me to help lock this kid up, I'll fight it. I'll give him work for the rest of his life if he wants it. I knew his mother. This means a lot to William. Counselor, if you fight me, I'll win."

Hanratty pulled his huge frame out of the chair. He pulled his pants up high on his hips, and Jackie might have laughed if the situation wasn't so ridiculous.

"High and mighty fucking people," Peter said.

Mary Ellen held her hands out in front of her, but William had also gained his feet.

"Gentlemen," Mary Ellen said, "please, let me finish. I didn't want to have to read this, but, please, let me continue."

Mary Ellen was fighting to regain her composure. She nervously shuffled the papers before her, and Jackie knew there was little chance she'd be strutting across the room again.

"What concerns me the most about Jackie, and what I had failed to tell you, is this." Again, she shuffled the papers before her.

"Jackie is an unbelievable reader. He devours books at a rapid pace. Also, he believes that society has failed him, and he *has* shown signs of wanting to strike back." Mary Ellen looked directly at Hanratty. His breathing had returned to something close to normal, and he nodded.

"As I was saying, members of the lower class live for the moment. Jackie perceives himself as eternally poor and surely doesn't have the emotional surplus to sustain him beyond the moment. Jackie possesses an almost unbearable tension between the ideal and reality and between the desired adherence to the norms of a larger society and the insistent demands of his own mind."

"I don't know what the hell that means," Peter said.

"Well, simply put," Mary Ellen said, "Jackie will be unable to function in society. He theorizes about a total restructuring of society. The plight of the poor has reared its head time and again in conversations with Jackie. He once told me he didn't believe crime could be reduced to a tolerable level unless those who felt excluded from society were allowed the chance to become full-fledged participants with a stake in preserving the American way of life. When I pressed him for an answer on how this might be achieved, he didn't hesitate. He said it could only be accomplished through violent means. Look at the Oklahoma City bombing. It's imperative that we don't ignore the warning signs. Jackie doesn't feel that Billy was responsible for what happened in that trailer. Instead, Jackie believes Billy was a victim. I believe that Jackie will feel very comfortable living a life of crime and violence."

"That's bullshit," Peter said. "He sounds like a thoughtful man to me."

"Precisely," Mary Ellen said, "and he's going to fight for a greater purpose in life. He possesses the capacity to be an above-average thinker, but, I'm telling you, Jackie is overly concerned with fostering feelings of negativity. He spends a lot of time reading works that can't possibly benefit his already battered psyche."

Jackie couldn't help smiling. For years, he had worked hard to understand why his family was left to fend for themselves, and, try as he might, he had never found the reason. Jackie knew that Mary Ellen would never fully understand his feelings, but he also knew that it was ridiculous for her to believe that he'd act violently.

"Jackie spent months reading the account of the Starkweather murders in Nebraska. On the same lampshade where he'd written his words of desperation, he scribbled Starkweather's words. *Sir, I guess there's just a meanness in this world.*"

"Jackie feels it's important to understand why Starkweather committed these acts. He's not concerned with the horrific nature of the murders. What's more alarming is that Jackie read the account of the social activist Samuel Melville. If you remember, Melville was convicted of randomly bombing social institutions in New York."

Mary Ellen stepped away from the lectern. She walked directly in front of Peter.

"It's my professional opinion that the choice to go into a life of crime is imposed upon the criminal as a reaction to what they perceive the world to be. Jackie Gregory, given his violent life and terribly tragic past, pictures the world as a fish bowl where his actions are magnified. You must agree that every member of society searches for a niche, and those who perceive themselves to be poor are no exception. I may quell my desire for adventure by taking a trip to the Gulf of Mexico, while the poor fulfill their desires through crime. Jackie passionately reads about guns. He studies murderers and their victims. When he does talk, it's about being socially active and restructuring society. He does not, in my opinion, have the emotional surplus to see beyond a single moment."

"That's your opinion," Peter said.

"Jackie's a danger to society. His future is bleak, and he speaks of the destruction of hope and the eventual realization of his fears. The most we can hope for is that this time bomb doesn't go off sooner, rather than later. Jackie is a picture of hopelessness. He suffers from severe disillusionment, psychological unreadiness, and cultural deprivation. Where can he find his niche? He smiles his crooked grin, and the death of his family is something he blames on the world. Jackie wants to make up for those deaths."

Mary Ellen made one more trip to the back of the lectern. She theatrically piled her papers.

"Mr. Hanratty and Mr. Bennington, if you'll take responsibility for this boy, there's not much I can do. I beg you to carefully weigh your options and consider your choices, because, like it or not, Jackie is a desperate man. And, as he's said, desperation has a way of exploding into pain."

Peter stood up slowly.

"Thank you for your opinion," he said. "His mother was working for me when she died, and William has always felt responsible for not protecting her. We're going to protect this boy, now."

# CHAPTER TWO

Although summer hadn't quite made an exit, Jackie closed his jacket around him. He stepped out into the intersection of Howard and Green Streets and glanced at the address card in his hand. He looked up at the number of the first house in his search for seven-two-three Howard. Jackie returned the card to the pocket of his jeans, ran his hand through his hair, and smiled. No matter what had been said back in that room, he was alone, and that's the way he wanted it to be. A thought crossed his mind, and Jackie held onto it, wondering why it seemed significant. *Every minute it keeps changing to something different.*

Jackie struggled with the thought for four blocks and shook it from his mind only when he arrived at the duplex that would be home. The idea of change seemed strange to him. He allowed himself a moment of hopefulness regarding his place to start life anew.

*It doesn't matter what I expected. This place is a dump.*

He walked up the front steps, taking it all in. He heard the faint sounds of a domestic squabble coming from the downstairs apartment, and he considered his new housemates for a moment.

*John and Anita Lopez and their son Oscar,* Jackie remembered.

Jackie looked at the house, itself. It was a standard box home with white, flaking paint. Jackie understood that state housing wasn't painted every season.

Jackie opened the screen door, believing it might open into a mutual hallway. Instead, he stood face-to-face with, whom he guessed was, Anita Lopez.

" 'Lo?" the woman said.

Jackie nodded, looking to the address card.

"Hi, I think I'm living upstairs. How do I get there?"

The woman smiled. Although she wasn't pretty by anyone's standards, behind the extra weight she wore on her hips and through the exterior of her tired eyes, Jackie recognized a sort of forgotten beauty.

"The stairs are to the right."

She pointed toward a door Jackie hadn't even noticed. It was hanging from its hinges.

"Thanks."

A piercing scream came from inside the room, and the unmistakable sound of a childhood skirmish blasted through the apartment. Anita turned and a child about five-years old came into view.

"Goddammit, I'm talking," the woman yelled. "I'm sorry," she said to Jackie.

Jackie smiled and shrugged. The child continued to scream.

"Shut up, or your ass'll be bleeding when your father gets here."

The child only screamed louder.

"Goddamn neighbor kids," the woman said as way of explanation, and she slapped the child hard across the side of the head. The cry of the child almost dropped Jackie to his knees.

"Lady, if I ever see you slap that kid again, I'll make *your* ass bleed."

The woman considered Jackie's words for a moment, then slammed the door in his face. Jackie turned and walked away.

\*     \*     \*

Jackie cautiously opened the door to his new home. Mary Ellen had described the room to him, but Jackie held his breath as he opened the door. He was glad that he had.

The last tenant had obviously left in a rush. The floor of the room was covered in old newspapers and food wrappings. The furniture consisted of a folding chair, an old stove, and an even older refrigerator. These simple necessities were scattered among the debris.

Jackie's eyes centered on the water-stained walls. Everything about the place seemed oddly familiar, and Jackie recognized the smell of human defeat. Still, he wore his crooked smile as he surveyed the apartment.

His bed was a mattress stuffed into the only closet in the place. Jackie pulled the mattress out, and it fell to the floor with deep stains looking back at him.

Jackie sighed deeply and moved to the bathroom. His first sight was of a broken mirror. The sink was full of discolored water, and the porcelain of the toilet bowl was dark brown.

"Not exactly as you described it, counselor," Jackie said as he pulled the bathroom door closed.

The cleaning of the place would be a considerable chore, and the two broken windows in the living area presented even more of a problem.

*Every minute it keeps changing to something different.*

Although Jackie shook his head as he closed the front door, his crooked smile was firmly in place.

*     *     *

His first stop was the neighborhood service center. Rossetti had agreed on his release only under a number of conditions, and a weekly trek to the center on Church Street was mandatory.

Jackie caught the cross-town bus, realizing that the center was just a few miles from the trailer park where Alan and Anna were killed. As he hung onto the pole, he closed his eyes and fought the images from entering his mind. He was looking forward to the first day when the image did not return. The bus pulled to a stop, and Jackie whispered his daily mantra, "Someday I'll be able to forget."

The neighborhood service center was an office building. Its neighbor to the right proclaimed that a beautifully written, professional resume could be had for ninety-nine cents, and the office to the left was owned by Magical Maria, a palm reader. Again, Jackie smiled. *Résumés, palm readings, and the help center. A shopping plaza for the poor.*

There was a venetian blind inside the front door. A crooked sign hung from the blind in such a way that the sign read open/abierto when the slats were turned one way and closed/cerrado when opened the other way. Although the closed sign was in his face, Jackie saw people moving about inside the place. He tried the door, hoping the place was, indeed, closed, but the knob turned in his hand. He stuffed his hands into his pockets and stepped through.

Jackie's eyes were drawn to Dorothy Robinson's nameplate in the center of the desk. Dorothy, an imposing, unsightly woman was seated behind the desk. She was having a rather heated discussion with a tall, skinny, black man. Without taking another step inside, Jackie smelled alcohol on the man.

"I was in here last week, and you told me I'd get a check on the fifteenth. I gets here, and you gives me the same shit." The man dismissed Dorothy with an emphatic wave of the hand.

"I'm not telling you again," Dorothy said, "you're drunk and you've been drunk every day for the past week. You come in here disrupting my office, and I can't do nothing for you."

Dorothy stopped the man with the sound of her booming voice. The man was nearing the door, and Jackie felt like turning away.

"May I help you?" Dorothy called to Jackie.

"She can't fucking help you," the black man said. Jackie stepped out of the way of his breath.

"Fucking, fat-ass bitch. Nine mother-fucking days I be waiting."

The man was directly in front of Jackie.

"They don't give a shit. I could die, and she wouldn't give a shit."

Jackie heard the sound of Dorothy's chair against the wood of the floor. Like a bolt of lightning, she was behind the black man.

"I've told you thirty times, Theodore, don't come in here drunk."

Dorothy had Theodore by the collar and the back of the pants. She pushed him across the floor to the front door. She pulled the door open with a grunt and shoved the skinny man to the sidewalk. The sign on the blinds clanked to the ground.

"I'm suing you, you fat, fucking bitch," Theodore screamed.

Dorothy bent down and plucked the sign from the ground. She brushed by Jackie and tossed the sign on her desk before plopping down in her chair.

"May I help you?"

Jackie extended his paperwork without a word.

"This is the standard statement of introduction. I give the same speech to everyone who walks through the door. It don't mean a thing, but here goes. We're here to help you help yourself. We'll offer you friendship and a service you can't get on the streets. No matter what time of day it is, the service will find a way to help." She looked to his name on the paper. "It's nice to meet you, Jackie Gregory. I hope we can get you going in the right direction."

Jackie nodded and smiled.

"Oh, great," Dorothy said. "I got another talker. Just sit down and I'll get a file going for you."

Dorothy scribbled across the top of Jackie's paperwork. He sat, looking to the floor. In a matter of seconds, his attention wavered far away from the scene at hand. He thought of the confrontation between Dorothy and Theodore, wondering what sort of sympathies this woman could offer, given what she'd seen in her lifetime.

As he watched her sign the forms, he wondered how many times she had to throw a drunk man into the street. It was a joke, and Jackie knew that Dorothy Robinson, the woman entrusted to welcome him back to society, was ten years beyond caring. She had already made up her mind about Jackie, and, no matter how many philosophical or psychological questions she asked, she considered him just another lazy man who couldn't take what was his. She'd never understand what was in his heart. She'd never know what it felt like to feel his pain.

"Hey, dream-boy," Dorothy called, snapping Jackie to the present. "Take these forms through those doors for your interview." She pointed to the doors at the left of her desk. "Good luck."

Jackie nodded and smiled.

*　　*　　*

He pushed through the doors and was greeted by a bustle of people moving from one partitioned wall to another. A short man with a nearly bald head moved to Jackie and took the forms from his hand.

"I'll be right back," he said, walking away.

Jackie stood in place, looking at the six interview offices. The entire scene was too much to believe, and he thought of running back out through the front doors. The man returned and extended his hand.

"I'm Vincent Paglia."

"Jackie Gregory."

Jackie looked directly at the man's obvious attempt to cover his balding head. A few strands of hair grew long on the right side of the man's head and were tossed to the left. Vincent's hand instinctively moved to the top of his head, and he motioned Jackie to a chair behind one of the partitions.

"I want you to know you made a friend today. I'll be here whenever you need me, and there's no need to ever make an appointment." Vincent smiled again, and Jackie offered his life-long stare. "The function of the neighborhood help center is two-fold. It's designed to form a bond between us and to offer monetary assistance. It's a state-funded organization that doesn't pride itself on profit and loss. It's simply a service by, and for, you."

Jackie sighed audibly. He wished the guy would spare him the happy talk.

"In your case, we're going to try and work to derail any self-defeatist attitudes you might have. I'm also to report any serious behavioral problems which might come up. Hopefully, we won't have any of those." Vincent leaned back in the chair, his bright smile still in place. "We'd like to give everyone as much money as they might need, but as you might have gathered from Theodore's explosion, we're often understaffed and

100

overloaded. We're able to offer stipends, but sometimes things we promise aren't always available. Do you see where I'm coming from?"

"Yeah," Jackie muttered.

"Okay, well, before we go on, let me tell you what we can offer." He grabbed a sheet from his desk. "We offer homemaker help, legal assistance, emergency loans, funding for education, state welfare, and a number of other services."

"Don't waste our time," Jackie said. He slumped back in his chair. "I have a job and money from a trust fund that the good people of Connecticut put together when my mother and brother were murdered. I don't want a handout."

"I understand," Vincent said, "but I'm required to go through the list."

"Why?" Jackie asked. "Don't you know I'm human? I know what welfare's about. There isn't one bone in my body that wants a penny from you. Don't you understand anything about human pride? Don't you know some of us don't choose to be children of the state?" Jackie's voice cracked. The years of living under the shelter of his father's life rushed to the front of his mind. "I didn't choose the life I've had to this point, but you can keep your counseling and your free lunches, because I'll make it on my own."

Vincent bowed his head.

"Do you mind if I ask you a few questions?"

"Whatever," Jackie said.

"Do you have a problem with alcohol abuse?"

"No."

"A history of drug abuse?"

"No."

"Have you experienced any psychological problems?"

Jackie got to his feet.

"I guess you could say that," Jackie said.

Vincent pointed toward the chair.

"Please, sit down, Mister Gregory."

"When I was twelve, I shot a man eight times. He'd just killed my brother, and I had watched my mother die. Of course, this was after my father had a heart attack trying to provide for us." Jackie paced in front of the desk. He was aware his outburst was the most he'd ever said on the subject. "Yeah, I might have a few leftover, psychological problems, but for you to bring me in here and ask a hundred standard questions is a little ridiculous, don't you think? Have you ever been a ward of the state, Vincent? Did you ever go to bed thinking there ain't a person in the world who cares if you live or die?"

Vincent was as white as the sheet of paper he held in his hands.

"It's not your fault," Jackie said. "Just sign my form, and let everyone think you've done your job. In the meantime, I'll come and see you like a good boy and make a life for myself around all of this."

Jackie ducked behind the partitioned wall. Vincent held the form in his hand with a look of utter disbelief in his eyes.

"I'll call if I need you," Jackie said as Vincent signed the form.

Jackie brushed past Dorothy, who was re-hanging the welcome sign. He stepped out into the bright sunshine.

*        *        *

Jackie heard a soft knock on his apartment door. He'd been standing over the kitchen sink trying to scrub away the stains. He shut off the water and shook his hands quickly.

"Who's there?" Jackie called. He grabbed a dish towel and wiped his hands.

"Tony Miller."

Jackie opened the door with the image of Miller from all those years ago etched upon his mind.

"Tony Miller," Jackie said. "I spent a lot of time trying to remember your first name." Jackie ushered Tony in with a wave of the hand.

"You remember me then?"

Jackie paused for a moment to allow the memory of Tony Miller as a young man fade into the back of his mind. He extended his hand, and Tony shook it quickly.

"There's not much I don't remember," Jackie said.

Tony looked around at the apartment and faced Jackie with a look of disgust.

"This place is a shithole," he said.

"Tell me about it," Jackie said. "They went through this long, drawn-out deal about how I was a danger to society, and then they turn around and dump me into this place."

"That's not all they dumped you into," Tony said.

Jackie went to the kitchen sink. He took a paper cup from the drainboard.

"You want a glass of water?" Jackie asked. "It's about all I got right now."

"Naw, I'm fine," Tony said. His hand rested on his gun, and, for a moment Jackie wondered why the cop was there at all.

"Like I said," Tony said, "the state didn't do you any favors."

"I know, I'll never get this clean."

Tony moved to the folding chair and sat as Jackie drank down two glasses of water. He turned to Tony with a grimace on his face.

"It's awful," he said, and Tony laughed. "You were a lot younger-looking last time I saw you."

"So were you," Tony said, laughing again.

"You been keeping Connecticut safe?" Jackie asked.

"Actually," Tony said, "I've been spending a lot of time chasing down Peter Hanratty."

"Peter?" Jackie asked. "Why are you chasing him?"

"He's a bad man," Tony said. "He's even worse than Billy Barth, because he's in control."

"What the hell are you talking about?" Jackie asked. He jumped into a sitting position on the kitchen counter.

"Just what I said," Tony said. "And I need you to help me."

"Help you with what?" Jackie asked.

Tony stood up. He walked around the apartment as though he were appraising the property.

"I heard about your years with the state," Tony said. "I guess I'd better cut right to the chase."

"What chase?" Jackie asked.

Tony moved to a couple of feet from Jackie. He sighed and shrugged his shoulders. For a brief instant, Jackie was sure Tony was everything a cop should be.

"For a lot of years now, Peter's been supplying half the east coast with drugs. I know he runs a gambling operation on the west side and a couple of whorehouses uptown. He sells guns, he steals money, the whole shebang. Man, you name it, he does it."

Tony paced the floor.

"On the other hand, he's been honored at every state dinner for the past twenty years. He tells the New Haven police force what kind of wood makes shingles. He manipulates everyone he meets."

"Everyone but you, right?" Jackie asked.

"I tell you, kid, he's got a lot of loyal people around him."

Jackie jumped from the counter. He smiled and shook his head.

"What do you want from me?"

"I want to get him." Tony slapped the inside of his left palm with his right hand. "To be honest, I'm at a dead end. I have a feeling that part of the reason Hanratty gave you a job is that he's trying to ease his conscience from having dealt with Billy Barth in the past."

"I don't need this," Jackie said. "Besides, he seems all right."

"He seems all right to everybody. He's no fucking good."

Jackie wasn't sure what to think of Miller's accusations. The man seemed passionate enough in his quest to tackle Hanratty, but it made little sense.

"Why would you come to me?" Jackie asked. "Why doesn't the FBI go after this guy or something?"

"They're afraid of him, everyone is."

"I don't need it," Jackie said with a wave of his hand.

"I think you do," Tony said. "I did a little research, and I think you're a rebel without a cause."

"You've got to be kidding me," Jackie said, laughing.

Tony's face showed determination. "I'm dead serious."

"You make this sound like an adventure," Jackie said. "I wrote a few papers during high school, and everyone has me pinpointed as a revolutionist."

Tony shook his head. He moved through the apartment like a trapped mouse. His hand never moved from his gun holster.

"I know you," Tony said. "From all those years ago, I've known you. You've had it rough. You don't want to see other people go through what you went through."

"You're losing me," Jackie said.

"Am I really losing you? I think I'm on target. I'm telling you, New Haven's a good city, but it's a city run by a bad man. You can help me stop him."

"If what you're saying is true," Jackie said, "it's been going on for a long time. What am I supposed to do? Am I going to be like Mighty Mouse? Yeah, I don't want to see people living poor, but what can I do?"

The room slipped into silence. Jackie grabbed a cleaning rag and scrubbed at the stains on the refrigerator. His thoughts were moving a mile a minute, and he turned it all over and over without understanding what was happening.

"Do you remember how your father looked when he was trying to make ends meet?" Tony asked.

Jackie didn't respond.

"Do you know why people like Billy Barth are allowed to evolve?" Tony moved closer to him.

Jackie closed his eyes tight and wished he could be left alone.

"You know what I'm talking about," Tony said.

Jackie continued to work at wiping the grime off the front of the refrigerator. For a second, he felt as if he might cry. Finally, he turned and tossed the cloth into the sink.

"I recall everything about that day," Jackie said. He felt as if his voice might fail him, and he strained for each word. "My brother and mother were killed, and every day I'm reminded of that. Tony, I've hung onto that thought with all the bitterness and pain my heart can muster, and, I swear, one day I might just rip it all out of the center of my chest. I am really thinking about cutting my shirt open, ripping my heart out, and getting rid of it."

Jackie laughed nervously although he felt as if he were going to cry. Tony's gaze was riveted to the floor.

"But I can't get rid of it, and I know it. Billy's dead, and I pulled the trigger and watched his blood splatter the wall. I knew what was happening, and, as amazing as it sounds, I knew how I'd feel for the rest of my life. Right at that moment, I knew I'd feel like this forever."

Jackie's voice faded to a whisper, and he turned away.

"I don't regret a thing about killing that man. When I was with the state, they tried to get me to relive it so I could forget. I relive it every day, and I'll never forget it. I don't have nightmares about the blood. If there's anything I regret, it's that there weren't more bullets. I've suffered a lot, and I'm going to suffer until they put me in a grave. But I deserve to live some kind of life."

Jackie couldn't speak for well over a minute. He walked through the kitchen area, and, although his fist was clenched, he felt a cleansing through his heart and mind.

"I remember my father being alive. I was by his side when we loaded the car for that trip. I'll never forget the look of pain on my mother's face when you told her you found Dad. God let me live through. Sometimes, life is too ridiculous to live."

Jackie felt the tears stinging the back of his eyes. He hadn't cried since the day his mother died, and he fought the tears again.

"I wonder what I can do with my life to make it worth more than my father's," Jackie said.

"I can give you a few ideas," Tony said.

# CHAPTER THREE

Just as he had done seven years previously, Peter instructed his chauffeur to wait by the curb for the cross-town bus. On that day long ago, Peter had gone to greet Anna in order to put on a show for the community and the New Haven Police Department. This morning, his motives were the same.

He watched Jackie exit the bus. Peter couldn't help remembering Anna's first morning, and the similarities were striking. Jackie approached the side of the limousine and glanced up for a moment, but he stuffed his hands deep into his jacket pocket and walked by with a faraway look already settling in his eyes. Peter scrambled out of the back seat.

"Jackie," he called into the crisp morning air. Nearly every person on Church Street turned to face him, and Peter instinctively adjusted his tie. A few of the people turned to see who would answer the call, but most moved on in casual indifference. Jackie turned at the mention of his name, but the expression on his face was the same. He walked to the car where Peter extended his hand.

"Good morning, Mister Hanratty," Jackie said. He shook Peter's hand sternly.

"Please, call me *Peter*."

"Good morning, Peter."

Peter waved his palm to the limousine.

"How about a ride on your first day?" Peter said.

"If it's all right, I'd rather walk," Jackie said.

Peter was a little confused by the expression on the kid's face. Didn't Jackie understand that Peter's influence was the reason he was out in public in the first place?

"It's quite a ways," Peter said. Again, he waved his hand in front of the car door.

"A limo isn't my style," Jackie said, a slight smile crossing his lips.

"Very well," Peter said. "But, as your new employer, I'd like the chance to talk with you before you begin your day."

"I'll be there early enough," Jackie said. He glanced at his watch. "I'd better get going, too. See you at the office."

Jackie walked away, knowing that he had left Peter in a state of confusion.

Just walking into the parking lot of the Hanratty headquarters reminded Jackie that Peter was a multi-millionaire. The four-story, brick building with the Hanratty name painted in red letters above the entrance was easily the best-kept structure in New Haven. The front grounds were flawlessly landscaped, and a garden complete with railroad ties and a water fountain drew Jackie's eye.

*It's like working at the Taj Majal.*

The furniture in the front lobby was better suited for a first-rate hotel, and Jackie stood looking at another door and a sliding glass window that looked in on a pretty woman in a long, black dress. The desk she sat behind was marble. The woman smiled brightly, and Jackie was struck by the fact that her eyes also seemed to smile.

"May I help you?"

Jackie glanced to the nameplate on the desk. He couldn't piece together what he wanted to say to Cynthia Marie Austin.

"The construction trailers are down the street," she said.

"I have an appointment with Peter Hanratty," Jackie finally said.

"Are you Jackie Gregory?" Cynthia asked. The smile returned to her eyes. She slid the glass open and extended her hand.

"Yes," Jackie said. He shook her hand.

"I've been waiting to meet you," Cynthia said. "Peter told me the story about you, and I've been curious."

Jackie didn't have time to respond. The front door opened, and Peter stepped through with all the grace his huge frame would allow.

"Jackie. How'd the walk go?" He placed his huge hand on Jackie's back and held the door until Cynthia buzzed them in. "You know, I was thinking, it is a nice day for a walk. I should walk more often."

Jackie didn't answer.

"Come into my office," Peter said as they stepped through the doors into a lobby area suited for ballroom dancing. "Would you like some coffee?"

"Yes," Jackie said.

"Cynthia, set us up with a couple of coffees."

Cynthia stepped away from the desk and moved to a room off to the left.

"She's my most prized possession," Peter said.

Jackie nodded, but he was fairly sure Cynthia probably didn't appreciate being called a possession. She probably also hated the fact that she had to fetch the coffee.

"Really, she's something else," Peter said. "What do think of her? She's single, you know."

Jackie rubbed his hand across his chin as if he were chasing an imaginary itch.

"Did you want to talk about work?"

Peter clapped him on the back and laughed boisterously. "You'll get over the shyness. You'll start thinking about Cynthia the way the rest of us do."

Cynthia emerged carrying two mugs of coffee. She locked eyes with Jackie for a split-second.

"Now that I think about it," Peter said, as though Cynthia were still out of the room, "you two would be a great couple."

The half-grin returned to Jackie's face. In some strange way, he felt as if Peter were testing him.

"I don't think Cynthia is yours to give away," Jackie said. He took the coffee from Cynthia. She looked at Jackie as if he were a god of some sort for having stood up to Peter.

"I hold a high regard for respect," Jackie said. "I don't think talking about us as a couple shows respect for either one of us." Jackie looked directly into Cynthia's eyes. "Tomorrow morning I'll fetch your coffee." Jackie looked to Peter with the smile still on his lips. "What will I be doing for you?"

They entered the office and Jackie immediately thought that it was worth more than any space Jackie had ever called home. The desk was at least three feet wide. The surface of the desk was glass, and, without even studying it, Jackie knew the frame was made of gold. There was no way any man deserved such luxury. Jackie scanned the room quickly as a sickening feeling worked its way through his body.

The left side of the room was home to a wall-to-wall bar stocked with every brand of alcohol imaginable. Jackie visualized evenings of pure overindulgence as the fat man sat behind the desk, drinking himself into oblivion while watching the wide-screen television in the back corner of the room.

"I see you looking at all of it," Peter said, "and you've got to remember, I worked hard for this. I see no reason why you can't get the same sort of things out of life."

Jackie lowered himself in the seat across the desk from Peter. He thought better of mentioning what he actually thought of the way Peter had set up his life.

"When do I get to work?"

"Relax, enjoy your coffee. Tell me about yourself."

Peter waited for a moment, but Jackie sipped from the coffee mug and looked straight ahead.

"I know the basic information, but I'd like to know the real you."

Jackie's smile was now full, and he hid it behind the coffee cup.

"They said you were a little difficult when you were with the state. I'm an employer, and I'd like you to tell me why you were gruff with your superiors."

"It's a long story," Jackie said.

"Your counselor thinks you might be dangerous. What did they do that got you so upset?"

Jackie left Peter waiting a moment before responding. "That's all behind me," he said, finally. "I'd rather not discuss it."

"I can respect that," Peter said. He rolled a pencil around in his chubby fingers and looked long and hard at Jackie. "You were a good student, correct?"

"In academic matters," Jackie said.

"Well, I have to tell you, this isn't just a job. I'll be helping you get an education."

"I'm a little confused as to why," Jackie said. "You could've just let me rot away in state housing."

"Like William, I feel responsible for what happened to you as a child. You're going to find that we're good, decent men who want to make a difference."

Again, Jackie nodded in approval. Peter sipped the coffee.

"Come on," Peter said, getting up as quickly as his girth would allow. "Let me show you the warehouse. It's rather impressive."

Peter led Jackie through a tall door that held signs warning against unauthorized personnel. They moved down another small hallway and an even larger door that was marked as an emergency exit. Peter pushed the door open and waved his hand for Jackie to pass, and the two men stepped outside into the cool morning air. Peter pointed toward a massive warehouse some three hundred feet away. "That's what's called a self-storage warehouse. It's an old concept that is more popular these days. Fortunately, I've pretty much captured the market in New Haven."

They walked on, and Jackie became aware of Peter's labored breathing.

"The basic premise behind an operation such as this is that we work with other corporations. They contract us to store their equipment in order to keep it safe from the elements, and we, in turn, promise to have it ready for them at a moment's notice."

"I never thought about it," Jackie said, "but I suppose there's a need for that sort of thing."

"You're goddamn right there is," Peter said. "Some of this equipment has been here for ten years. Other folks use us as a short-term facility, but, either way, I make a killing."

Jackie was going to great lengths to try and remember that Peter wasn't just a businessman. The conversation with Tony was in the back of his mind, and, no matter how interesting it all seemed, Jackie had to focus on the fact that Peter was adept at speaking out of both sides of his mouth. They walked in silence for a short time, and Jackie knew it was so Peter could catch his breath.

"Our responsibilities to our customers are two-fold. First of all, we have to make certain that the equipment isn't damaged or stolen. I have men who tag the equipment when it comes in, and that gives us a point of reference to work from when we need to recover the piece."

"What kind of equipment are we talking about?" Jackie asked.

"Just about anything. Right now, we have everything from a thirty-ton industrial press to a personal computer system we're storing for IBM. You'll see what I mean when we get inside. But that does bring me to the second point. We have to expedite the materials to the owners when the need arises. If we don't pay close attention to the customer, our operation isn't worth a fuck."

Jackie nodded in agreement. He was becoming mesmerized by the professional tone to Peter's voice, and he now knew how the man was able to dupe the entire city.

"I don't tolerate any sort of incompetence when it comes to satisfying the customer."

They stood before the front door. Peter took three deep breaths of air and patted his stomach. "I make that walk about ten times a day," he said, "but it doesn't seem to be helping."

Jackie followed Peter through the front door and stopped abruptly when Peter moved to a thermostat off to the right.

"This is regulated and watched very closely. Most of the machinery in the storage area can't be exposed to warm temperatures, and it's our job to ensure that the conditions are hospitable."

Jackie nodded in understanding.

"The position I've always had in mind for you is a tough one," Peter said. "You'll work hard and go to bed real tired."

"I'm not afraid of working hard," Jackie said.

"At the same time," Peter said, "you'll face tasks that challenge the upper part of your anatomy." Peter pointed to his right temple. "Let me show you that aspect of it."

Peter led the charge to another room that seemed non-existent until they were right on top of it. The door swung open on a very fat man sitting slouched over a pile of paperwork.

"This is Rick Montgomery," Peter said. "But that isn't important, because Rick's on borrowed time. You'll be taking his place because Rick never gets his fat ass out of that chair. Isn't that right, Rick?"

Rick grunted an unintelligible sound, and Jackie felt instant sympathy for the man.

"Where's Ben?" Peter asked.

"He's out in the house," Rick managed. The ringing telephone interrupted the exchange, and Peter picked it off the receiver without hesitation.

"Good morning," he said, gruffly.

Jackie turned his attention to the office. As he took in the overall setup, his eyes settled on a Garfield cartoon that poked fun at the fat cat. Garfield's name had been crossed out and replaced by Rick's.

*The poor bastard.*

Jackie's quick scan of the office area was shattered by the sound of Peter's booming voice.

"Those lousy motherfuckers!" Peter screamed into the telephone. Jackie glanced at Rick, who showed no sign of having heard the outburst.

"I'll kill those lazy sons of bitches! Sons of bitches! You tell them to meet me in my office in ten minutes, both of those bastards! Son of a bitch!" Peter slammed the telephone down as hard as he could. His hands were on his hips, and he moved around the room looking down at the floor, with curse words and little droplets of spittle escaping. His face was bright red, and his entire body shook. Every breath seemed as if it might be his last, and Jackie instinctively backed away.

"Those miserable bastards! You trust someone to do a fucking job, and they fuck you over." He slammed his fist on the desk.

Jackie realized he was seeing the other side of Peter Hanratty, and he wondered if the mayor or the city's police officers had ever had the pleasure of watching Peter throw a fit. Slowly, Peter's breathing evened out, and he looked to Jackie.

"Jackie, I apologize, but I'm going to have to head back to the main office for a couple hours. Introduce yourself to Ben when he comes in, and he'll go over everything with you. Later on, I'll send Cynthia for you, and we'll talk about the things you've seen."

"Okay," Jackie said.

"And welcome to the team," Peter said, extending his hand to Jackie. "Hey, fatso, show Jackie the paperwork."

"Fuck you," Rick said as the door closed and Peter was out of range. "That man's a living hell." His fat face was contorted by a grimace. "I'm going to the labor board when this is over." He stood up and tugged down on his shirt in an effort to cover up the slabs of fat. He took a couple of steps toward the door and peered out through the glass.

"I'd go to the cops if I thought they'd do anything," Rick said. "I can prove he's doing fucked-up things around here." Rick looked to Jackie as if to gauge the reaction his statement might have made.

"And he calls me fat. Shit, I bet that fucker weighs twenty more pounds than I do."

Jackie thought it might be a close call, but he simply looked away. He was sure it was best to stay quiet and take in all of Rick's rant.

"You aren't going to want this job. Nothing you ever do will be good enough. When I first got here, I used to help unload the trucks. I used to be in the warehouse all day and was down to about two hundred pounds, but when I got back in here at the end of the day, Ben would have the paper work fucked up."

Jackie nodded sympathetically.

"Besides, Peter hates me because I'm close to Cynthia. He doesn't want anyone talking to Cynthia, because he thinks she's his."

Jackie wasn't sure what to say, but he found it peculiar that Rick might be close to Cynthia.

"It wasn't nothing like that," Rick said, laughing. "Cynthia and I got to be friends, and we started talking about some of the things going on here."

"What things?" Jackie asked.

"Put it this way," Rick said. "I made a remark to Cynthia that I thought there were drugs going in and out of here. I know she told Peter, because ever since he's been calling me a fat pig and making fun of me in front of everyone."

"What made you think there were drugs?"

Rick pondered the question for a full minute. He chewed on the pencil eraser and wrestled with the question.

"I really don't know," he said. "Maybe I was just trying to get Cynthia's attention, if you know what I mean, and I made some things up."

"I see," Jackie said softly. He didn't believe a word Rick was saying.

"It's a clean business," Rick said, letting out a snort and turning back to his paperwork.

"I'd like to see the warehouse," Jackie said, realizing he wouldn't get much more out of Rick.

"Let Ben take you. I'm too busy."

*     *     *

Ben Potter was an intimidating man. His six-foot-seven-inch frame moved through the door, and Jackie immediately gained his feet. Ben wore a dark mustache and beard, and his quick smile set Jackie at ease.

"Good morning, I'm Ben Potter. I run this little operation."

Jackie shook hands with Ben and introduced himself.

"I know who you are," Ben said. "I've worked side-by-side with Peter for fifteen years, and you're well known around here. Peter speaks very highly of you, as does William."

"I appreciate that," Jackie said.

"Have a seat for a minute," Ben said. Jackie followed the instruction like an obedient dog. "I have to tell you a few things." Ben hesitated for a moment and then moved to the spot directly behind Rick's chair.

"There's a couple of lessons to be learned here," Ben said. He placed his hand on Rick's shoulder. "If you're loyal to Peter, it'll pay great dividends. If you cross Peter, you'll pay for it, right, Rick?"

Rick shrugged and tossed the pencil on the desk. He squirmed under Ben's grasp. Jackie instinctively understood that Ben wouldn't be providing information about Hanratty's criminal activities.

"I understand perfectly," Jackie said.

"Let's go see the warehouse," Ben said. He opened a file drawer, extracted a pair of safety glasses, and held them out to Jackie.

"You're going to enjoy seeing the operation," Ben said. He opened a huge, gray door at the back of the office, and Jackie followed him out into the massive, warehouse area.

"How high's the ceiling?" Jackie asked as he looked up to an overhead crane and the roof of the building in the distance.

"A very interesting question. We get a lot of visitors who see the traffic we do, and they think it's a simple concept. A lot of times they'll ask you a question of that sort to gather information. I don't think we should give them information that might allow them to compete, do you?"

"Sorry I asked," Jackie said.

"I know it sounds paranoid, but that's life here at Hanratty's. We can't forget that every question should be answered with Peter's best interests at heart."

"I see," Jackie said.

Ben laughed heartily, slapping Jackie on the back.

"All right," Ben said. "Let's get the show on the road."

Ben guided Jackie toward a work area bustling with activity.

"You see that guy there?" Ben asked. He pointed to a short, muscular man with a dark mustache and sweat racing down his face. Jackie nodded. "He's doing the job you'll be doing. His first responsibility is to look at the piece of equipment closely so he can document any damage. Some of this stuff comes in from across the sea, and it could be pretty banged up before it gets here."

"What's this shipment?"

"These are press parts for Ford Motor Company. The biggest piece weighs about twenty ton. There's about four hundred additional pieces."

Jackie nodded again.

"With that many pieces, it's important we mark them correctly. Joe's making notes on each tag to distinguish the pieces. Then he'll mark it in a log book and turn it over to the girls up front. They'll print out a ticket and send a confirmation notice to Ford."

Ben stepped back and allowed Jackie to watch the operation for a moment. The huge overhead crane buzzed, and Jackie was transfixed by the entire procedure. Joe signaled the crane, and the huge hook dropped to his feet. Two men worked to place the slings on the hook, and in a matter of minutes the huge press piece was in the air moving across the warehouse.

"We're going to store that in the west corner. Joe'll mark that on the ticket too; and, when Ford wants it, they'll give us the tag number, and we'll chase it down."

Jackie couldn't help but smile. The whole operation was smooth, and a number of thoughts immediately jumped to the front of his mind. If Peter was involved in illegal activities as Tony had insisted, this was the perfect cover. Secondly, the new job was going to be more than a challenge. It was going to be downright enjoyable.

# CHAPTER FOUR

They made their way back to the office. Rick was munching on a chocolate bar and he ignored their entrance, concentrating only on the candy.

"What you saw out there is half the job," Ben said. "You'll also be counted on to keep precise records and to handle ordering equipment and supplies. It might seem tedious to you and you'll wonder how I can possibly expect you to get all the work done. But it's extremely important."

"I understand," Jackie said.

A soft knock at the door interrupted Ben's speech and Rick's candy break. Rick pulled himself out of the chair long enough to open the door. It was the first bit of work Jackie had seen out of Rick.

"Excuse me," Cynthia said, "but Peter would like to see Jackie if you're done."

Cynthia looked directly at Ben, and Jackie took a moment to see how Rick was reacting to her presence. The look of desire in Rick's eyes was fascinating. He watched Cynthia's lips move as she talked and the movements of her hands as she spoke with Ben.

"I'll see you in the morning," Ben said as he thrust his thick hand out for Jackie to shake.

"Thank you," Jackie said. He turned to Rick. "It was nice to meet you."

"The pleasure was all mine," Rick said, with a trace of sarcasm. "Good-bye, Cynthia," he smiled, but she didn't respond.

\*     \*     \*

"We haven't been formally introduced," Cynthia said. They were outside the warehouse now, making the same walk Jackie and Peter made earlier in the morning. Yet, this time, Jackie was having trouble concentrating on anything other than the physical presence of his companion.

"I'm Cynthia Austin," she said. "You can call me *Cindy* if you want, but I kind of prefer *Cynthia.*"

"*Cynthia* it is," Jackie said, and he couldn't help but think Cynthia Marie Austin was beautiful. She had long, dirty blonde hair and those smiling blue eyes. Yet, beyond all of the physical beauty, it was more the way she moved and talked and twirled the pen in her hand as they walked. Something about her mere presence stirred emotions inside of Jackie.

"Thank you, for this morning," Cynthia said. "The way you stood up to Peter was kind of shocking. You must know him pretty well to talk to him like that."

"It wasn't a big deal," Jackie said.

"Knowing the way people run scared from him it is," Cynthia said.

"I know he's the boss, but why is everyone so afraid?" Jackie asked.

"It's a long story, but be careful. If you mention I said that, I'll deny it." Cynthia laughed, and Jackie was drawn to her eyes once more.

"Did you know your eyes shine when you laugh?"

"Thank you," Cynthia said. "That's a nice thing to say."

They reached the front door, and Cynthia swung it open.

"Just remember," she said in a whisper, "if you do your work and mind your business, Peter won't bother you."

"With all due respect," Jackie said, "I'm not afraid of anybody."

Cynthia's face crinkled in a look of confusion and wonderment. She studied Jackie for a moment and, finally, offered a huge smile. Her bright, smiling eyes sent a wave of emotion through Jackie's body.

\*　　\*　　\*

Peter sat with his back to the door. He didn't turn around when Jackie entered the room nor when Jackie cleared his throat in an attempt to get his attention. Jackie stood in place just inside the door, taking in the surroundings of the majestic office. Finally, he cleared his throat a second time, and Peter swung around in the chair.

"Jackie, how'd it go?" Peter stood and waved a hand at the unoccupied seat in front of the desk. "It's a little early, but how about some lunch?"

Peter walked across the room to the refrigerator off the bar. He extracted a platter of lunch meat and a loaf of bread.

"We'll make our own sandwiches, if that's all right," Peter said. "I don't really care to eat sandwiches a stranger prepares. Heaven knows where some of these people have their hands." Peter laughed boisterously. He set the meat down on the desk.

"Help yourself," Peter said.

"So, tell me what you think," Peter said. He was halfway through his second salami sandwich before he had even bothered to ask. "Do I run a neat little business here or what?"

"It's very neat and very well organized."

"That's it in a nutshell," Peter said. "We're an organized company. Organization breeds success, and we've had a great deal of success. You think about it, and all the great people in this world have had a carefully laid-out plan on their way to success." Peter took another healthy bite of the sandwich, and a glob of mustard fell to his hand.

"It's important to set goals and work toward them. A solid work ethic is what separates a successful man from a common laborer." Jackie felt as if he'd been slapped across the face. He thought of his father and how their goals were centered on mere survival.

"You take a man who sweeps a floor for a living," Peter said. "That man can't see beyond the floor in front of him, and he'll suffer forever within his dreary life. He doesn't have the organization, the spirit, or the drive of a man like me."

Jackie felt the color drain from his face. The image of his tired and hurting father coming in from work burned at the front of his mind.

"I beg to differ," Jackie said. "You told my counselor, yourself, that some of the most intelligent people in this world sweep floors for a living. Honest people who get up and go to work every day to feed their family don't have to apologize for anything."

"I know," Peter said. "Don't get me wrong. I just think you want to be more of a success."

Jackie shook Peter off again. He hadn't expected to get into a philosophical chess match with Peter, but he couldn't let it go.

"When I was in the orphanage, I used to keep my mouth shut, but I don't think success has anything to do with what other people think. I can be a success without your approval."

Peter smiled for a moment and then began to laugh, as though he were mocking Jackie.

"Listen, go home today, and work on getting your apartment straightened away. Take a few minutes to think about everything you saw here and come back tomorrow ready for work. Success isn't breaking your ass to put dinner on the table. When you stop arguing with me, I'll see what I can do for you, but, right now, you're just another employee."

Jackie felt his eyes glaze over. He bowed his head and fought against the urge to argue.

"Remember something," Peter said. He paused for effect and slowly got out of the chair. "The state wanted to keep you locked away. I carry a lot of influence in this town. I stood up for you, because I liked your story. I expect you to work hard for me."

"I'll be ready to work," Jackie said, and, before Peter could speak again, Jackie extended his hand, offering his crooked grin.

The sounds of the New Haven night made their way from the streets below, but Jackie's attention had long ago drifted from thoughts of the outside world. He was back in the orphanage once more. He was traveling down the road to the hotel room with his family, trying to make sense out of everything the world had offered him to this point in time.

His mind brought back the sounds of Peter's cursing screams into the telephone, and in his mind's eye the images of his new co-workers flashed before him. They all seemed to carry an intense, absurd fear of Peter. Money, power, and greed wasn't what the world was supposed to be about.

Finally, Jackie's mind brought him the image of Cynthia and her shining eyes. For the first time ever, Jackie felt his heart stir in an odd manner. He drifted toward sleep, honestly believing he was on the verge of building a new life.

# CHAPTER FIVE

It was nine o'clock on a Saturday morning, and Jackie sat at his kitchen table. He sipped his coffee and concentrated on the newspaper. The lead story was an account of a speech made by President Clinton, and Jackie had a hard time believing the words of optimism. The article spoke of an economic rebirth and the goal of removing the homeless people from the streets of the nation. It was more of the happy, political bullshit Jackie noticed in nearly every article about the topic.

"You aren't going to wish people off the streets," Jackie said to the article. "You've got to give them a purpose."

A knock on the door made Jackie jump in surprise. He swung the door open to face Tony.

"Morning, I see you got the paper."

"Yeah, I read it for entertainment purposes." Jackie said. "Clinton amuses me."

"I know what you mean," Tony said. "But there's one in there that ain't much fun." He flopped his paper down on the table. It was folded open to a story about a drug scandal in New Haven.

"Let me tell you a little story," Tony said. He pulled a kitchen chair toward him and sat down on it backwards. "Read the account of what happened to a drug dealer last night, and then I'll put a little spin on it."

Jackie pulled the paper to him and looked blankly to the words of a story which he had already glossed over.

"Read it over," Tony said. "I'll get some coffee."

Jackie read the article, and, by the time Tony returned to the table, Jackie was ready for Tony's version of what happened.

"It's a neat little piece, isn't it? Let me give you the background. Jeremy Hagar is your average dope dealer, right? He went to the streets with thirty grand worth of a designer drug called fentanyl. He thought he was selling heroin to the good people of New Haven, and instead there are about eleven people dead this morning. Hagar sampled the product, and he's dead, too. Big deal, right? You sell drugs, you die, right?"

Jackie wasn't sure what Tony was getting at, but he sat back and sipped his coffee, knowing the story would come to him.

"I'll give you a scenario," Tony said. "We've been following Hagar for a long time. In fact, we even busted him a couple a times on petty shit." He slugged at his coffee, and a look of intense anger showed on his face.

"Hagar wanted to be a basketball player. He loved the Boston Celtics. He wanted to be the black Larry Bird. When I interviewed his mother, she said she thought her son would be able to escape crime and drugs. Well, Jeremy got sucked right in to all of it. You know who sucked him in, don't you?"

"Let me guess," Jackie said. "You're thinking Hanratty, right?"

Tony paced the floor.

"Not exactly, Peter doesn't like to get his hands dirty."

Tony stood directly above Jackie's shoulder. He turned the page of the paper and pointed emphatically at another small piece.

"Right there's a story about a man called Frank Patterson."

Jackie scanned the article, which spoke of a man found on the west side with six bullets in his chest.

"Patterson was also under our watchful eye. I personally followed the guy around for a week. He always had the goods, and he usually contacted a kid on the streets to sell for him."

"A kid like Jeremy Hagar?"

"Exactly like Hagar. Anyway, my guess is that Patterson was the guy who contacted poor Jeremy. He told the kid he'd be selling heroin and he'd be able to keep a little for himself and make himself a couple of bucks in the process."

"Except it wasn't heroin?"

"No, it was fentanyl, and when you try and cut that like heroin, it'll kill you. It's a hundred times more potent."

"Hagar sold it like heroin and killed his customers, right?" Jackie asked.

"Twelve kids like Hagar died, and about a hundred and twenty more got their stomachs pumped. Last night, I was driving down the street with a bullhorn telling anyone that might have taken it to come out and get medical attention. Luckily, the cramps were so bad that most of the people who took it were flopping around like fish on the streets."

"You got a connection between Peter and Patterson?"

"Yeah, I got one connection," Tony said. "Patterson's dead, and that's Peter's normal way of dealing with something like this."

"That doesn't give you much," Jackie said.

"What it does give me is a picture of that fat bastard sitting back hearing about the mix-up and ordering Patterson dead."

Tony slammed his fist on the table. "You see what I'm going through? We were watching both of these guys hoping to drill them about who was supplying the shit, and now I got two corpses to try and interview."

Jackie looked to the floor as a wave of nausea worked its way from the pit of his stomach.

"I've been there almost two months, and I haven't seen a thing," Jackie said.

"I didn't imagine you would," Tony said. "But this is a big story, and maybe somebody'll slip up. Lean on that Cynthia girl. She's got access to what he knows, I know she does."

"I don't think Cynthia's like that. She'd never hurt anyone."

"I'm not saying she would, but, goddammit, someone's got to know something."

*     *     *

"So you gonna' tell me what it was like?" Cynthia asked.

Jackie glanced to his lunch tray. He toyed with the idea of picking up the hamburger and avoiding the question, but he was having a hard time ignoring the anxious look on Cynthia's face.

"It must have been exciting, or at least interesting."

Jackie allowed the statement to hang in the air. Interesting and exciting weren't the words he'd use to describe his time in the orphanage.

"It wasn't your typical childhood," Jackie said. He picked the burger from his plate and took a bite.

"How is it?" Cynthia asked.

Jackie smiled in spite of himself. "You're asking a lot of questions today, aren't you?"

Cynthia smiled and flicked her hair away from her face with an exaggerated flip of her head. She leaned to Jackie and rested her chin on her hand, smiling the whole time.

"Now it's my turn for a question," Jackie said.

"Shoot," Cynthia said as she batted her eyelashes for effect.

"I heard something out on the floor about this guy named Frank Patterson," Jackie said. "What do you know about that?"

Cynthia's face immediately changed expressions, and Jackie knew she understood what he was talking about.

"Don't even speak about something like that," Cynthia said. "If someone even heard you mention his name."

Her voice faded to a whisper. Jackie took another bite of the hamburger.

"It's good," he said as he put it on the plate.

"What's good?" Cynthia asked. She wasn't the same person she'd been just moments before.

"The hamburger," Jackie said playfully. "Come on. You act so different when Peter's name comes up."

"I'd rather talk about other things, that's all." She leaned back in her chair. "Now, tell me, were there girls there?"

"Were there girls where?" Jackie asked.

"At the orphanage," Cynthia said. "Have you ever been in love?"

Jackie sipped his soda through a straw, never once taking his eyes off of Cynthia's smiling face.

"Why would you ask a question like that?"

"Because I think you dig me," Cynthia said.

"I what?" Jackie asked, as if exasperated by the line of questioning.

"You dig me. You like me. You want to be with me all the time."

Jackie's eyes found the plate.

"I'm not sure about all of that."

Cynthia extended a leg under the table and playfully kicked out at Jackie. "A girl can tell," she said.

Jackie pulled his leg away from her, and a strange sort of nervous tension began building inside him. He wanted to get away from it but couldn't. He pushed the tray across the table, and a half-smile found his lips.

"I have to get back to the warehouse. I'll see you later."

Jackie stood up, never taking his eyes from Cynthia. He hoped he was wrong and she didn't know anything about Peter's dealings, but he doubted it. He walked away with a heavy feeling in his heart.

"Hey, Jackie," Cynthia called.

He turned to face her.

"I dig you, too," she said, with a bright smile.

Jackie carried the smile with him through the rest of the day.

*    *    *

Jackie set up the apartment in the same fashion his mother and father decorated their home in Savannah all those years ago. There weren't any fancy pictures on the wall, and, although he could afford it, he didn't own a television or a stereo. Instead, Jackie lived with the bare essentials. He owned a bed, a lounge chair, a clock radio, and a couple of folding chairs around a small kitchen table.

Jackie lay on the bed, listening to the sounds of the family in the apartment below. They always seemed to be having trouble dealing with one another, and the loud piercing screams of Anita Lopez shook his heart. There was genuine hate in her voice, and night after night, it was too much to take.

"You fucking bastard!" she screamed over and over. She was obviously drunk, but she wasn't yelling to herself. "You don't give a shit about the kids. You lay around all goddamn day expecting me to take care of everything. I ain't putting up with it no more. I'll have you thrown out of here so fast your fucking head'll spin."

Every night it was a variation on the same theme, and what tore at Jackie's heart were the sounds of the children in the background. Some nights, he felt like taking the children away from the pain. Instead, he simply listened.

"Go to fucking bed," the husband shouted back. "I can't take the bitching anymore, go to fucking bed!"

Jackie was never really sure when the shouting would stop or how the situation would be resolved. In all likelihood, they'd shout themselves to sleep in the middle of their drunken reality and they'd wake up the next day amidst the same nightmare.

*It's a hell of a way to raise children.*

As the screams finally died down, Jackie went back in time to his own childhood. He drifted back to his days at the orphanage and how the counselors would try to get him to grieve. Jackie knew he'd never be able to explain it. Instead, he talked to God.

*I never could tell them what it meant to be poor. God, I'm feeling sorry for myself, but I couldn't ever explain why it felt like everyone else was better than me. There's so many people alone. Sweet Jesus, why are there so many of us alone?*

Jackie thought of the children in the apartment below. Every day was a struggle to fight to find a way through the screaming.

*God, how can I help those kids? I know what it feels like to be alone, and I don't want them to feel that way, too.*

The screaming stopped and, somewhere along the way, Jackie felt himself drifting toward sleep. His mind offered him the image of Peter sitting in his office, ordering

123

Frank Patterson's death. All at once, Jackie jumped from the bed and ran to the bathroom. He threw up into the sink, and, in the middle of it all, he swore that somehow he'd make a difference.

*    *    *

The following Saturday, Jackie spent the early part of the day outside a 7-Eleven store around the corner from his apartment. He'd made a few small purchases, including a cup of coffee, the morning paper, and a loose-leaf notebook in which to store the thoughts that randomly entered his mind. Ever since he was a boy, Jackie kept a journal, and his private thoughts were often times what got him in trouble with the counselors.

Despite the December chill in the air, Jackie leaned against a telephone pole in front of the store. He watched the people rush by him into the store. He sometimes felt as if he could enter the minds of the people as they went about their day.

On this particular morning, there was an overweight woman carrying a twelve-pack of toilet paper, three teenage boys sharing a story about a basketball game, and a solitary old man who searched the parking lot for something missing.

*Everyone's looking for something.*

He noticed Tony rounding the corner thirty feet away. Jackie walked in the direction of his apartment. The coffee spilled from the top of the cup and ran down his hand, and Jackie sipped at it as he followed Tony. There was a sense of purpose in Tony's steps, and Jackie wished he had information for the man. Tony was a cop who wore the uniform the way it was supposed to be worn. He fought the fight for good against evil and was losing to a man because of greed and corruption. Jackie felt a strong surge of pride. Despite all he had to face, Tony fought from day to day, one minute at a time.

"Tony," Jackie shouted.

Tony stopped on a dime, spun on his heels, and moved his hand to his holster. He dropped his hand to his side when he saw Jackie.

"What's up, partner?" Tony asked when Jackie got close enough.

"Not much," Jackie said. "I didn't get you a coffee, sorry. I'm a little short of supplies."

"That's all right," Tony said. "Let's just get inside, I don't know if I want Peter to know I speak with you on Saturday mornings. He might never let you in on his little secret."

Jackie stepped to the door, opening it quickly.

"So how is the scumbag behaving?" Tony asked as they stepped through the front door.

"I don't have anything," Jackie said. He set the paper and notebook on the table. "I know half the employees hate his guts, but you'd never get one to admit it."

"That's the stone wall around the castle."

"I have some thoughts on it, based on conjecture," Jackie said.

"Of course," Tony said.

"Since last week, when you told me about Patterson, I've brought it up to a few people. I didn't say much about it because I don't want to make anyone anxious. But I've gotten the same reaction every time."

"It's fear, right?" Tony asked.

"Yeah, extreme fear," Jackie said. "It's a terrible way for people to live, but anyone near Hanratty cowers as though he could snuff their life out with a wave of his hand."

"He can," Tony said.

Jackie went to the cupboard and removed a coffee mug. He poured half of his coffee into it and extended it to Tony.

"I'm pretty sure you're right about Patterson. Peter did it, but there isn't anything out there to tie him to it."

"Nothing," Tony said, sipping from the mug. "You got anything?"

Jackie shook his head.

"Nothing but the fact that I'm pretty much convinced you're right. There was a fat kid there before me, and he made a reference to drug running. Ben and Cynthia seem to know what's going on, too, but Peter's bulletproof."

"We'll find something sooner or later," Tony said. He paced the bare floor. His level of intensity was what drew Jackie to him.

"You have to get his trust," Tony said. "He makes mistakes, man. He fucked up that fentanyl thing, and I know he fucked around with Barth all those years ago, too."

Jackie felt a deep gnawing in his heart. The thought of Billy Barth and Peter Hanratty working together made sense for the first time.

"You're going to have to be as nice as pie," Tony said.

"One problem," Jackie said. "The guy repulses me."

"Understandable," Tony said. "I know it, but you have to get it done."

*　　*　　*

Jackie spent the remainder of Saturday afternoon as if he were at the orphanage. He read an obscure novel by Beth Holmes entitled *The Whipping Boy* and selected passages from a Bible, worn from daily use. When Jackie wrote his thoughts into the spiral notebook, the writing was fast and furious. He was aware his new friendship with Cynthia was fueling his thought processes, yet the dark sentiment of his earlier writings was also present.

*Life is a pain sometimes. It is often weary and tiresome with an emphasis on living day to day, taking what you can from your fellow man without being caught. You look from here to there for something you can cling to, and there are moments when you feel it within your grasp. It's as if it's right there in your hands, and you're finally making a connection within your heart. Then it disappears. The wind of life carries it far away from you, and it's gone forever.*

*The time we've spent together is etched upon my mind. Every laugh we've shared comes back to me, and then it's just carried away. I know I'll never be close with someone again. I can't ever feel love in this heart because of what I've lost.*

Jackie sat alone as the sun drifted in the sky making its daily descent. It was early evening before he decided he should make an attempt to rejoin the world. He was a couple of feet away from the door, with his mind on a small pizza from the corner shop, when he heard a knock. He opened it without thought and was faced with Cynthia's smiling eyes.

"If you'd get a telephone," she said, "I wouldn't have to come across town to talk to you."

"Yeah, but if I got a phone it'd ring."

Cynthia laughed nervously, and Jackie waved her into his home.

# CHAPTER SIX

They sat across from one another in a corner booth of Sammie's Pizza Palace. The shop was dimly lit but alive with the sounds of a jukebox and the hurried conversation of six patrons. Cynthia rubbed her hands, which were numb with the coldness of the night. Jackie, as usual, took in his surroundings. He noticed everything from the sauce stain on the waitress' apron to the color of the scarf at the feet of the elderly woman at the table across the room.

"This place claims to be the first pizza joint in the world," Cynthia said.

"It's not, though, is it?" Jackie asked.

"I don't know," Cynthia said, "but they get a lot of mileage out of it. Their bacon, onion, and cheese pizza is, like, the best-known pizza in Connecticut."

"I know how to pick the place," Jackie said.

Cynthia rubbed her hands together and smiled.

"I feel like I'm on a date," she said with the excitement of a thirteen-year-old.

"I've never had a date before," Jackie said.

"I think it's great," Cynthia said, "but if we're going to make a habit of this, we should, maybe, drive next time." Cynthia laughed, reaching across to pat Jackie's hand.

"I'm sorry if your toes got cold," Jackie said. "It's a clear night, though. I thought a walk would be nice."

"Nice?" Cynthia said. "If it were any nicer we'd be in Alaska. Nice is when it's eighty degrees."

"What're you doing living in Connecticut?" Jackie asked.

Cynthia stirred her soda with a straw and looked reflectively to the floor. A Springsteen song played in the background, and it looked to Jackie as if she might cry.

"Someday I'll have a house on the beach with servants bringing me drinks while I get a tan," Cynthia said.

"Not working for Hanratty you won't," Jackie said. "He likes to tie his money up in himself."

Cynthia didn't look up to meet his eyes. Her mood seemed to darken. "I have all these stupid dreams. I want a home, family, and car. Sometimes I wonder where all the dreaming and wishing is getting me."

"There's nothing wrong with wanting more," Jackie said.

"I know," Cynthia said, "and it's not like I'm unhappy, but sometimes I wish I had a family or someone there all the time." Cynthia smiled brightly and moved up in her seat.

"There's this town called Clinton. It's just like so nice. It's real colorful, and the birds are flying all over the place. I want to take you there someday. Anyway, whenever I get to Clinton, I feel like the world is perfectly balanced. Most other times, it feels like I'm chasing my own tail."

Jackie laughed. He wanted to pull her close to him. He knew what it was like to chase his tail.

"You'll get what you want and more," Jackie said. He patted her hand. "What happened to your family?"

Again, Cynthia's eyes found the floor.

"It was only Mom, Dad, and little old me," she said. It looked as though she were speaking to her napkin. "All they ever did was fight. They tried to stick it out for me, but, when I was fourteen, my father figured he'd better get out or he'd wind up killing us both. He lit out down to Texas, and me and Mom high-tailed it to Florida. We talk once in a while, but it's not a family." Cynthia bowed her head and fought back the tears. "I don't know why I'm bitching. Look what you went through."

The pizza-toting waitress saved Jackie from answering.

"It looks awesome," Cynthia said, and the tears in her eyes were replaced by a look of happiness. The waitress lowered a piece of pizza onto Jackie's plate, but he hardly noticed. He couldn't take his eyes off Cynthia.

\*     \*     \*

"I can't believe I ate so much," Cynthia said as they walked out into the cold night air.

"You're telling me," Jackie said. "It was like a blur in there. You ate like you were possessed, I only had one piece."

"Cut it out! We each had three pieces. God, did I really?" Cynthia laughed, and Jackie joined her.

"You put on a real show," Jackie chided.

"Well, I'd hate to freeze to death on an empty stomach. You know, I'd stay warm if you put an arm around me."

Slowly, he draped his arm across her shoulder and pulled her to him. They walked in silence for a few moments, and Jackie thought about how warm she felt on his arm. For one of the first times in his life, Jackie began the conversation.

"Isn't it an amazing world when you think about it?" He fixed his gaze upon the star-studded sky.

"It really is," Cynthia said. "It's even more amazing that we screw it up." She sighed lightly.

"There's this guy at the warehouse who always has a nasty scowl on his face. Every time I say hello or ask him how it's going, he tells me how miserable his life is. At first, I used to try to say something encouraging, but now I just walk by. I think it's kind of sad, you know?"

"It really is," Cynthia said. "Guys like that make it harder than it has to be."

The sounds of traffic carried the tone for the next few moments, and Jackie couldn't help but feel a certain peacefulness in the night.

"We all make our own reality," Jackie said. "We shape our lives and arrange 'em any way we want. We can rearrange them, too, when things are lousy."

"So, if that guy is miserable forever, it's his fault."

"Exactly," Jackie said, "Sometimes it's easier to stay down, because you don't have to worry about falling."

Cynthia's eyes moved toward the sky. She squeezed tighter to Jackie and slipped her arm around his waist.

*     *     *

It was a little after seven o'clock on the morning of December twenty-second when Jackie entered the front door of the Hanratty building. Although he wasn't scheduled to begin working until eight, Jackie was usually the second Hanratty employee to start his day. He had never once shown before Peter.

Jackie went through his morning ritual of turning on the lights, starting the coffee-maker, and warming up the copy machine. It wasn't that he was trying to make points with Ben or Peter, he just enjoyed the solitude of the deserted offices and knew it was a privilege to go to work.

Jackie paused for a moment outside Peter's office door. He heard the muffled sounds of a telephone conversation and wished he knew what made Hanratty tick.

Power and money seemed to be the only driving forces behind Peter's existence. To Jackie, it seemed to be an awfully lonely life. Peter had never married, he didn't seem to have any close friends, and there weren't ever any long, business lunches or golf dates. It was as if the business were the man's only interest.

Jackie entered the office he shared with Ben. He quickly gathered his thoughts for the day ahead. His responsibilities were fairly consistent from one day to the next, and it was comfortable to be able to structure his day as he saw fit. For the most part, Jackie spent the morning tracking the previous day's activity and completing the extensive paperwork. In the afternoon, he concentrated on supervision and documentation of trucking activities. It was more responsibility than he'd imagined, but it was satisfying work.

Jackie sorted through the paperwork. He assigned job numbers for billing purposes and made a neat stack of the items to be typed or filed. A few minutes before eight, Jackie made his usual jaunt toward the coffee machine. With his mug firmly in hand, he stopped by Cynthia's desk and set the paperwork by her telephone. As he did each morning, he took a post-it note and scribbled a morning greeting. He turned to walk away when a simple slip of paper on the corner of her desk caught his eye. In Cynthia's now-familiar handwriting there was a short note addressed to Peter. "Bennington knows about Patterson," it said.

Three different thoughts fought for time within Jackie's mind, and he read the words over and over to engrave them in his mind. He thought of stuffing the note in his pocket, wondered about Cynthia knowing of Hanratty's criminal activities, and considered forgetting he'd even seen the note.

Although he barely remembered his retreat, Jackie was back in the spot behind his desk when Cynthia stopped by to wish him a good day. Even as her eyes shined their radiant look of happiness, Jackie felt the coldness of his past.

"Are we doing lunch?" Cynthia asked.

"Definitely," Jackie said. "I'll meet you in the cafeteria at noon."

Cynthia made a quick exit, and Jackie looked to the paperwork. Somehow he'd have to find a way to hide the disappointment.

*     *     *

They sat in their usual places in the company cafeteria. Cynthia sat in front of a salad she hardly touched. Jackie tried the meatloaf and was sorry he did.

"What's wrong with you?" Jackie asked as Cynthia moved a tomato wedge back and forth across her plate. She almost seemed to be racing it from side to side.

"It's you. You never tell me how you feel."

Jackie set his fork on the plate.

"What do you want to know?"

Cynthia looked as if she might cry. "I'm so stupid," she said. "I thought we'd get closer and you'd tell me everything that happened when you were young."

"I don't talk about it," Jackie said.

Cynthia pushed the plate away as tears filled her eyes. "Friends talk about those kinds of things. It hurts that you won't talk about it."

Jackie looked away from her tear-stained eyes. It was too much to comprehend.

"I feel selfish, too," Cynthia said. "Instead of worrying about how you really feel, I'm more worried about the fact that you don't trust me."

"It's hard bringing it into casual conversation," Jackie said. He was having a difficult time focusing on Cynthia's effort to console him, knowing that she'd written the note to Hanratty.

"Last night, I couldn't sleep, and I kept thinking about you and your family. Jackie, I want to help you."

She was in the midst of a full-fledged, crying session. Jackie leaned across the table and flicked a tear away from her cheek.

"You've helped me," he said softly. "Besides, it's done, and I can't undo it. It's hard to think about the past when going forward is so complicated."

The tone of his voice seemed to have a calming effect on Cynthia, who wiped her tears away. "What're you doing for Christmas?"

"I don't have any plans," Jackie said with a slight smile.

"We should be together," Cynthia said. "We should be closer. What else do we have?"

"That's a very attractive way to put it," Jackie said, with a laugh. "What else do we have?"

# CHAPTER SEVEN

Jackie stood on the bottom step of the police station. A light snow fell around him, and he stuffed his hands into the pockets of his jacket. He watched the traffic pass by and didn't even see Tony's approach.

"Hey, partner, what's going on?" Tony asked.

Jackie turned in time to see Tony pulling up the collar of his coat.

"Yes, and a Merry Christmas to you, too," Jackie said.

"Sorry," Tony said. "The fat pig has me a little worked up today."

"When doesn't he?" Jackie asked as they walked to Tony's car. "What I got can be summed up in one word, *Bennington*."

"Bennington?"

Tony's face took on a look of doubt. A snowflake touched down on his right cheek and melted away before Tony could bring his hand up.

"I saw a note on Cynthia's desk this morning. It said, *Bennington knows about Patterson*."

Tony shook his head in denial.

"It's got to be a mistake. Bennington doesn't even leave his house anymore, he's a fucking recluse."

"He's got a telephone, doesn't he?" Jackie asked. "Maybe he picked up the word on the streets."

Tony stopped walking, and Jackie could almost see the thoughts rolling around in his mind.

"He's a good cop," Tony said.

"It's all I got," Jackie said, shrugging.

"I'll check it out, but Cynthia surprises me. I didn't think she'd be stupid enough to leave a note out in the open."

"Maybe she wanted me to see it," Jackie said.

Tony considered it for a moment and quickly dismissed it.

"You can't protect her," Tony said. "Some of the most dangerous people in the world have blonde hair and nice asses."

Jackie couldn't think of a suitable response.

"What did it say?"

"Bennington knows about Patterson," Jackie said.

"It was in Cynthia's handwriting?"

Jackie nodded and Tony repeated the message over and over as if the more times he said it, the closer he'd get to a clue.

"Let's talk to William," Tony said.

It was the last thing said between the two men before they pulled into Bennington's apartment complex.

* * *

William was dressed in a T-shirt and pair of jockey shorts. The television set was on in the room just off the kitchen. Jackie thought of how old William looked. Nonetheless, he offered a smile to his old acquaintance. William ignored the greeting and moved about the apartment as if he were still alone. He returned to the living room, sitting down in front of the television.

"What's on the tube?" Tony asked.

William gestured toward the couch. The place seemed clean enough, in a lived-in sort of way, and William also appeared clean and healthy. It was his manner that was peculiar.

"It's some goddamn game show," William said.

Jackie and Tony sat on either end of the couch. Jackie thought back to the days long ago when William had walked with them along the sound.

"What're you doing here?"

"We thought it'd be nice to visit," Tony said.

"Tony, don't bullshit me," William said with a look of complete annoyance. "You don't pay social visits."

Tony forced a laugh.

"I guess we can't fool the old owl," Tony said. He, again, tried a slight chuckle, but William wasn't buying it.

"It's Hanratty," Tony finally said.

"Of course it is," William said. He picked up the remote control and snapped the game show to darkness.

"What is it now?" William asked. Tony looked at Jackie. They already knew how William would respond to the accusation. For the first time, William's eyes found Jackie's face.

"I came across a telephone message to Peter from his secretary," Jackie said. "It said that you know something about the drug death of Jeremy Hagar and the murder of Frank Patterson."

William shifted in his seat. He seemed to be trying to read what Jackie knew about it. "I do know about it," he finally said.

"Hanratty's involved, right?" Tony asked hopefully.

"No," William snapped. "I know that it's bullshit. Peter didn't have anything to do with it, and he offered to help me find out more about it."

"Why of course he did," Tony said sarcastically. Tony plopped back against the couch in complete exasperation.

"Once again, you're chasing the wrong man. Let me tell you something. Since I left the force, I've had the time to take a good look at Peter's business, and your preoccupation with this man is ridiculous. He's always been a good friend and a fine businessman. He's been good to me, and he's been good to people like you." William pointed in Jackie's direction.

Tony sighed loudly. He looked to the blank television screen as if he wished the game show would magically reappear.

"I've worked with him for the last few months," Jackie said, softly, "and I think you're wrong about him."

William looked as if he'd been punched. "I've known him all my life!" he screamed.

"Yes," Jackie said, undaunted by the scream, "and that's why you're looking at it through rose-colored glasses. Sir, you don't want to find anything. I appreciate what you did for me, but he's not the man you think."

William considered the words for a moment and emitted a low growling sound that reminded Jackie of a wild animal.

"Everyone's a penny-ante detective. I'll be fair with you guys. Tell me what you have, and I'll shift allegiances."

Neither Tony nor Jackie could answer.

"You don't have nothing, because there ain't nothing there!"

William sat back in the chair. His breathing was heavy, and he flicked the television back to life. Tony stood up, looked to the television set, to William, and finally back to Jackie. It was past their time to leave.

"I think you know you're wrong," Jackie whispered.

He got to his feet, turning to the door. As he looked back, Jackie saw tears in Bennington's tired eyes.

\*    \*    \*

The temperature seemed to have dropped twenty degrees while they had been in the apartment. Jackie pulled his jacket tight to protect himself from the chill. The snow fell lightly around them, and the silence of the night added a shivering exclamation point to the thoughts in Jackie's mind.

"So what're you doing with the rest of the night?"

"I don't know," Jackie said. "I'll probably just spend the night thinking about everything."

"That's not exactly a typical Christmas thing to do," Tony said.

"I've never been typical," Jackie said, and the two men stood silent.

"We'll come up with something," Tony said. He was trying to convince himself.

"Why do you think he'd lie for Peter?" Jackie asked. He wiped a snowflake away from his right eye.

"I've my theories," Tony said. "If you'll make me a cup of coffee when we get to your place, I'll let you in on a couple of them."

\*     \*     \*

They sat on folding chairs in the center of the living room. The single lamp in the center of the room did little in way of illumination, but Jackie turned on the small clock radio near the window. The apartment was comfortable enough for their uneasy words.

"William's wife died tragically," Tony said. "He had a tough time of it, as any of us would." He sipped at the coffee.

"Are you married?" Jackie asked.

"I got a wife, and my first kid's on the way," Tony said. "If anything ever happened to Margaret, I'd shoot my head off."

Tony looked to the floor.

"When William's wife died, he became a basket case. His world caved in, and he forgot about everything that was ever fun."

"He was at the mercy of the world," Jackie said.

"Exactly," Tony said.

"Well, I know how that feels," Jackie said.

"As you also know, people on the brink often look for a hero," Tony said.

The remark instantly brought to mind thoughts of Cynthia, and Jackie shrugged them away.

"If there's one positive thing to say about Hanratty, it's that he's always there when the chips are down."

135

"There's always a piece of heaven at a disaster site," Jackie said.

"Yes, exactly," Tony said. "Peter counts on that, too. He's always around when people are most vulnerable. He kept William alive. He made William look forward."

Tony sipped his coffee. "Peter was at the center of every disagreement William and I ever had. What's more, Peter also got William cleared when he was in trouble over you."

"How's that?" Jackie asked.

"The leaders of the community were ready to hang William, because he'd given your mother the gun that killed her."

"It killed Billy, too," Jackie said.

"How'd you ever handle that?" Tony asked.

Jackie teetered back on his chair. He shook his head from side-to-side, allowing a grin to crease his lips.

"I learned a lot about life in a short time. If you're poor and alone in this world, you're at everyone's mercy. Yet you know that's not really an excuse for just plain, bad living. It wasn't Billy Barth, either. He was a result of the world we were forced to live in. Everything about my life up to that point led to those few minutes in the trailer. It started with the desperation in my father's walk, speech, and everything about his entire existence."

Jackie caught Tony's eye. He was certain he was still grinning, and, for a single, fleeting moment, he felt that Tony didn't care about any of it. For over a minute, there was only the sound of laughter from the apartment below. Jackie knew their party would turn into a drunken argument.

"So why are you helping me bring Peter down?" Tony asked.

Jackie sighed as if he were about to completely bare his soul.

"I can't stand what he stands for."

"Me either," Tony said, nodding slowly.

"Can we get him?" Jackie asked.

"If there's a way, it rests with you," Tony said. "Somewhere along the way, he might trust you enough to let you into his inner circle. The only reason why Peter pulled you out of the institution is because he wants to be known as the man who saved you."

He gained his feet and headed to the kitchen. He rinsed the cup and left it in the sink.

"Have fun reading and thinking."

Tony showed himself out. Jackie didn't move from the chair for over an hour.

*    *    *

It didn't snow on Christmas morning. Instead, the clouds hung low in the sky thick, dark, and threatening. Yet, in a strange way, they offered a feeling of comfort. The clouds seemed to hold Jackie close, protecting him against the world and offering a peaceful feeling. Somehow he pushed the thoughts of Billy and Peter far away. He thought only of Cynthia and what their friendship could mean.

"You look outstanding," he said to Cynthia as she opened the door. Cynthia was wearing a white and red dress. Her hair was tied back in a ribbon, and her smile was bright. Jackie handed her a gift.

"You have to put it under the tree, silly," Cynthia said.

Jackie was immediately overwhelmed with the scent of their dinner. The soft sounds of Christmas music rang in his ears. The apartment was decorated with wreaths and pictures of Santa Claus and his reindeer. In the far corner of the room was a medium-size Christmas tree without a single bulb out of place. Jackie took it all in within a matter of seconds and felt the smile on his lips.

"It's my first real Christmas," he said.

Cynthia stood directly in front of him, and they were close enough to touch. Her eyes looked directly into his, and for a moment the feeling of loneliness was gone from Jackie's heart.

"Would you like something to drink?"

"What do you recommend?" Jackie asked.

"I'm going with the egg nog," Cynthia said.

"Of course," Jackie said, and the tears welled up in his eyes.

*    *    *

William also noticed the low-hanging clouds dominating the morning sky. The clouds didn't offer him comfort.

William was overwhelmed by the anxiety the day offered. He'd formulated his plan for over a month, and, with any luck, he'd bring the city to its knees. At one o'clock the shit wouldn't just hit the fan, it'd knock it over.

William's movements were precise and deliberate. The planning was flawless, and the proof was indisputable. Peter would, at least acknowledge that much, and together they'd decide on the next step. William also anticipated the resentment and hate. It came with the territory of accusation.

William cleared the breakfast dishes from the table. He thought of his wife and how she'd cleaned up after him every day they were together. This morning, he wiped the table neatly and spread the letters, confessions, and tape recordings out across the table. He gazed at a picture of his wife and whispered a silent prayer, hoping that she'd watch over him.

He sat reading over the notes. He sipped bourbon and water and looked to the clock. It was a hell of a way to spend Christmas Day, yet if all went according to planned, Peter would be in jail for Christmas next year.

Like clockwork, the doorbell rang at precisely one. William looked to the ceiling and quickly wiped his brow. For no good reason, he looked through the peephole, and he shook his head at Peter and the bottle of whiskey. William knew Peter was also carrying two shot glasses with the year engraved on them. He wiped his eyes before opening the door to his friend.

"Merry Christmas," Peter bellowed, extending the whiskey.

"I know we don't normally exchange presents," William said, "but this year I got you something."

\*     \*     \*

They sat side by side on the couch. Their presents to one another rested in their laps. Jackie felt awkward, but deep-down he wasn't sure what he should feel. It had been a lot of years since he felt as if someone cared for him, and the thought of Cynthia inviting him into her home was almost too much.

"You open first," Cynthia said. Her smile was broad enough to take control of the entire moment. Jackie protested, but the smile stopped him dead in his tracks. There was no way he'd win an argument.

The gift was wrapped in red and green, and Jackie held it up to inspect the wrapping job. "You fared better than I did," he said with an uncomfortable chuckle.

"Stop stalling, and open it," Cynthia said excitedly.

For an instant, Jackie thought of the lonely Christmas Days he'd spent at the orphanage. He wondered about the people who'd be alone this year and thought of William Bennington.

Jackie shrugged the thought from his mind. He turned the box over in his hand, in search of a seam. Finally, he tore the paper away and was left holding a box with *The Gap* written across the front. He tried to remain graceful and in control. He removed the lid and peered down at a heavy, dark blue sweater. He held it up in front of him.

"Do you like it?" Cynthia asked.

"Of course I do," Jackie said, and without warning, he leaned and kissed Cynthia. She kissed back, and Jackie closed his eyes in an effort to wipe away the pain of those Christmas Days at the orphanage.

"It's your turn," Jackie said as the kiss was broken. "Oh Come, All Ye Faithful" played in the background. Jackie couldn't think of a better way to present his gift.

Cynthia didn't hesitate. She ripped the wrapping paper aside and let it drop to the floor. She offered Jackie one more smile before looking down.

"Oh, my God," she said. She held the cloth-bound, gold-laced Bible out in front of her. "It's beautiful."

"Everyone should have one," Jackie said, "and it comes with a story, too."

Cynthia's left hand rested on his right knee, and she clutched the Bible to her chest.

"I was in the mall," Jackie said. "I had the Bible in mind as a gift, but when I took it to the cash register the lady seemed surprised I'd be getting such a serious gift for a young woman."

"No way," Cynthia said. "It's beautiful."

"Anyway, it made me think I'd better play it safe and buy a more conventional present, too."

Jackie extracted a small package from his front pocket and Cynthia tore into it with the same delicate fury. She held a bottle of *Obsession* perfume in her hand.

"That has a pretty descriptive name for the way I feel about you," Jackie said.

Cynthia returned Jackie's kiss.

\* \* \*

"What the fuck is this?" Peter asked. He sifted through the proof, tossing the papers aside one by one. "This is absolute bullshit. Are these more of Tony's lame attempts to set me up?"

"Tony isn't involved, and, Peter, you know it's anything but lame."

"You better think hard about what you're saying. This is serious business. Do you understand what I am to this town?" Peter's face was a deep shade of red.

"I think I understand it now, yes," William said. He poured a shot of whiskey. "It broke my heart to find out about this." He passed the bottle to Peter, who took it without a word.

"Let's see how close we are to the truth," William said. He walked slowly around the table, sipping his drink. He sat directly opposite of Peter.

"Go ahead," Peter said, pushing the papers away.

"There was a young man on the streets named Jeremy Hagar," William said.

"Never heard of him," Peter said confidently.

"You probably haven't, but let me tell you about him. Jeremy wanted to be a basketball player. He found a good way to make money running drugs, and he knew a man named Frank Patterson."

Peter shrugged his shoulders.

"You were always at the top of the ladder," William said. "Through a rather extensive marketing plan, you got the drugs to Jeremy."

Peter offered only a blank stare.

"Humor me," William said. "Let me guess what happened three weeks ago."

"Why not?" Peter said. "All you're doing is guessing."

William sipped the whiskey, but his mouth felt completely dry.

"On December third, Patterson contacted Hagar. They met in their designated spot, and Patterson gave Hagar a heroin substitute called fentanyl. Jeremy never knew the difference, and Patterson never thought to check the potency. In the end, it cost both of them their lives. Jeremy cut into the profits, and, along with a lot of other people, he dropped dead. Patterson was ordered shot to death in case he ever thought of opening his mouth."

William sized up Peter, and neither man dropped their stare.

"Am I close?" William asked, and Peter laughed boisterously. Again, William took a slug of the whiskey as if it were providing him with the strength to go on.

"Do you even care about the kid who died?" William asked. "Do you care his mother's only wish was that he go to college and make something of himself? Peter, the woman is devastated. She said that the only reason Jeremy would've dealt drugs was because of the money."

Peter yawned loudly, waving his hand over his mouth as if to emphasize his boredom.

"You never really gave a fuck about anyone, did you?" William asked. The anger was beginning to crest in William's heart and mind. "You only pretend to have a warm exterior."

"Thank you," Peter said, offering a wide grin.

"You do whatever you please," William said, "and if you make a mistake you atone for it by killing people."

There was very little to go by in Peter's face, and William wondered how far he could push it.

"I've researched this," William said. "I know the name of the man who pulled the trigger, and I know Ben Potter directed the killing on your orders."

"I don't have to listen to this," Peter said. He waved his hand at William but made no motion to get out of the chair. Instead, he poured another shot of whiskey into his glass.

"That's right, get comfortable," William said. "I got a lot more for you."

*     *     *

Jackie had never had Christmas dinner with all the trimmings. As he ate the ham, baked potato, and cauliflower, he thought of the children at the orphanage.

"This is the best dinner I've ever had," he said, laughing nervously. "Everything is perfect."

"I'm not the greatest cook in the world," Cynthia said, "so I'll accept that without an argument."

Empty plates covered the table, and the music softly played in the background.

"Can I get you coffee?" Cynthia asked.

"No thanks, I drink too much of it."

"How about a glass of wine?" Cynthia asked.

"Maybe in a little while," Jackie said. He turned his gaze away from Cynthia to the bright lights of the Christmas tree.

"It's pretty hard for me to open up," Jackie said, "but I want you to know that you're kind of a symbol."

Cynthia shook her head, and a huge smile crossed her face.

"That's very romantic. I've never been a symbol before."

"I've spent so much time alone, and the words ain't always there when I'm looking for them. But, Cynthia, I want to live a real life. I'm tired of just surviving. You're kind of a symbol of beginning again."

"You mean you dig me, right?" Cynthia asked.

Cynthia's smile was transferred onto Jackie's face.

"I just want a little happiness. I want to make my life worth something."

"Will you ever tell me what it was like at the orphanage?"

"There isn't much to tell. I confused the counselors, but I was just trying to stay alive. I was in a complete shell, and I wanted to study and get on with my life. I didn't have any desire to talk to anyone about anything. It's easy for people to say they care, you know?" Jackie felt a twinge of sadness at his own words and the realization that no one had truly cared for him since the day in the trailer.

"Those counselors say the right things to collect a paycheck. The bottom line was I had to believe in myself before I left that place, and I do. Now, I just want to try and make it so there aren't as many kids like me walking around."

Jackie stopped short, smiled, and reached for Cynthia's hand.

"You just want a new life?"

"I really do," he said.

"I want to be a part of it," she said, and she slipped her arm around his shoulder.

\*　　\*　　\*

"We've been friends a long time," Peter said. He allowed the words to hang in the air. William bowed his head, and the magnitude of what was happening choked the words back into his body. He wondered if he could let Peter walk away unscathed.

"Remember the nights when you, Debbie, and I would sit up and talk and laugh? We drank Jameson's by the gallon. Debbie drank some kind of wine, right?"

"She always drank white Zinfandel."

"Yeah," Peter said, laughing, "that real sweet shit."

"She had a way of being able to stop us before we went completely overboard," William said.

"She was a hell of a woman," Peter said, and again the words hung in the air.

"Debbie was the best," William said. He was nearly in tears and made a move toward the Jameson's.

"I miss her a lot," Peter said. "There isn't a day that goes by that I don't think of her."

William was in tears. "The thing about it," he said, "is I miss the little things more than anything else. I miss the way she walked around the house. I miss the sound of her gargling before we went to bed. I miss the way she used to eat everything on her plate separately. She'd eat all the potatoes, all the corn, and then all the meat. She never mixed them and it used to drive me crazy. But now I really miss it."

"You guys didn't do everything right," Peter said. "But you definitely did more things right than wrong."

"You're goddamn right we did," William said. He took a swig of the whiskey, and, when his eyes cleared and he focused on Peter again, he saw the gun for the first time.

"I'm sorry," Peter said, "but I can't let you tear me down."

"It doesn't have to be like this," William said.

"No, it doesn't," Peter said. "Yet, when I was a kid, I saw a poster hanging in a gun shop. The poster was red and yellow and the darkest shade of ominous blue you ever saw." Peter aimed the gun at the center of William's forehead.

"There were two vultures sitting on top of a hill, and they were looking down at a field of people. The caption said, *Patience my ass, I'm going to kill something.*" He took a slug of whiskey, grimacing as it went down. "My friend, I never forgot that cartoon. You've always known I'm an impatient man. I know you're a proud man. There's no other way."

William begged Peter with his eyes, but deep-down he knew his life was over. No one heard the shot, and the bullet made a very small hole in the center of William's forehead.

# CHAPTER EIGHT

At nearly midnight, Jackie stood under the threshold of Cynthia's apartment door.

"I had a great day," Jackie said.

"One more kiss would make it perfect," Cynthia said, and Jackie didn't hesitate.

"Are you sure you don't want a ride?" Cynthia asked.

"I like to walk," Jackie said.

"It's almost midnight, and it's cold."

"If I get cold, I'll think of you," Jackie said, and Cynthia stepped back.

"God, that's corny," she said in mock horror. "Watch out for the bogeyman."

"I already beat the bogeyman, once."

Cynthia pouted with her eyes. "Can I have *one* more kiss?" she asked. Jackie shook her off.

"If I kiss you again, I might not leave," he said.

"You don't have to," Cynthia answered.

Jackie kissed her quickly and backed out the door with his smile firmly in place.

\*     \*     \*

He walked back to his apartment with her image etched upon his mind. It wasn't just her physical presence. Her entire outlook on life was refreshing. The way she smiled at him and held him close made him feel needed for the first time in his life. It occurred to Jackie that just holding life close could take the sting out of his nasty memories. He ran the last quarter-mile back to the apartment, and, as he turned the key in the lock to his door, he looked to the darkened sky.

"Thanks, God, for giving me something I'm afraid to lose."

\*     \*     \*

Peter didn't run away from the scene. He walked from William's apartment with the next order of business already in mind. He whistled a Christmas tune realizing that he'd have to get someone to clean up his latest mess. He wasn't about to entrust it to anyone other than his two most trusted employees.

Peter walked past his waiting limousine. He turned the corner on Mission Street. He took in the sight of the 7-Eleven store and its huge neon sign that proclaimed it was open twenty four hours a day. His breathing grew heavy, and he abandoned the Christmas song until he was inside the store. He walked straight to the magazine rack where his two best men stood with their backs to him.

"Clean it up," Peter whispered. "Leave the body but not the evidence."

Peter began whistling once more. He plucked a bag of corn chips off the front counter and turned to watch Ben Potter and Tony Miller leave the store.

"How's your Christmas going?" the girl asked as she rang up the purchase.

"I've had better," Peter said, but he couldn't help smiling. His best friend was gone, but new friends were just a few dollars away.

*He brought it on himself.*

He ripped open the bag of chips, dipping his fat hand into the bag.

\*       \*       \*

The first knock on the door stirred Jackie from his slumber. He heard the second knock and, as he turned over in bed, he believed it was another drunken brawl in the apartment below. The third knock, however, propelled him from the bed. Jackie opened the door and was faced with Tony in full uniform.

"What's wrong?" Jackie asked. The look in Tony's eyes was enough to freeze water.

"William's dead," Tony announced. "He was shot to death in his apartment."

Jackie's heart dropped to his knees, and he had trouble hearing the rest of Tony's words.

"I was trying to call him all day," Tony said.

The words swam through Jackie's mind.

"Finally, I went over there, and he was sprawled out on the kitchen table."

It couldn't be true. Somehow, it just couldn't be true.

"It was one bullet in the center of his head."

The nightmare of his life was starting all over again.

"He died before he knew what was happening," Tony said. "Let me in, we'll figure it out together."

"I can't," Jackie managed. "Tomorrow."

Jackie shut the door and slumped against the kitchen wall. How did Tony know if William had suffered? How could anyone understand the terror unless they were there?

He sat in the dark for a long time before gaining the strength to get off the floor. A little more than two hours after learning of William's death, he sat in a folding chair with a notebook in his lap. He scribbled the words quickly and read them over and over until the morning light came shining through his window pane.

"*There is no barometer within us that measures the amount of pain we can withstand. A red light will not flash on inside of us when we know we've had enough. The pain of life will divide you into pieces and eat away at you until it consumes you to the point of utter despair. And, still, there is no kill switch. The pain grows, and there is no level of enough. It seems as if God has placed me on this earth for the sole purpose of dying, and, still, I must continue, because I have no idea how much pain my heart can absorb.*"

# CHAPTER NINE

It hardly mattered that it was the day after Christmas or that William had been killed. At nine, Jackie was expected in Mary Ellen Rossetti's office for his monthly visit. He arrived at ten minutes before the hour knowing he couldn't pull off the charade that life was perfect. He pictured William denying knowledge of Peter's wrongdoing. If William held fast to Peter's innocence, then why his sudden death? Maybe it was Tony who was responsible for what had happened. Perhaps Tony had gone back to discuss it with William, and his anger had gotten the best of him.

Jackie dismissed the thought. Tony wasn't anything if he wasn't honest. He was insane in his desire to tear Peter down, but he wouldn't do it at William's expense.

Mary Ellen entered the waiting room at precisely nine. Jackie was in a chair in the far corner of the waiting room, and Mary Ellen strode past him to the inner offices without so much as a nod in his direction.

Mary Ellen stopped at the front desk, and the receptionist pointed to Jackie. He stood up slowly, and Mary Ellen spun on her heels and offered a beaming smile.

"Good morning," she said.

"How are you, Miss Rossetti?" Jackie asked.

Mary Ellen allowed the question to pass. She sized up Jackie for a moment, and her smile never dimmed.

"How about we go inside and talk?" she asked.

Mary Ellen held the door, and Jackie walked beside her down the corridor toward her office.

"So how you holding together?" Mary Ellen asked.

"I'm doing all right," Jackie said. He thought of asking if she'd heard about William but decided that the less he offered, the better.

They entered a small office which held only a desk and two chairs.

"Have a seat," Mary Ellen said, and Jackie complied. "How's your apartment? Do you have everything you need?"

"All the comforts of home," Jackie said. He would've laughed had he been in a better mood.

"Is your job okay?" Mary Ellen asked. "Are you making enough money to get by?"

"Everything's super."

"Any trouble fitting in with the other workers?" Mary Ellen asked.

"None," Jackie said. He slumped back against the chair, and Mary Ellen emitted a slight groan. She set the pencil down and moved the notepad to the furthest point on her desk.

"Jackie, my job is very precise, and, despite what you may think, it's also very important. You're making it difficult to make an evaluation of your progress. Your one-word answers aren't enough, and this is a crucial period for you."

Jackie stuffed his hands into his jacket pocket. He knew of no other way out of the situation and began speaking in a low, clear voice. "I haven't missed a single appointment with you or the help center. I haven't been absent a day of work, and I eat three square meals a day. I drink too much coffee and read strange books, but I'm as close to normal as I can get." Jackie licked his lips, pausing to see if his words were being accepted.

"My apartment won't be featured in *Better Homes & Gardens*, but it suits me. I'm not a social butterfly and won't ever be, but I'm in control of what happens and that's more than you can say for a lot of people." Jackie smiled slightly knowing that he'd surprised her with his words. She jotted notes on the pad, but didn't speak.

"I've heard good things about your work," she finally said. "Jackie, I want to be wrong about you. I really do."

She offered a smile and flipped to the next page. "Let's talk about what happened to William," she said. Jackie looked away.

"How has his death affected you? Do you think his death has anything to do with you?"

Jackie didn't respond.

"Had you spoken with him since your release?" Mary Ellen asked.

Jackie was on his feet and moving to the door.

"Please talk to me," Mary Ellen said. "It's important I know how you feel."

"Have a nice day," Jackie said. He opened the office door and stepped into the hallway. He felt as if he might throw up, and he moved down the hall quickly, swearing that his days of counseling were over.

\*     \*     \*

Tony swung the office door open and poked his head inside. Peter was at the bar, with his back to the door.

"Come in," Peter said, without turning to face his new colleague.

"I have everything," Tony said. He tossed William's notebooks and tape recordings on the desk. "We really cleaned the place up."

"Good. You want a drink?" Peter asked. "You've earned it."

"I suppose," Tony said, sitting in the chair in front of the desk. Peter poured a shot of whiskey and moved it across the desk.

"Isn't this partnership better then fighting?" Peter asked. He drained his glass. "How about the police force? What's the word about town?"

"Oh, they're up in arms, of course," Tony said. "The thing is, I'm leading the crusade, and your name hasn't been mentioned. The word around the department is sympathetic toward you. They know how much you loved William."

"You're in charge of the investigation?" Peter asked gleefully.

"You can't be touched," Tony said, raising his own glass.

Peter contemplated the statement for a moment.

"Don't ever think I can't be touched," Peter said. "I thought William would always be loyal, and look what happened. This position in life comes with certain risks, and sometimes the good guys change sides real quick. Do you understand where I'm coming from?"

Tony nodded. He drained the last of the whiskey from his glass.

"Tony, let me tell you something," Peter said thoughtfully. "Everyone has a price, but William couldn't be bought. You, as a point of reference, had to buy into it. You saw the things I could offer and set aside your petty beliefs and bought into it, didn't you?"

Tony nodded once more, but Peter knew he was uncomfortable.

"You had your price because your wife's pregnant and you're getting strangled being an honest guy, right?"

"I suppose," Tony finally said.

"Yeah, you suppose. Now, how about Jackie? What will his price be?"

"He doesn't know anything," Tony said.

"I should have never stood up for that kid." Peter said. "Do you think he'll ever compromise his principles?"

"I doubt it," Tony answered.

Peter leaned back in the chair and closed his eyes for a moment.

"I have an idea that might throw the kid off for a while," Peter said.

"You shouldn't have any trouble setting him up," Tony said. He took Peter's glass and headed toward the bar.

"My sentiments exactly," Peter said. "I've kept Mary Ellen Rossetti's phone number handy for such an occasion. That bitch would love to get hold of that kid."

# CHAPTER TEN

Jackie issued hand signals to the driver, and the tractor-trailer moved smoothly back into the warehouse. Jackie stopped the driver with a quick wave of the hand, and the other workers moved into position at the back of the truck.

Jackie wore a Dallas Cowboys T-shirt and faded blue jeans. The hard hat on his head didn't slow the sweat that poured down his face. It wasn't overly warm in the warehouse, but Jackie hadn't taken a break all morning. The bustle of activity kept his mind from wandering to thoughts of William's death.

The truck driver stepped down and made his way to Jackie.

"What do you have?" Jackie asked, picking up a clipboard. The long-haired driver handed the paperwork to Jackie without so much as a word. Jackie examined the paperwork and shouted to the workers.

"Take off the pallets in back. Use the fork-truck, they don't weigh nothing."

One of the men nodded, and the sound of the gate being raised on the back of the truck nearly drowned out the sound of Peter's booming voice.

"Jackie!"

Jackie turned and watched Peter's slow approach. He nodded and slowly backed away from the driver. Instinctively, Jackie wiped the sweat from his brow. Much to his surprise, his mind was devoid of any thoughts of hatred for Peter.

"Jackie, can I speak with you a minute?"

Peter waved a hand toward the head dispatcher's office and Jackie followed.

"Look at this mess," Peter said. He motioned to the chaotic state of the room. "Rob's a pig."

Jackie dabbed the sweat on his forehead. He sat in the chair beside the desk.

"You're probably wondering why I'd call you in here," Peter said.

Jackie shrugged. He was thankful for the break.

"You've been here a little while, what do you think of our operation? Also, do you have any thoughts of learning more about the business?"

Jackie moved forward in the chair. It was the perfect opportunity

"Of course, I'd like to learn more," Jackie said. He was surprised by the enthusiasm in his voice. Peter leaned across the desk and pushed the button on the intercom.

"Cynthia, send Danny in please."

"Right away, sir," Cynthia answered. Jackie shuddered at her patronizing tone.

"Danny's a little obnoxious," Peter said with a chuckle, "but he's a good man and one of my most trusted employees. You can also be a trusted employee for many years to come."

"Thanks for the chance," Jackie said, mimicking the patronizing tone he'd heard from the other employees.

"Danny has a strange way of looking at life. He talks non-stop about anything he can think of, but he knows enough not to let his mouth get him in trouble."

Jackie wasn't sure what Peter meant, but, before his mind was able to fully dance around the thought, the door swung open.

"Hey, boss," Danny said, bursting on the scene. He walked straight to Peter with his right hand extended. "Happy Tuesday," he said. Danny spun on his heels facing Jackie. "You've got to be Jackie."

Jackie half-rose out of his chair, but Danny's hand was thrust out.

"Sit down, I'm not the freaking Pope."

Jackie smiled at the tall, thin man with the long, greasy hair and the unkempt beard.

"Are you a Cowboys fan?" Danny asked, pointing to Jackie's shirt.

"Actually, no," Jackie said. "I don't know much about football."

"They're a great team," Danny said, "but not for me, I'm a Buffalo Bills fan." Danny laughed uproariously, and, although Jackie had no way of knowing what was funny about the statement, he smiled in spite of himself. Peter watched the scene with a look of amusement in his chubby cheeks. Danny leaned against the back wall.

"So what's up?" he asked. He searched his front pocket for a cigarette and pulled a crumpled pack out, extending it to Jackie, who shook him off.

"All right," Peter said, "if we're all settled now." He paused for a moment as Danny lit the cigarette.

"I called you here to introduce you as partners."

Danny laughed, and Peter looked startled.

"Sorry, I was thinking about my last partner. Peter, you remember Mark Thomas, right?"

Peter nodded and smiled.

"What a freaking geek," Danny said. "Remember when you sent us to New York?"

Peter shrugged, but his smile didn't dim.

"We were cooped up in a hotel, and I'd been sleeping for about an hour. Anyway, I turn around in the bed and the freaking guy is sitting on the heat register. Every minute or so he reached into a bucket on the floor. Finally, I couldn't take it anymore, and I asked him what he was doing. He said he was watching ice melt."

Danny howled in laughter, and Peter laughed nervously.

"That guy's got to be dead somewhere," Danny said.

Peter allowed the moment to pass.

"Jackie isn't Mark Thomas. He's a level-headed kid with a lot of drive and ambition. He's familiar with our warehouse procedures, but he doesn't know much about what goes on in the real world. There are things we do that go unnoticed by a great many people."

Jackie's mind instantly turned to thoughts of William, and he had to work to hide his anger.

"We often make deliveries to our customers who not only pay for storage, but also need us to help them to haul the goods."

"I understand," Jackie said.

"On this particular assignment, we'll be making a delivery for a company called GT General. They're a construction outfit out of Brooklyn that's replacing press components in the General Motors plant on the outskirts of New York."

Peter tapped his hand off the desk and pointed a finger toward Danny.

"Danny's job is to get you and the cargo to New York in one piece. Jackie's job will be to make certain the paperwork is in order. We want a smooth transfer of ownership to the people at GT General. It's an easy assignment, but it's also a necessary one. I'm counting on the two of you to make it happen. You'll receive your hourly wage for the duration of the trip, and I'll handle all expenses. Any questions?"

Jackie's mind was a whirlwind of thought. He examined the possibility that it might very well be a legitimate business trip, but it felt too much like a test.

"I don't have anything," Jackie said.

"We'll be fine," Danny said. He put his cigarette out on the wall and moved to the desk.

"What route are we taking? I'm not going through that butcher job you sent me on last time." Danny turned to Jackie. "They told me my permits would be set all set, but I ended up spending three freaking hours at the state line, staring at a tremendously fat broad who ate thirty freaking donuts while I waited."

Danny laughed uproariously and pointed an accusing finger at Peter. "That's how this guy keeps you in place."

"When Jackie is sure he understands everything, we'll work out the permits."

Peter offered Jackie a stern smile.

"You have to make sure the paperwork's in order. Danny'll explain it as you go, but you'll get it. You leave tomorrow morning, and you'll be gone for a day or more."

"I understand," Jackie said. He rose to leave.

"Glad to have you aboard," Danny said, shaking Jackie's hand again. "Don't worry, we'll do great."

Jackie turned to the door. He felt Peter's eyes burning a hole in his back. It all appeared civil enough, but Jackie couldn't help feeling queasy.

*     *     *

Jackie stared at the paperwork. He couldn't concentrate, but, thankfully, the telephone took him away from it for a moment.

"Hi, Jackie," Cynthia said.

Jackie smiled into the mouthpiece. "How's it going?"

"Typically irritating," Cynthia said. "How about dinner tonight at that pizza joint?"

"I'd love to."

"You're leaving in the morning, huh?"

"How'd you know?" Jackie asked.

"I know everything," Cynthia said.

The comment caught Jackie off-guard, and he hoped it wasn't true.

"What's wrong?" Cynthia asked.

"Nothing. I was thinking about you stuffing pizza in your mouth."

"I'll see you at eight, smart-ass."

Jackie replaced the receiver, and the usual worried smile worked its way onto his face. The telephone rang again.

"Don't worry," Cynthia said. "This isn't another social call. Line one is Tony Miller for you."

Jackie wondered what Tony was thinking calling him at work.

"Meet me at Rip's Tavern at six o'clock," Tony said.

"Okay," Jackie said, and the line went dead.

＊　　　＊　　　＊

The Tuesday evening crowd at Rip's was fairly thin. There were a few well-placed couples working on dinner and two construction workers at the bar, drinking their dinner at a furious pace.

Jackie did a quick scan of the area before sitting at the bar in a seat facing the television.

"Can I help you?" a small, dark-haired girl asked. She studied Jackie's face, almost daring him to try and order alcohol.

"I'll have a Pepsi," Jackie said.

The girl appeared disappointed.

"What brings you here?" she asked. "You didn't come here to watch television and drink Pepsi."

"That's exactly what it is," Jackie answered, and she walked away. Years of practice allowed Jackie to be alone when he wanted to be.

The front door snapped open, and Jackie instinctively turned on the stool to face it. Peter walked in flanked by Ben and another man whom Jackie didn't recognize. Jackie swung his stool back to the front of the bar and dropped his head away from their line of vision. They walked past him without a sign of recognition and continued to the back corner of the room.

Jackie took his hand away from his face a few moments later. He got off the stool and skirted his way to the door. He reached for the front door just as it opened. Jackie nearly smacked heads with Tony.

"Peter's here," Jackie whispered, and Tony backed out of the bar and into the street.

"What's he doing here?"

"It's not a big deal, he didn't see me."

The cold, bitter air hit Jackie directly in the face. "He wants me to go on a run to New York."

"I know," Tony said. "I got a strange phone call from Mary Ellen Rossetti."

Jackie stopped walking. "My counselor? What's she calling you for?"

Tony stuffed his hands in his jacket pocket. He looked squarely into Jackie's eyes.

"Peter called her," Tony said. "He said you're depressed over Bennington. He told her he'd get you out of town until the press got off the story."

"What're you talking about? I don't follow you."

154

"He's setting the table," Tony said. He began walking again, and Jackie marched in step beside him. "He's painting a picture of despair, so if something happens he'll be covered."

Jackie didn't respond right away. He did a mini-pirouette and then froze in place. "What's he up to?"

"I wish I knew. I've never been able to figure him."

"Should I not go?" Jackie asked.

Tony took a moment to consider the question.

"No, you have to go. He's testing you, and, if you back out, he'll know he can't trust you."

They continued moving toward Tony's car. "You have to go prepared." Tony turned the lock on the driver's side door. "Before you go, I'll find out what you're up against."

Jackie waited for Tony to open the side door. If there was one thing Jackie knew for certain, it was the fact that he'd be lost if it weren't for Tony.

*   *   *

Dinner was over, and they sat on the couch in Cynthia's apartment. Jackie ran the earlier meeting with Tony over in his mind, but he wasn't about to share it with Cynthia. She huddled close, with her right hand on his left thigh. Jackie looked at the side of her face as she stared blankly at the television screen. A break in programming ended the silence.

"You're being quiet tonight," Cynthia said. "Even for you."

"I'm thinking about the trip," Jackie said.

"Will you miss me?" Cynthia teased. Jackie didn't answer, and Cynthia caressed his thigh. "It's not a big deal. It's just a short trip."

"Actually," Jackie said, "I don't know. I have no idea what this guy wants from me."

Cynthia sighed audibly, and her hand came away from Jackie's leg. "You don't have to analyze everything."

Jackie stood up. At that moment, he felt like walking away, but something made him stay. "Bennington's dead, and Peter knows all about it."

"That's ridiculous," Cynthia said. She quickly moved from the living room to the kitchen. It was as if she were making a conscious effort to avoid Jackie's eyes.

Jackie followed Cynthia into the kitchen. Her head was bowed, and she mindlessly walked to the refrigerator and opened the door. Jackie wasn't sure if she were crying, but he knew his words upset her for some reason. He stepped behind her and wrapped his arms around her waist. Cynthia eased back into his embrace.

"I read somewhere that you should never apologize," Jackie whispered into her right ear. "The guy who wrote that was a moron. I don't want to upset you. You're the one person I can't lose right now."

Cynthia held the door open. The refrigerator light was the only light in the room.

"You looking for more pizza?" Jackie whispered.

Cynthia swung around. She was still in his arms but her handle on the door was lost. It slowly swung shut. "No more pizza jokes." She kissed Jackie hungrily.

*     *     *

Jackie walked toward his apartment. He knew Cynthia had some link to what happened to Bennington, but he didn't want to believe she was completely involved. For some reason, he felt that he needed to shield her from the pain.

Tony sat with his back pressed against the front door of the apartment. He looked at his watch and shook his head. Jackie turned his key in the door as the sounds of the battle in the apartment below raged on.

"I should arrest that family on fucking principle."

"You talk about prisons being crowded, now," Jackie laughed. "If you arrest people for being ignorant, half the world would be in prison."

Jackie swung the door open, and they stepped inside.

"They've been screaming like banshees for the last hour. They swear and scream in front of the kids like they aren't there."

"That's every night," Jackie said. "Some nights, I cry for those poor kids."

They were just inside the front door. Tony seemed totally preoccupied with the sounds of the fight below.

"You need a license to drive a car, but any dumb bastard can have a kid. My wife's pregnant, and all I think about is how miserable this world is, now. I'm tired of fighting all the time."

"We're still fighting it, aren't we?" Jackie asked. He tossed his keys on the counter and flipped on the overhead light.

"Of course, we're still fighting it."

Tony looked around nervously.

"Are you ever going to fix this place up?"

"It's as decorated as it's going to get," Jackie said. He hung his coat on the back of the chair. "You want a drink?"

"No," Tony said. He walked through the apartment. He was taking stock of Jackie's meager possessions. He picked up the Bible, turning it over slowly.

"You seem lost tonight," Jackie said.

"I don't think you should take the gun," Tony said. He looked reflectively at the Bible.

"What gun? What're you talking about?"

Tony placed the book on the kitchen table.

"I was thinking of giving you a gun for tomorrow. Maybe it's better if I don't."

Jackie saw the internal battle brewing inside of Tony. "I'm not taking a gun," he said. "I promised myself I'd never hold a gun again. I'm not going to let this guy scare me."

Tony paced the wooden floor of the living room. He didn't seem to be in much of a hurry to discuss his plan to expose Peter. The longer Tony was silent, the more certain Jackie became that there wasn't a plan. Jackie sat on the counter and worked his bottom lip over between his forefinger and thumb. He allowed five minutes to pass before he spoke.

"Tony? What's going on?"

"I don't know," Tony said. "I've never been able to figure Peter out."

"No," Jackie said bluntly. "I can't buy it anymore. You aren't telling me everything. I know you're trying to protect me, but I need more than this. Something's going on."

Tony did one more pace around the room before sitting backwards on the folding chair. He appeared to search his mind for the right combination of words. "You're right. I'm not telling you everything, and I'm not sure I can. I'm tired of fighting. Maybe you should get out."

"For months you've been preaching this act about how good prevails over evil, and, all of a sudden, you don't know."

Tony shrugged and gazed to the floor. His hands were coupled, and he looked like a beaten man.

"Just tell me the truth," Jackie implored.

"The truth is, I think he's going to kill you. Maybe not tomorrow or next week, but he doesn't trust you, and killing you will keep you out of his way."

The words didn't stun Jackie as Tony may have thought.

157

"Well, the plan is still the same," Jackie said. "I'll make him think he can trust me."

"Maybe we should just give it up," Tony said.

Tony was on his way to the door. Jackie stared after him blankly. Tony faced him with his arms outstretched and his palms showing.

"I'm still going."

"I know," Tony said. He walked out the door.

\*     \*     \*

They moved steadily down Interstate 95. The traffic heading south toward New York City was building, and their trip had already been delayed by a stop at the McDonald's off the interstate in Meridien. Danny was discussing Bill Clinton with a stranger, arguing that Clinton was destroying the country. The exasperated stranger finally shrugged and walked away.

"That's the pulse of this country," Danny said as he and Jackie returned to the confines of the truck cab. "No one knows what's going on anymore. They have their pulse on a small portion of the freaking world, and, as long as their own little corner is tidy, they've no idea the rest of the world sucks."

Danny barely stopped to take a breath of air. "I bet that guy lives in a house he hasn't paid for and drives a car he doesn't own. Him and his wife probably drop the kids at daycare and travel two hours to get to work. They probably get drunk on the weekends and try to save enough money to see a movie."

"Yeah, things are bleak," Jackie said.

"Bleak! Freaking-a-right they're bleak, and it ain't gonna stop. We're living off credit cards. We spend our time catering to a boss or the freaking whims of a lying, cheating president. We don't know what the hell's going on anymore. It's more than bleak. It's downright scary."

Jackie listened intently. Danny's incessant chatter would carry the travel portion of the trip.

"I want to be honest," Danny said. "Hanratty wants to see if he can trust you. He talked to me after you left. He was all secretive and shit. Now, me, that ain't my way. I'm a straight-shooting kind of guy, and I shoot straight with everyone, even Peter. You want a smoke?"

Jackie shook him off.

"Good, these'll kill you'."

Jackie waited for Danny to continue. For the first time, he thought he might learn something about Peter.

"He wants me to fill your head with stories," Danny said, laughing. "That man's a real joke sometimes. Anyway, he wants me to tell you about drugs and all this other shit to see if you'll go running to the police. I don't know much about you, but I'd take that as a compliment. You got the fat one scared. Of course, that ain't hard to do anymore. He's so freaking paranoid these days his shadow makes him jump."

Danny took a couple of drags on the cigarette and exhaled through his nose. His eyes remained on the road, and his mouth stayed in motion. "'Course, I ain't gotta make up stories when it comes to Hanratty. Even though he thinks no one knows about him, everyone does. He deals drugs and kills cops and robbers alike. He's so deep into this shit he's got to keep buying people off. It's funny, but, like I told you, ain't no one around anymore who sees past the freaking nose on their face. Peter's the same way. For all his money and power, he's just everyone else."

Danny flicked his ashes onto the floor.

"How does he get away with it?"

"Money, my boy," Danny said. "Money's the key to everything."

A quick nod was all Jackie could manage.

"And it's only freaking paper. All this fuss over paper!"

Danny tossed his head back and laughed.

"Peter's got us all in his back pocket."

"I'm not in his pocket," Jackie said.

"Yeah, you are," Danny said. "He signs your check and keeps you right where he can watch you."

Danny took another draw on the cigarette. His left eye closed slightly to dispel the smoke. "He's got it over all of us, you, me, the police, congress, all the way down to the chick at the front desk. We owe our whole existence to Peter. Do you remember that fat kid Peter fired?"

"Rick Montgomery?" Jackie asked.

"Yeah, Rick, never learned the rules. Well, you know what happened to Rick?"

"I can't say I do," Jackie said.

"His fat body washed up on the beach of the Long Island Sound, and they ruled it a suicide. Of course, Peter was right there telling everyone how sad he was. I'm not surprised you missed it, though it didn't carry much weight, so to speak, on the six o'clock news."

Jackie felt his stomach tighten in a knot.

"He thought he could beat the man. He called Peter a fat fuck to his face, and he couldn't keep his mouth shut about Cynthia and Ben."

"Cynthia and Ben?" Jackie felt the blood drain from his face.

"Yeah, Ben was fucking around with her, and Rick told everyone. Cynthia and Ben are as untouchable as Peter."

Jackie was convinced he was about to vomit.

"Don't tell me you got a thing for her, because that'd be suicide."

Jackie shook Danny off.

"The place is a freaking soap opera, and your character can be canceled at anytime."

"Jesus," Jackie said.

"Keep your nose clean, kid. Stay away from thinking you can bring Peter down, and you'll be fine. In fact, you can make a nice living. That's all I do. I shoot straight with Peter, and I'm shooting straight with you. If I have a gripe with someone, I let 'em know. If you're going to have an attitude with Peter, I'll tell him. If everything's cool, I'll tell him that, too. What I tell him is up to you."

Danny lit another cigarette.

"Are we running drugs now?" Jackie asked.

"I couldn't tell you," Danny said, with a laugh. "A long time ago, I told Peter I'd go anywhere and do anything as long as he covered me. Once in a while, I think about it, and it scares me. But I figure I'm pretty safe. No one's dumb enough to challenge him outright."

Danny shrugged and turned his attention back to the cigarette.

"You'll let me look through the load if I want to?" Jackie asked.

"Sure," Danny said. "Be my guest, but I'll have to tell the fat man."

"I don't want to know," Jackie said, although it was killing him inside.

"It's pretty scary when you figure out reality, isn't it?" Danny asked.

Within a matter of minutes, Danny turned the conversation into a monologue about the upcoming football season. Jackie nodded occasionally and smiled every so often, but basically he tuned Danny out, letting his mind race to a fury. It was inconceivable that Peter was allowed to twist and turn and end lives on a whim. It was as if the man were a god. At least Danny's dissertation solved a bit of the puzzle.

Jackie couldn't stop thinking of Cynthia. It was too much to think about, and New York was only twenty miles away.

*     *     *

Cynthia was biding her time. It'd been a year since she'd begun trying to rid herself of Peter. Meeting Jackie was enough to inspire her to make the move, but she'd have to prepare to face the consequences of crossing Peter.

She packed her car with personal items and carefully moved about the office, rehearsing the plan over and over. Now, it was just a matter of pulling it off. She knocked on Peter's door.

"Yeah, what is it?" Peter bellowed from behind the closed door. Cynthia entered slowly.

"What?"

Peter's tone bordered on impatience and irritation. Yet, she had to confront him, and there was no turning back.

"It's me," Cynthia said.

"What?" Peter asked. Cynthia ran the silent pep talk through her mind. She needed to be direct and strong. She would have to turn away and not look back.

"I'm quitting. I'm pregnant, and I'm moving to Florida with my mother."

For a moment, Cynthia thought that he knew she was lying, but he moved to comfort her. Cynthia turned on the tears.

"You're pregnant? How could you let that happen?"

Peter directed her into the chair in front of the desk.

"I don't want to talk about why," Cynthia said in between sobs. "I just want to get on with life."

Peter draped his arm around her shoulder. He actually bent to his knees beside her chair. "Cynthia, let's think it through." Peter's voice drifted to a soothing whisper. "There's no reason to jump into anything. There's things we can do. Who's the father?"

The question was crucial to the plan, and Cynthia jumped all over it. "It's none of your business!" she shrieked. Peter reacted exactly as she had imagined.

"No, you're right. It's none of my business. I don't need to know."

Cynthia had him right where she wanted him and continued with the attack.

"What can you do? Make me unpregnant? How can you make it better?"

Peter was stunned. He held her, but the words wouldn't come.

"This guy doesn't want to hear anything. He wants me to leave him alone. I'll go back to my mother. She's the only one who'll help."

"You're wrong. There's people here who love you. I'll help you get through this. The people you work with are your family." Peter's voice crackled with emotion.

"I don't want to leave, but I have to."

The crying part had been easier than she thought. The tears continued to flow. "It's not Ben, is it?" Peter asked.

Cynthia had banked on the question, and she jumped all over it. "You son-of-a-bitch!" she screamed as she leapt to her feet. She fought back the urge to slap Peter across the face and moved to the door in a run. "How could you ask me that?"

Peter was too stunned to move. Cynthia swung the door open, banging it against the back wall, and escaped into the lobby.

"Cynthia!"

She didn't look back. She scooped her personal belongings off the desk and escaped through the front door. Peter wasn't in any position to chase her, and Cynthia heard him calling her name even as she sat down in her car. Tears flowed down her cheeks.

# CHAPTER ELEVEN

Jackie felt like a million other anonymous men who'd entered New York for the first time. The nervousness and apprehension built inside of him as he gazed at the world outside the window.

"This place is amazing," Danny said. "This is the George Washington Bridge. I have no idea how many people go over this bridge every day, but it's an amazing number."

"Everything's massive," Jackie said.

"Even bigger than you imagined, right? No matter what people tell you about New York, it still catches you by surprise. It's just enormous."

Danny lit a cigarette and steered the tractor-trailer through a blur of cars.

"When we get down into Manhattan, you'll be amazed by the famous places you see. Macy's is on one corner, and there's Madison Square Garden and Radio City Music Hall. It's freaking unreal."

Jackie was grinning in spite of himself. Having Danny along for the ride provided him with a trip to New York that he'd never forget.

\*     \*     \*

Danny backed up to the docks.

"This is where the unloading and sign-over procedure takes place. Don't sweat it, it's a piece a cake."

An armed security guard tapped lightly on Danny's door. "Danny, my boy," he said, with a smile as bright as day.

"Hey, Doug, how's it hanging?" Danny asked. He shoved his hand out the window, and Jackie watched the two men exchange a rather elaborate handshake.

"Who's the kid?" Doug asked.

"Jackie Gregory, he's one of Peter's pet projects."

"That's the way they all start, isn't it?" Doug asked with a laugh. He leaned into the truck, and Danny backed out of the way to give Jackie a line of sight. "You checking the load?"

Jackie glanced at Danny and then looked back to Doug. He knew exactly what was riding on his answer. "I don't need to check it," he said. "Whatever's back there is back there."

"Smart boy," Doug said.

He smiled broadly as he walked away from the truck. Danny went for another cigarette, and Jackie leaned back against the seat, closing his eyes. "Is this it?"

"It might be," Danny said. "Sometimes Doug has instructions about another stop, but it hardly ever gets real complicated. In fact, usually I just drive straight out."

Jackie shook his head in wonderment over how Danny could be so casual.

"It's just the way it is, kid," Danny said. "We deliver goods from here to there and back, and we sign the papers saying it's legit. All we have to do is stay out of the way."

Danny took a drag on the cigarette as Jackie did a slow burn.

"Get comfortable, sometimes it takes awhile."

Jackie sat back as the thoughts in his head fought for expression. He swallowed hard and tried to keep it locked away.

"This is wrong." Jackie said. "This is how it is, but it's not how it should be. Danny, you could be smuggling drugs that a kid might get or a gun someone can use to kill. You're running it across state lines, and you sit there smoking a cigarette. It ain't the way it is. Don't you have a conscience?"

Danny flicked the ashes to the floor.

"I had such hopes for you," he said in a patronizing tone. "This is the way the world rolls, kid. Peter's got the power, and better men than you've tried to bring him down. Now, they're either working for him or dead."

Danny paused and looked curiously at Jackie. The rage burned deep behind Jackie's eyes.

"I told you, you're free to jump back and take a look. Hell, you're free to go to the mayor, but this is life. The rich get richer, and the poor get poorer. Nothing you come up with is going to change it."

"Bullshit," Jackie said. He opened the door and stepped down.

"Kid, go back there and you're as good as dead."

"Dead's a shaky term," Jackie said. "Some people die a long time before you put them in the ground, and a snake squirms after you cut it in half. You tell me when something dies."

Jackie slammed the truck door. Danny's voice rang out across the parking lot, but Jackie walked to the back of the truck without turning back.

\*     \*     \*

Cynthia wasn't sure how much time she'd have before Peter came after her, but she wasn't taking any chances. Losing this game with Hanratty would be way too permanent. She exited the parking lot as if all the king's horses and all the king's men were giving chase. Although she was less than a mile from her apartment, she continued to check the rear-view mirror every ten seconds.

Cynthia was about to throw her entire life away, and she knew it was the perfect move. As the thought occurred to her, she considered Jackie. Cynthia knew he was her way out of Peter's grasp. Everything about Jackie's life was fascinating, and the closer she got to her apartment the more excited she became over the prospect of gaining her freedom.

She pulled the car into the lot and slammed it into park. For three years, she had worked side by side with Peter. She ran toward the front door with her mind intent on grabbing the bags she had packed the night before.

Peter had counted on her for anything and everything. *I was so goddamn stupid.* Cynthia turned the key in the front door. She pushed the door open and took a quick look around at her, now bare apartment. She lifted the first box from the floor and stepped back out through the front door. *I listened to Peter without judgment, while he killed people all around me.*

Cynthia tossed the box into the back of the car.

*He killed Patterson and Bennington and had the gall to hand me the evidence.*

The thoughts rolled through her mind, and, as she ran back to the house for the second box, the tears raced down her cheeks.

*Jackie showed me it could be different. He taught me to respect myself.*

Cynthia leaned in, grabbing the second box of clothes. Her next thought sent a shiver up her spine, and she tried to fight it back. She thought of the night she'd spent with Ben because Peter had asked her to do it.

*The son of a bitch used me like a whore.*

There was no stopping the tears. She recalled Ben pawing at her, expecting her to respond because Peter had told him she would.

Cynthia tossed the second box into the car. She got in behind the wheel. It would have to be a clean break. The details of her plan sifted through her mind.

*I can't ever turn back.*

\*    \*    \*

Jackie didn't have a plan for forcing his way into the back of the truck, but he knew he had to look.

"Who do you think you are?" Doug shouted.

"I'm doing my job," Jackie said. "I'm seeing what we delivered across the state line."

Doug tossed his head back in an exaggerated laugh and stepped directly between Jackie and the back door.

"Get out of the way," Jackie said.

"Let me explain something to you."

"Just back up," Jackie said.

Doug moved forward. He was bigger than Jackie, and his eyes glistened with anger. Jackie reacted quickly, pushing Doug in the center of his chest. Much to Jackie's surprise, the push sent Doug sprawling backward onto the pavement. It appeared to be in slow motion, and the only sound to echo through the parking lot was Danny's slamming door.

"You just put the last nail in your coffin," Danny said.

Doug was still painfully quiet from his spot on the ground. He looked at Jackie in shock and disbelief.

"Are you all right?" Danny asked.

"Get him out of my sight," Doug said.

"Don't worry about it," Jackie snapped back. "I'll go as soon as I see what's in the truck."

"Get the whole fucking truck out of here!" Doug screamed. He regained his feet and charged at Jackie like a bull. He stopped inches short. "I don't want anything. Take it back, and explain what happened. When they find your fucking body, I'll make a special trip to piss on your grave."

Danny edged between Jackie and Doug. Danny's hands shook as he struggled to keep Doug out of Jackie's face.

"Come on, Doug, think about this. It's a lot of money, and he *will* kill the freaking kid. We've been friends for a long time, we've seen a lot of shit. Come on."

Doug took a step back. He appeared to calm down, but all at once he lunged forward again.

"I should kill you myself! Ain't a man alive gets away with pushing me. I ain't about to let a snot-nose kid do it."

"I know, man, come on," Danny said. He held the front of Doug's shirt. Jackie continued to stare Doug down.

"The kid's freaked out. He's a little confused. I'll straighten him out."

Doug broke free from Danny's grasp. He took a walk around the lot with his hands on his hips. Jackie followed Doug's every step, preparing to defend himself.

"Get him off the property, and I'll think about taking it. If he so much as sneezes, you can take the truck back. Hanratty can have that bastard shot ten times for all I care."

Jackie walked across the lot. Danny called for him, but Jackie walked quickly as if distance would solve the problem. Danny ran to Jackie's side. "Man, what're you trying to pull?"

"Nothing," Jackie said. "I'm not going to be a part of this. It's wrong, and you know it."

Jackie continued walking. Danny stood in place, and, when he spoke again, his voice bordered on hysterics. "Stop for a freaking minute and listen to me."

"I'm just getting away."

"Then get away, but don't do it like this. Hanratty won't like this one bit, man."

"I don't care," Jackie said. "No one should be allowed to live like Hanratty does."

"Come back," Danny called. "We'll work something out."

"The only reason I'd come back is to take Hanratty down," Jackie said.

"Then go the other way," Danny called back.

\*       \*       \*

Cynthia stood in front of the locked door of Jackie's apartment. She'd written a note explaining that she was taking up residence at The Quality Inn under the name of Kellie Beaman. She mentioned that she needed to talk to him, but she didn't want to just slide the note under the door. Hanratty probably hadn't made the connection between the two of them, but it wasn't worth the risk.

Cynthia descended the stairs two at a time. The Lopez family at the bottom of the stairs was her only hope. She knocked on the door, and it was opened by a gap-toothed boy about ten years old.

"Hi," he said. "My mother ain't home."

"That's okay, honey. Do you know where the landlord lives?"

The child shook his head.

"Is your daddy home?"

"He's home, but he's sleeping. He was drunk today." The child made the statement in such a matter-of-fact way that Cynthia actually groaned.

167

"It was his day off," the child said, as if adequately explaining the situation.

"I see, well, thank you."

"Jackie might be home," the kid said.

For the second time in the conversation, Cynthia was caught by surprise.

"You know Jackie?"

"Yeah, he's a good guy."

The kid smiled, exposing three missing teeth.

"He brings us candy and lets us stay there when mom and dad are fighting, even when he ain't home."

"How do you get in?" Cynthia asked.

"Come on, I'll show you."

*     *     *

Jackie strolled through the streets in confusion. The crowd carried him from one corner to the next as he contemplated the rich businessmen mixing with the common, street bums.

New York was a collage of sights and sounds the likes of which he'd never encountered. He worked hard to take note of each thought that entered his mind. His thoughts no longer drifted to Peter as the city offered a glimpse into something new and exciting.

Jackie stopped at the streetside stands. He examined the merchandise as if he were ready to buy and walked away when confronted by the vendors. The thought that his life was irrelevant occurred to him time and again. He couldn't help but think of the hopes and dreams of millions of people that had started and ended right there. Jackie felt like an ant on the hill doing a dance among a million other ants. Although his life was all he had, it meant precious little to anyone but himself. He'd thought that Cynthia cared, and the realization that she probably didn't propelled him to the bus station. He had to find her. Jackie walked the streets knowing that life was too long of a haul without some sort of connection.

*     *     *

"I stick the card in here like this," Oscar Lopez said.

Cynthia backed away from the door, and the library card fell to the floor.

"It doesn't work all the time," Oscar said. He bent to pick up the card.

"Jackie lets you do this?"

"I told him, and he didn't say anything." Oscar's deep, brown eyes searched Cynthia's face for an answer. "Sometimes I gotta get out of there." Oscar looked to the bottom of the stairs, and Cynthia felt her heart breaking. He turned away to work on the lock.

"Jackie's apartment is kind of empty," he said. "I don't stay too long, because there ain't much to do."

The card found its way between the latch and the door, and Oscar turned the knob. The door popped, and Cynthia looked in on the emptiness of Jackie's world.

"I told you it worked," Oscar said.

Cynthia could not repress the urge to rub her hand through his hair. "Come on in. Maybe we can find where Jackie keeps his candy. You should have some candy." She wished she could take away all of Oscar's pain.

*　　*　　*

The bus bound for New Haven was scheduled to depart at five o'clock. Jackie sat in a window seat, hoping the seats beside him would remain vacant, but even before the bus was half-filled a middle-aged woman and a small girl sat beside him.

"Is it all right?" the woman asked.

"Of course," Jackie said. He looked to the child and smiled. The girl's return smile sent a shiver of happiness through Jackie's heart and mind.

"For a minute I thought I missed the bus," the woman said. "My husband would've killed me."

"These buses never leave on time," Jackie said, just to have something to say.

"Do you live in New Haven?"

"Yes, I suppose I do. I was in New York on business. It'll be nice to get back."

The woman looked inquisitively at Jackie. "You seem young to be on business."

Jackie shrugged, but he was drawn into conversation with the woman.

"Sometimes I feel a lot older than what I am."

"Life's like that sometimes." The woman looked away nervously.

"My mommy and I were shopping," the girl said. "I got a doll and a dress."

The girl grinned at Jackie, and he nodded his approval.

"It was a shopping extravaganza," the woman said. Her eyes darted to the packages at her feet. "My husband's a firm believer in keeping a fresh outlook. He knows spending money on clothes makes me happy."

"We all need a fresh outlook," Jackie said.

"My name's Rosemary," the girl said.

Jackie smiled again.

"I'm Jackie."

He extended his hand, and Rosemary shook it as a puzzled look creased her eyes.

"Jackie's a girl's name."

"Rosemary, that's not nice," the woman said.

"It's okay," Jackie said. "I thought it was a girl's name, too, but my mommy and daddy liked it."

Jackie found that the mere mention of his parents' lives was enough to conjure up feelings of regret. "How old are you, Rosemary?"

"Six," she said. She flipped her hair back away from her left shoulder as a woman five times her age might do. Her two front teeth were missing, and Jackie couldn't help smiling.

"Six going on twenty-four. I'm Donna Lewis, and you already know Rosemary."

"It's a pleasure to know you," Jackie said.

The bus pulled away from the terminal, and Donna glanced at her watch.

"A little after ten, that's not bad."

Donna seemed content to dwell on her statement for a moment. "Life's too much of a rat race, anyway. We shouldn't worry about ten minutes here or there."

"You're right," Jackie said.

"It's funny, my husband sends me on these trips, and I always end up talking the ear off some poor stranger. He says I'm going to get robbed or raped or something. I guess he's right, too. You read the paper and watch the news and start believing it can happen."

Jackie nodded, offering his crooked grin.

"I tell him life's not all bad. There's a billion nice people, you know? Besides, you got to live, right? You have to trust someone enough to talk to them."

Just as he had smiled at the innocence of Rosemary, Jackie found himself taken with the presence of Donna.

"You're right, there are things worth embracing."

"What's that?"

"It's another lesson I need to learn," Jackie said. "It's easy to feel bad about life and forget the cute smiles and warm people you meet along the way." He smiled at Rosemary. "Let's see your new doll."

In the middle of the chaos, Rosemary offered the smile he needed.

*　　*　　*

Cynthia took her time looking over Jackie's moderate possessions. She struggled with the pain of life that Jackie's bare apartment offered. Yet there was also a part of her which admired the simplicity of his existence.

"Jackie doesn't have any toys," Oscar said.

Cynthia had almost forgotten that the child was still in the room. Still, the lack of toys was indeed powerful.

"He doesn't even have a television."

"Jackie reads a lot. Do you like reading?"

"No," Oscar said, crinkling his nose. "I don't know the words."

"You have to practice," Cynthia said.

Oscar shook her off. He bit the black licorice that he had retrieved from the kitchen cupboard. "Sometimes Jackie gives me the whole bag."

"This time we'll save some for later," Cynthia said.

She looked over the titles of the books that Jackie had collected. She wanted to find one with a bookmark. Although she was drawn to Oscar's life and this was an opportunity to understand Jackie better, she had to get going.

"Why's Jackie so nice?" Oscar asked.

Cynthia wasn't ready for the question, but she knew that Oscar didn't know what it felt like to be treated right.

"He doesn't yell like my Dad. I wish Jackie was my dad, but we'd have to get a television."

Cynthia's eyes swelled with tears. She was crying for everything wrong in Oscar's world. She reached out and pulled him to her.

"You can have the whole bag of candy."

As she left, Cynthia placed the note in the front page of Jackie's tattered Bible.

# CHAPTER TWELVE

Jackie's first step off the bus was wrong, and his ankle twisted under him, sending waves of pain through his body. He stepped quickly to regain his footing, and his mind did a dance around the symbolism attached to the turning ankle. It was an observation he couldn't dismiss. Maybe he should have stayed away, but there was work to do. The time for hiding was behind him. Still, in all, he was having trouble focusing his determination. He wasn't sure if his return was due to courage or desperation.

Although he didn't know why, Jackie decided to head to his apartment. It was the only home he knew, and, until he formulated a plan, he'd have to establish a pattern within his mind. He needed clear thinking and the power of his convictions to carry him through.

Jackie noticed that Oscar had been there. He headed to the cupboard, noticing the missing licorice bag.

Jackie poured a glass of milk and grabbed a handful of cookies. He sat in the folding chair, and his eyes found the ceiling. He half-expected the door to blast open and Peter to enter in a a rage. Instead, he munched cookies and sipped milk. He wondered how long life would seem so weary and tiresome.

He rocked back and forth on the chair and thought of Cynthia. As much as he wanted to believe that her life was not entangled with Peter's, he couldn't fool himself any longer. When he'd first seen the note, he'd known she was involved.

"I should've known better," Jackie whispered. In order to find value in his self-condemning thoughts, Jackie picked up his Bible.

He stuffed the last cookie into his mouth. He set the milk on the floor and lifted the book from the shelf. He immediately saw Cynthia's note, and his heart jumped. The feeling of connection returned.

\*     \*     \*

Even though the workday was over, Hanratty's offices were a bustle of activity. Peter held the telephone to his ear. Danny was on the line, and Doug was waiting on hold.

"Where the fuck is he now?"

"I don't know," Danny said into Peter's right ear. "He went to the freaking moon for all I know. He was half-cocked about calling the police, the mayor, and the

President. I couldn't calm him down. I tried to reason with him, but he kept saying it was your ass, not his."

"All right, Danny, don't worry about it. I'll find the bastard."

"You want me to straighten things out with Doug?"

"No, goddammit! Just get your ass back here. Do what you're told!"

Peter slammed the receiver and hit the second line, but Doug had disconnected.

"Son of a bitch," he muttered. He called the temporary girl.

"Get Tony Miller and Ben Potter."

"How do I reach them?" the girl asked nervously.

"Holy fuck, forget it."

His breathing grew heavy. He pushed back away from the desk and stepped to the bar. Before he even finished pouring the whiskey into his glass, the office door swung open, and Tony stepped inside in full uniform.

*　　*　　*

Jackie entered the hotel lobby. He scanned the area for a sign of Cynthia. He made his way to the front desk, and an overweight, middle-aged woman, greeted him with a smile.

"Kellie Beaman's room number, please."

"I'm sorry, I can't give out that information."

The woman sounded as if she worked for the CIA. Jackie offered a smile. "I'm supposed to meet her here. Is there a way to get in touch with her?"

"Use the beige telephone to call her, and she'll come down and escort you in. It's for security.

Cynthia answered on the first ring, asking if it was Jackie.

"It's me," Jackie said, and the line went dead in his ear.

Jackie returned the receiver to the cradle and walked nervously around the lobby. The woman watched his every move so Jackie sat down and flipped through an issue of *People* magazine with Oprah Winfrey on the cover.

Cynthia made her appearance from the left side.

"What's going on?" Jackie asked. The sight of her was enough to calm him inside.

"We have a lot to talk about. Let's go upstairs."

Cynthia turned on her heels and led the way toward the elevators.

"Before we get into any of it, I'm really sorry."

Jackie didn't respond.

＊　　＊　　＊

"What the fuck do you mean you want out?" Peter said. He stood nose-to-nose with Tony. He tossed the half-filled glass of Irish whiskey into the corner of the room.

"I can't live this way. I thought I could handle it, but I can't even sleep. My wife's pregnant, and we just bought the house. I need the money, but I can't do it anymore." Tony's voice trembled, and his hands shook violently.

"You're pathetic," Peter said. "The big, bad cop who tried to bring me down is crying, because he can't live with himself."

Peter filled a fresh glass with Jameson's. The feeling of excitement was almost overwhelming. He loved watching Tony tremble in fear. "Would you like a drink?"

"No, thanks."

Peter made his way back behind the desk. He set the drink down without taking a sip, and he held his chin in his right hand as if he were contemplating the meaning of life. "There are two ways out." Peter took a healthy swig of the whiskey. "The obvious way, of course, is in a body bag, but that's probably not your first choice."

Tony's eyes were riveted to Peter's face. His hands were still shaking.

"Would you like to hear the other option?"

"Yes, sir."

"Now you're calling me fucking sir. You tried nailing me for years, but when you got a little taste of money, you jumped sides. You didn't want out when I was supplementing your bullshit salary, did you? You didn't want out when Margaret got pregnant. You stayed when you needed a down payment for the house, didn't you?"

"I can't think straight anymore," Tony said.

"Everything I ever gave you was offered with trust, wasn't it? I thought it was an unbreakable trust, and now you're defying me. This is fucking wrong."

Peter sipped the drink as tears welled in Tony's eyes.

"That's right, cry, mother-fucker," Peter said. He pulled himself out of the chair, moving behind Tony.

"I have a very straightforward way of doing business, and I don't tolerate defiance." Peter tried to keep his voice even, but he couldn't catch his breath.

"I'll offer you another way out. You have to make amends for defying me. You realize I can torture you for the next twenty years, because you've nowhere to turn. You have thought of that, haven't you?"

Tony nodded, bowing his head.

174

"You have to give me something for your freedom." Peter paused in order to dramatize the moment. "The people who cry hardest for freedom usually put themselves in their cages."

Tony nodded once more, and Peter wanted to slap him in the head.

"Jackie's becoming a thorn in my side. He's a minor annoyance but an annoyance, nonetheless. He's hell-bent on making my world difficult after all I've done for him." Peter moved to the front of the desk. He picked up his drink, pacing in front of Tony. "There are a lot of men that can be bought and sold. You know that, right?" Peter didn't wait for an answer.

"This kid answers to a higher set of principles. He won't be bought, and he's trying to make up for his father's miserable existence."

Peter placed his chin inches from Tony's face, which was wet with tears. "You're going to bring him here so I can rest a little easier."

Peter brought the drink to his lips, draining the glass. "How about a refill?"

Tony took the glass from Peter's hand. His eyes never left Peter's face, and as he pulled himself out of the chair, he stumbled ever so slightly.

"I'm not going to kill him. I just need to get him off my mind. I contacted his counselor, and it'll be easy to tell her that Jackie's not cutting it. I should have left him locked up."

Tony extended the drink to Peter.

"Is this an acceptable arrangement for you?"

"I don't have a choice," Tony said.

"You're right. Please, sit down, I'd like to bring Ben here to discuss our arrangement."

Tony slumped in the chair.

"Relax," Peter said. "In a few days, it'll be all over, one way or another."

\*     \*     \*

Jackie followed Cynthia to her room. He still hadn't broken his silence and was concerned with what his first words might be. He thought of Cynthia with Ben and the lies that she'd told him. As if she were reading his mind, Cynthia turned to him.

"I'm in the middle of all of it. I'm not free of blame, but I need to be free of it now."

She pleaded with her eyes, and Jackie thought he'd melt under the weight of her stare.

"If you want me on your side, you have to tell me everything."

Cynthia went to the dresser in the far corner of the room. Jackie stood inside the doorway with his hands stuffed into his front pockets.

"You can come in." Cynthia pulled out a pile of documents and three cassette tapes. She placed them neatly on the table facing the window.

"I'm trying to figure out if I'm staying."

Cynthia looked up from the documents. She brought her hand up across the top of her head and clutched the back of her neck.

"I'm sorry I'm hurting you, but this isn't how I wanted it to be."

Cynthia sat down in resignation. "I've thought about this a long time, but you're the only one who ever gave me a reason to get out. I pretended Peter wasn't a bad guy. I told myself he wasn't really doing what I *knew* he was doing."

Jackie leaned against the wall, squeezing his eyes closed. He wanted to make the world disappear.

"I couldn't do it anymore. Jackie, please, sit down."

"It's Ben that's bothering me. A lot of people are in Peter's web, but I can't believe you slept with Ben."

"So that's what you think? We've spent all this time together, and you think I'd do something like that?" She jumped from the chair as if sprung from a trap.

"You've closed *me* out. You never once told me about your family. You didn't tell me what you knew about Peter, and I'm supposed to tell you who I've slept with? Jackie, look at me! You know I couldn't do something like that."

"I didn't think you could cover up murders, either."

Cynthia swept the papers off the desk. "I don't give a shit! I'm putting my life on the line here. Do you know why?" Cynthia was crying, but Jackie didn't open his eyes.

"I'm doing it because of you."

A wave of life swept through Jackie's body, and he slowly opened his eyes. He blinked away the first tears since his father's death.

"I have the nerve to get out, because I love you," Cynthia said.

Jackie dropped down to his knees and allowed the tears to fall.

\*     \*     \*

The temporary girl ushered Ben into the office.

"Afternoon," Ben muttered, going straight to the bar. "What the fuck's going on around here? I heard Cynthia quit, and where the hell's Jackie? Peter, you're getting awful lax in your old age."

Ben poured a glass of vodka. "So, what's up?"

"Plenty, they're defecting one after another today."

Peter sized up Tony as Ben slugged down a quarter of the vodka.

"Tony's also a little disenchanted with our working relationship."

Ben struggled to hold the drink down. "You've got to be fucking kidding me. Looks like you've told him his options. He's as white as a ghost."

Ben and Peter laughed uneasily as they held Tony on the hook.

"You know, I'm not an unfair man. I've never kept anyone around against their will."

"No," Ben said, with a chuckle. "You've always released them."

Peter rose from the chair. "I've made an arrangement with our police officer. When he gets the job done, he'll be free to go."

Ben nodded as if it really could be tied up into a neat little package.

"I want him to find Jackie and bring him in. As you've heard, Jackie was unruly today, and we can't have that. "

"That's for sure," Ben said, taking a gulp of vodka. "The bitch is on his side too."

Confusion and rage fought for space in Peter's mind. "They're together?" he screamed.

"They've been thick as thieves for the past couple of months. That frigid bitch probably filled his head with all kinds of stories."

Peter felt a sharp pain in his chest. "That sneaky little bitch told me she was fucking pregnant!" Peter slammed his fist on the desk. "I'm fucked if she ever comes out with a story."

"She won't," Tony said. "She knows what'll happen to her."

Peter spun to face Tony.

"Listen, you dumb fuck, she knows everything! And Jackie's a righteous bastard. Those two can tear me down!"

Peter threw his second glass of the day. It shattered against the back wall, and the whiskey dripped down the wall onto the carpet.

"Goddammit!" Peter cried. "Find those son-of-a-bitches, and kill them, now."

\*　　\*　　\*

Jackie was on his knees just inside the doorway. Cynthia rocked him back and forth like a baby.

"We'll get through this," she whispered over and over. "I love you. We'll get through it."

The tears slowly subsided. Cynthia led Jackie to the bed, and they continued to hold each other, realizing that they were in for the fight of their lives.

"We have enough proof," Cynthia said, "but someone has to listen to us."

Jackie leafed through the papers in his lap. There were pages of notes implicating Peter in the murders of Bennington and Patterson.

"The cassettes are conversations between Ben, Peter, and Tony. I know where the gun is that they used to kill Bennington, but, if we trust the wrong person, we're both dead."

"How deeply is Tony involved?" Jackie asked.

Cynthia's uneasy laugh caught Jackie off-guard.

"He's been in bed with Peter for the better part of six months."

"You've got to be kidding."

Cynthia shook her head. "Peter lured him with the money. Jackie, I'm sorry, I didn't know what to do to get away."

"You did fine," Jackie said.

Their faces were just inches apart. The thought that Peter would probably chase them down and kill them was burning through his mind, but Jackie leaned and kissed Cynthia. They held it for a moment.

"Growing up, I had no idea what if felt like to be kissed," Jackie said. "I remember how much Mom and Dad loved me, but, like everyone else, I was always searching for acceptance. It's a shame we need money to feel accepted."

Cynthia's eyes grew wide, and she looked at Jackie with sense of awe.

"I don't always show my emotions, but I do love you."

# CHAPTER THIRTEEN

Peter sat alone. In the confines of his treasured home, with a vault for his belongings and a high-tech security system protecting his wealth, he sat in solitary confinement, trapped within the walls of his own existence.

He stared at the blank screen of his wide-screen television set. He sipped from the bottle of Jameson's in his lap, plotting revenge against his collapsing world. Why had everyone suddenly turned on him?

"I hold all their dreams in my hands," he slurred.

His mind twisted to the thought of Cynthia and his feelings for her. "She's like a goddamn, bitch dog that bit me when I fed her." He took a sip off the bottle. "I held her up when she had nowhere else to turn, and she bit me like a rabid, fucking Doberman."

Peter closed his eyes tightly. He took another heavy swig from the bottle and allowed the whiskey to work its way through his mind.

"I gave them their fucking worlds, and they all turned on me."

He was having a hard time breathing. The pains in his chest were stronger than ever before. Still, he sipped at the whiskey.

"I was Bennington's only friend. I offered comfort, and he shit on me."

Peter nodded as though the shaking of his drunken head confirmed his words.

"I picked Jackie out of the fucking orphanage, and, instead of thanking me, he pushed me to the limit."

Peter shook his head violently. The ache of self-pity gnawed at his heart. "I hate feeling like a poor man." He threw his glass for the third time that day. This time, he shattered the big-screen television in front of him. Glass sprayed across the room, and he looked at the set for a long moment, as if it, too, had defied him.

\*     \*     \*

Jackie didn't want to do it, but he had nowhere else to turn. He punched the numbers into the phone, glancing at Cynthia. She nodded as if to give him strength to make the call. He punched in the last number but quickly placed his hand on the disconnect button.

"She's won't help. She thinks I'm a time bomb. She tried as hard as she could to keep me institutionalized."

"I know," Cynthia said, "but she's our only hope. If she feels responsible for unleashing you on the world, she'll, at least, talk to you."

"I hope you're right," Jackie said. He punched the numbers in a second time. He closed his eyes and fell back onto the bed as the telephone rang in his ear.

"Hello?" Mary Ellen's voice reached Jackie's ear, and he nearly returned the receiver to its cradle. Something inside of him made him hang on.

"Miss Rossetti?"

"Yes, who is this?"

"It's Jackie. I'm sorry to be calling so late, but I need to talk."

"Of course," she answered.

"I'd rather not discuss it over the phone," Jackie said. "Can you meet me at the diner on Myrtle Avenue?

Jackie sighed heavily and waited as Rossetti considered the request.

"Dominick's, right? Is a half an hour too late?"

"No, that's fine."

Jackie placed his finger on the button to break the connection. He looked to Cynthia and shrugged.

"You had to do it," Cynthia said. "Don't worry, you can trust her."

"I hope so." Jackie said.

*     *     *

The ringing telephone vibrated within Peter's swollen head. He struggled to get his huge frame out from underneath the covers. He grabbed the receiver with a groan.

"What?" he asked.

"Peter Hanratty? This is Mary Ellen Rossetti. I just spoke with Jackie Gregory."

"Where is he?" Peter asked.

"I'm meeting him in an hour at a diner called Dominick's on Myrtle. If you care about him, like you say you do, maybe you can meet us there. We'll bring it all to a head."

"That's a good idea," Peter said, wiping the sleep from his eyes. The rage in his mind allowed him to focus his eyes. "Yes, let's bring it all to a head."

Jackie and Cynthia sat in the diner for nearly twenty minutes. Two cups of coffee were going cold in front of them, and they passed the documents that incriminated Peter back and forth.

"I'll do the talking if you want," Cynthia said. "I know she doesn't trust you."

"It ain't a matter of trust," Jackie said. "I just always kept to myself. I didn't give her the answers she wanted. I didn't have much to say."

Cynthia held the cup to her lips as she considered her next words.

"I was scared of everything." Jackie said. "I wanted to make the world right, but, honestly, I didn't know where I was half the time."

"It must've been horrible," Cynthia said. "We'll get through it. She'll know enough people to help us out."

"When this is all over, I want to get away, " Jackie said. "I'd like to go somewhere like Nebraska and become a short-order cook. I want to forget everything that's happened. I want a real life."

Jackie meant for the moment to be light, but Cynthia seemed to be pondering their future.

"We could get on a bus and run, now," Cynthia said, "but I know you, and I picture your parents the same way. You'll fight for your survival."

Cynthia reached across the table. Jackie looked to the spot where they were touching.

"That's why I wanted to be with you. You're giving me the strength to believe in myself and stand up to him."

Jackie wanted to lean across the table and pull her to him, but the smiling waitress interrupted his thoughts.

"More coffee?" she asked. She didn't bother to wait for Jackie's answer. She turned the coffee in his cup from light to dark brown.

"Thanks," Jackie said, and, in the same instant, his heart jumped at the sight of Mary Ellen Rossetti entering through the side door. She appeared lost as she scanned the tables for Jackie.

"She's here," Jackie said, as he poured cream into his coffee. Cynthia turned in her chair, following Jackie's eyes.

"She's beautiful; tall, dark, great shape. You must have been in love." Cynthia laughed lightly.

"She has an idealistic view of life. She thinks money and power rule the world. She never let me forget I was poor and socially deficient."

Jackie didn't have time to expand on the thought. Mary Ellen spotted him and offered a wave. Jackie instinctively waved back as though he'd spotted an old girlfriend at a high school reunion.

"This ought to be fun," he said. Cynthia gripped his hand tightly.

"Hello, Jackie," Mary Ellen said. Jackie nodded.

"I'm a friend of Jackie's," Cynthia said. "He's told me a lot about you."

Cynthia moved deeper into the booth, and Mary Ellen sat beside her, opposite Jackie.

"I'm sure he did," she said. For the first time since Jackie knew her, Mary Ellen seemed nervous. "I was surprised to hear from you. In my profession, I usually hear from a former client from a jail cell."

"It isn't a social call," Jackie said.

The waitress poured a cup of coffee for Mary Ellen.

"How can I help you?"

Jackie hesitated for a moment, and Cynthia jumped to his rescue.

"I've been Peter Hanratty's secretary for years."

Cynthia paused as if to solidify her credentials. Mary Ellen nodded in recognition.

"I know Peter inside and out, and everything Jackie's going to tell you about him is disturbing and accurate."

Mary Ellen sipped the coffee, leaving a bright red edge on the top of the cup. She smiled at Cynthia as if amused.

"When I got there," Jackie began, "Tony Miller, who's a cop, came to me and asked if I'd be interested in helping him bring down Hanratty for various criminal activities."

"It's a common practice for them," Cynthia said. "They want to see if they can trust new people. Hanratty wanted Tony to find out if Jackie was going to be trouble."

"I see," Mary Ellen said. Her smile hadn't faded.

"At any rate," Jackie said, "I told Miller I'd see what I could find out, and, being exposed to a lot of records, I, honestly, didn't find too much. Peter runs a good business, but there was Bennington's murder and the murder of a man named Frank Patterson. Suddenly things didn't add up."

Jackie fidgeted with the handle on his coffee cup. It was the most he'd ever said to Rossetti, but he had to trust her. "Peter asked me to go on a trip to New York with one of his drivers. Basically, it convinced me that something was going on. All of his employees are scared to death of him."

Jackie paused for emphasis. "Of course, we wouldn't have come to you without proof, and that's where Cynthia comes in."

Cynthia took charge of the conversation. "Peter doesn't do any of this by himself. He has a well thought-out plan. He's a tremendously lonely man who tries to gain as much power and money as he can. He's loyal only to himself and really believes he controls the entire city, and he might. He buys and sells people. He lets them live and decides when they're going to die. That's the only reason he rescued Jackie from you."

Cynthia didn't have the chance to back up her words with the evidence. Jackie cut her off in mid-stream. "Cynthia, it's Potter and Tony."

The two men didn't hesitate in their approach. Potter nearly knocked over a waitress who juggled a BLT sandwich and a glass of milk. Tony cut behind the table in front of the cash register and sat down on Jackie's right side. He didn't bring his eyes up to meet Jackie's.

"Let's not make a scene," Potter said. "Let's just head out of here, nice and quiet, and go see Peter. He wants to resolve this as quickly and peacefully as possible."

"I'm not going anywhere," Cynthia said. She was begging Potter to challenge her.

"Then I'll kill you where you sit," Potter said through a grin.

"Wait a fucking minute," Tony said. "Nobody's killing anyone. Let's just get up and leave as a group. We'll get it all out in the open without any trouble. There's not going to be any killing. I'm an officer of the law."

"You don't even know what the law is," Jackie said. "Laws preserve human life, not end it."

"All right, enough with the righteousness," Ben said. "Let's go."

Again, Ben looked directly at Cynthia, who did not back down.

"I'm not going anywhere. You're going to have to take me *and* the chair, or you *will* have to kill me. I'm not moving."

"Maybe we should meet with Peter," Mary Ellen said. "Maybe we can clear this up."

"Oh, God, you never really listened, did you?" Jackie asked. "We can't go anywhere near Peter. We'll find someone else who'll help us. There has to be one honest man in this town."

Tony's eyes remained riveted to the ground. Ben extracted a gun from his coat pocket. The twenty-two fit snugly in the palm of his hand. He cupped it so that Cynthia would see it and smiled at her.

"It'll be a pleasure to get rid of you. You're a smart-ass, smug, little bitch, and I wouldn't feel a moment's remorse." Ben cocked the gun. "Do we go, or do we have problems here?"

Jackie didn't have a plan. Mary Ellen sat back with a look of horror on her face. Jackie was suddenly struck with the thought that Ben couldn't possibly be serious. He wouldn't risk his neck for Peter. Even with all of Peter's connections, Ben couldn't possibly explain gunning down three people in a diner full of people. Tony wouldn't chance it, either. He looked like a beaten man, who was embarrassed and ashamed of himself. He'd sold out to the man he hated at the expense of his pride and dignity. Jackie had no way of being sure, but he had to take the chance.

Jackie gained his feet. He walked directly in front of Ben, placing himself between Cynthia and the gun. He held his hand out to Cynthia, and she grabbed hold. Jackie felt a slight tremor of fear but saw a look of quiet determination from behind Cynthia's eyes. She pushed her chair back from the table and, with Jackie's guidance, got to her feet.

"We're leaving," she said. "Are you coming with us?"

Mary Ellen stood slowly. She looked to Ben and cautiously backed away from the table. Jackie and Cynthia had already turned to the exit.

"You're all going to end up in the fucking lake," Ben said.

From the front door of the diner, Jackie saw Ben return the gun to his inside jacket pocket without looking back in their direction.

Jackie and Cynthia broke into a full run. Mary Ellen stood just outside the door as though she were trying to make up her mind about which way to go. Finally, she sprinted after them. The trio moved three full blocks away before slowing to a walk.

\*     \*     \*

Inside, Tony sat opposite of Ben, his mind racing a mile a minute.

"This is getting fucking ridiculous," he said, leaning back in his chair.

"You ain't kidding," Ben said. "Peter'll explode when he hears about this."

"Fuck Peter," Tony said. "He's losing his mind. He's got us chasing kids for Christ's sake."

Ben picked up the spoon and stirred his coffee in a maniacal manner.

"You needed money, and Peter gave it to you. He's never been anything but loyal. The only ones who ever had problems with him are the people who couldn't do their jobs."

"It's wrong," Tony said. "There's too many people involved."

Ben ran his hand through his shaggy beard. "Either you're loyal or you're dead, Tony. I'm going to stay alive and make money."

Tony sipped the coffee, feeling as if he were going to wretch.

"The gun is to your head," Ben said. "You took his money, and now you have to choose. Right and wrong is real clear here. You've always known the difference, so, if you think you can go back to what you had, give it a try. I'll see you at the funeral."

Tony rubbed his eyes with both hands. It wasn't supposed to be like this. "I hate Peter and all he stands for. I sold out, and if I have to die knowing I tried to atone for that, then I'll die. I had a choice, and I blew it. Now, if you'll let me walk out of here, I'll make up for it."

Ben smiled a wicked grin. "But will you make it to the door?" He reached into his pocket, bringing his hand up and placing the gun on the table next to his coffee.

"If you're going to shoot me, it'll have to be in the back," Tony said. "It wouldn't be right if I turned around."

"It's your choice."

The last thing Tony saw before turning around was the gun wrapped in Ben's right hand. He heard the unmistakable sound of the cocking gun. The chattering of the stunned diner patrons sounded magnified a thousand-fold in his brain, and Tony imagined that he felt the nozzle of the gun in the small of his back. He half-expected to hear the shot and feel the numbness in his body. He walked to the door, waiting for the shot to come. As he swung the door open, he felt the warm radiance of sunshine upon his face. He knew he'd made his first legitimate step away from Peter.

Once more, Ben slipped the gun back into his pocket. He took a last gulp of coffee and scanned the diner for a pay phone. It was time to get the big man involved again.

\*       \*       \*

"I think we'd better use the car," Jackie said. "I'm partial to walking, but this time the car'll come in handy."

Jackie held the door open as Mary Ellen slid into the back seat of Cynthia's car. Jackie sat in the passenger seat next to a visibly shaken Cynthia.

"Where can we possibly go?" Cynthia asked. "He'll have a hundred people looking for us."

"Go to the police," Mary Ellen said. "They'll help us. They really will."

Jackie knew Mary Ellen wasn't totally convinced, and it was as if she was waiting for Jackie's suggestion.

"Where should I go?" Cynthia asked, anxiously.

"Just get away from here," Jackie said. "We have to go to a place where he can't find a trace of us until we can come up with a plan."

Cynthia moved away from the curb as if she were a Hollywood stunt driver. They traveled well over the speed limit on Interstate 95 for a good five minutes before Cynthia looked to Jackie. Her knuckles were white on the steering wheel, and her voice cracked when she tried to speak.

"I hate feeling desperate."

"I'm used to it," Jackie answered. "I've felt this way for a long time now."

Jackie spun in his seat to face Mary Ellen. The counselor looked as if she were resigned to the fact that she was now a prisoner.

"There's no concrete answer for desperation," Jackie said. "The answer has to come from within."

*　　*　　*

Peter listened to Ben's words in disbelief. For the first time, Peter actually felt threatened by the situation at hand.

"We'd have been better off if you'd gunned them down," he said.

Peter paced back and forth behind his huge desk. "She's got enough on us to make us fry. She cleaned out the goddamn file cabinets. Do you realize the fucking scope of this?"

"I do," Ben said. "Peter, we have to think it through. We've been sloppy lately. There were too many people involved with Bennington and Patterson. We have to think straight this time, or it's over."

"I know what we have to do!" Peter said. He slammed his chair into the desk. "There's people in fucking California that'll go to jail if that bitch goes to the right people. We have to kill her. They all have to die!" He slammed his fist on the desk to emphasize the point.

"Don't panic," Ben said. "They're scared kids. The counselor is deathly afraid, and Tony's just trying to run. He won't say anything; he's in as deep as us. Believe me, they're going to run around in circles trying to figure out what to do. When they make a decision, we'll be right there waiting for them."

Peter moved back around to his chair. He sat slowly.

"As we speak, I have people posted outside every municipal office in the city," Ben said. "If they try to get anywhere with those papers, we'll have them in a second. I instructed all the men to bring them here. If we start shooting them like clay pigeons, we're dead."

Peter felt a sudden surge of pride. Ben was absolutely right. They couldn't take down the entire Hanratty empire. "Okay, first things first. I want you to personally go and get Tony's pregnant wife and bring her here. Secondly, post someone in front of their homes. I want them in the construction office, with the proof, inside of ten hours, or it's over. Ben, we're going down hard if we aren't careful."

"Yes, sir."

"Do you have any idea where they might go?" Peter asked.

"We'll begin with the obvious choices."

"Check all the choices!" Peter said.

"Yes, sir, but, Peter, you can do what you want with them after I bring 'em to you. I'm not going to kill them for you."

"You will if I tell you to," Peter said.

# CHAPTER FOURTEEN

The list of supplies seemed endless. Jackie wanted to believe that they'd planned for every possible circumstance. They were all off in opposite directions in search of the items on their unusual shopping list. Jackie really had no idea how long they'd have to be out in the woods in Clinton, but he did know that they'd have to figure out a plan.

Jackie walked the streets in search of the one item he needed to find to complete their mission. Although he honestly had no idea how he'd be able to find what he was looking for, he was glad that he'd sent Mary Ellen and Cynthia to the K-Mart for the other supplies.

*Where would a criminal look for a gun?* Jackie's fist was clenched in the pocket of his jeans. He'd give it half an hour.

\* \* \*

Cynthia was in charge of putting a roof over their heads. She stood in the center of the sporting goods department and remained surprisingly calm as the salesman ran through her list of options.

"We have three types of sleeping bags. They're all very durable and fairly warm. You're going to need a little warmth if you're camping around here this time of year."

"Any one will be fine," Cynthia said.

The salesman ignored her. "We have five different kinds of tents. We have one deluxe model that you could live in year-round. We have a varied selection of lanterns. In short, we could set you up for your vacation in a number of ways."

"It's not quite a vacation," Cynthia muttered, and the salesman cut her off with a laugh.

"What is it? A stakeout?"

Cynthia tried to appear calm, but the words in her head wouldn't leave her alone. "It's an introduction to nature," she said, and she smiled brightly, hoping the guy would keep his mind on his job. Instead, she read desire in his eyes.

"I want to make it comfortable for my husband," Cynthia said to get him thinking about the tent.

"Of course," he said. "We'll make your husband proud, and your credit card won't take much of a beating."

*   *   *

Twenty minutes into his search, Jackie saw a run-down man standing on the corner of sixth and Wright. The man scanned the streets with a set of wild eyes that got Jackie thinking that maybe he'd know where to go. He said a quick prayer, hoping he was reading it right.

"Hey, pal, I need a piece," Jackie said as if he looked for one every day of his life.

"What do you have on you?" the man asked, never once looking at Jackie's face.

"Hundred and a half," Jackie said.

The man feigned disgust. He looked to the sidewalk as if the gun might suddenly surface. "Wait here."

Jackie followed the man with his eyes. His new friend cut across the street and went through the front door of a dilapidated townhouse. Jackie waited in the corner telephone booth, but the wait was only a few minutes.

The man ran back across the street, motioning for Jackie to follow. He stopped in front of a vacant parking lot and held a brown-handled Colt .45 out for inspection.

"I have to get one-seventy-five. It's already loaded, man. You ain't going to get a better deal anywhere."

Jackie's eyes did a quick dance down the barrel of the gun. His mind twisted back to that day in the trailer. He felt the color draining from his face.

"Don't just stare at the fucking thing. You want it or not?"

Jackie fished the money out of his pocket.

"Kid, you kill a cop, you never saw me."

"I never saw you."

Holding the gun in his hand sent a shiver down his spine.

*   *   *

They traveled to the wooded area near Clinton. Jackie wasn't sure where they were headed, but Cynthia drove with confidence and calmness.

"How far away is this place?" Mary Ellen asked. She leaned forward in the seat. There was doubt in her voice.

"It's just a couple more miles," Cynthia said.

"The reason I ask," Mary Ellen said as she leaned into the front seat, "is that I've been considering this for the last few minutes, and I'm not sure what we're going to accomplish by camping in the woods. If Peter's the man you say he is, we aren't going to stop him out here. We're going to be sitting ducks. We won't be able to present the evidence, either."

Jackie considered the words of protest. He mulled over the reactionary mind that controlled Mary Ellen. He was sure she felt absolutely right. There *wasn't* a logical reason why they should isolate themselves in the woods. Yet, in a much more abstract way, Jackie knew that this was the right move.

"Did you ever watch the stars fill the sky on a clear night?" Jackie asked.

"Of course," Mary Ellen snapped.

"No, I mean did you ever *really* watch it happen? It's an amazing thing, you know? Did you ever just sit in the quiet, listening to night sounds? Did you ever breath and concentrate on the way the air enters your body?"

Jackie gauged the expression in Mary Ellen's eyes. She didn't have a clue of what he was talking about.

"There's so many miracles happening around us every day."

"What does that have to do with the situation we're in?" Mary Ellen asked.

Jackie leaned across the seat. He was inches away from her face. "Everything," he said softly. "It's what we're doing out here. I've had moments in my life when I truly needed clear thinking. There were times when I could go either way. I was in a position where a lot of times my next decision could either make or break me. Every time I ever felt thoroughly confused, I looked for a higher being to pull me through."

Mary Ellen's eyes softened. For the first time, Jackie seemed to be truly reaching her.

"I know what you mean," Cynthia said. "I got caught up in the game and forgot the big picture. Peter tossed money around and made me believe he was the world. My pockets were full, and I thought I'd be able to work it out sometime down the line."

Jackie was charged by Cynthia's words. Once again, she knew exactly what he was trying to say. "It's not a mystery or a philosophy," Jackie said. "It's more an idea of knowing what's in front of you and how you'll deal with it. My father was beat down by life. I think about him a lot. I remember his love and how we were his only true concern. He swallowed his pride and dignity to make sure we lived right. He was always coming up with a game plan, you know? He struggled right up to the day he died."

Silence took control, and Mary Ellen sat back in the seat, sighing loudly.

"He died thinking that, someday, we'd be able to enjoy watching the stars fill a summer night. All he ever wanted was for us to live a normal life chasing all the bullshit things everyone chases."

Jackie snickered at his sense of logic. The fact that his father was never able to provide from them was lost in the true dignity of the man. Almost on cue, Jackie caught sight of a clearing through the trees leading deep into the wooded area.

"That's the spot we're looking for." Cynthia navigated the car down a narrow path, and the car rocked as they headed down the makeshift road.

"This is perfect," Jackie said. He rolled down the window and let the air fill his lungs.

Mary Ellen sat quietly in the back seat. She appeared to be deep in thought, but she wasn't protesting anymore.

*   *   *

Margaret Miller was confused. Her husband's words came fast and furious, but he wasn't making sense.

"We have to get away," he said. "There's shit going on that could put us in real danger."

A wave of panic took control of Margaret's mind. What kind of danger could Tony have gotten them into? How would they solve it by running away? Margaret wished she could make it right, but she thought only of the unborn baby.

"Okay," she said softly, as a sob escaped.

"We don't have time to cry," Tony said. "Get a few things together. I'll be there in an hour. Be ready to go."

"I will," Margaret said. She sobbed once more. "Tony, I'm seven months pregnant. Tell me what's wrong."

"I know how fucking pregnant you are. Just be ready."

The line went dead in Margaret's ear. She sat on the couch in stunned silence, instinctively running her hand over her belly. Maybe it was just a tough case he was working on. Tony had been working a lot of overtime and hadn't been sleeping well, but she had no idea it was this bad.

Margaret looked around her home with tears filling her eyes. They'd dreamed all of this together. They picked out all the decorations and put it all together themselves and, now, this. The promise of togetherness lingered in her brain. The doorbell rang, and Margaret opened the door to two huge men who grabbed at her hands. They pulled her outside through the front door, and she realized her baby's life was in danger.

*   *   *

Jackie hadn't even noticed the day's slow transition into evening. They had worked the entire day away to set up camp in the wooded area. Although the sun had gone down without their notice, the tranquil feeling that Jackie had expected began to take hold. As the first few pieces of wood burned in the makeshift pit, their conversation shifted to a higher level.

"It's hard to believe that life was just like this years and years ago," Cynthia said. She sat cross-legged a few feet from the fire. Jackie was a few feet away, lying on his side, and Mary Ellen was directly across the fire with her legs stretched out before her.

"Before there were rules, boundaries, lawyers, and wars, people probably sat around the fire wondering what to worry about," Mary Ellen said with a chuckle.

Each of them considered the thought for a moment.

"They were probably happier," Jackie said. "Fighting for survival gives you a true sense of yourself."

Jackie knew that Mary Ellen was growing more comfortable with their situation.

"That's true," she said, "but people need to feel as if they're moving forward, somehow. It's only human to want to grow and expand." She paused for a moment to allow her thought to gain steam. "I think the people we're talking about probably were happy for a while, but they had to find something to keep them moving."

"Imagine feeling like you can't move forward," Jackie said. "Not being able to shake that feeling causes a lot of pain."

"Yes, there's a lot of anger because of that."

Again, their words hung in the air. The exaggerated bouts of silence before they spoke allowed Jackie to realize that they were actually talking and listening to one another.

"When I was in the orphanage, I read a lot. I mostly read about people and how they felt in certain situations, and I always tried to find myself in there. I'm not very good at figuring out how people should be living, but I know that, if you feel isolated from everything around you, you'll go crazy." Jackie sighed heavily. He turned onto his back and looked to the sky. It was a clear night, and the stars were just beginning to dot the sky.

"They bury five thousand anonymous kids a year in this country. They're kids who don't have anywhere to turn and nothing to hang onto. Sooner or later, they just die, you know? They don't feel like they're part of anything, and they don't have parents to speak of. So they turn up dead, like stray dogs."

Jackie could have been one of those children. "It isn't just kids, though," Jackie said. "There's so many people out there just walking dead. They go from moment to moment never really expecting anything."

Cynthia was also looking to the sky.

"Isn't it amazing that we take it for granted?" she asked.

"Life can become a mess, quickly," Mary Ellen said.

"What really gets me," Jackie said, "is how people get wrapped up in it. Peter's a complete mess, and his isolation comes from a whole different place. I came from literally nothing, and I'm able to see how screwed up his life is."

"That's probably why you can see it so clearly," Mary Ellen said. "You appreciate all the things that Peter wasn't ever able to hold sacred."

The sound of a far-off animal provided the background noise as their conversation stalled once again.

"Peter's controlled by his wants," Cynthia said. "All of us, to a certain extent, feel like we're owed something special. If you can't put those thoughts in perspective, they'll control you. I'm sure Peter hasn't had a non-manipulative thought in years, and the people he's dragging down with him need the connection, too. Chasing money blinds you, and, before you know it, you're struggling to find a glimpse of yourself."

They took in the silence of the night. Their eyes were turned heavenward, and Jackie's mind danced in circles.

"It's so easy to forget how much more is out there," he said.

*     *     *

The two men ushered Margaret to their waiting car. She dropped to her knees as the tears muddled her chance to understand what was happening.

"What do you want?"

The first man was in front of her. He grabbed a fist-full of her hair, pulling her to her feet. "Don't fucking fight me."

"Just tell me what's going on," Margaret pleaded.

"Your husband fucked up, big-time," the man said.

Margaret found the strength to get to her feet. "Let go of my hair!" She fought back the tears.

"Where's Tony? Is he all right?"

She was pushed in the back. She thought of the child inside of her, and it was too much to keep the tears from falling.

"We can't find the rat fuck," the man said. The second man held the back door of the car open.

Margaret stopped walking again. She turned to face the man behind her. His hair was long and greasy, and his fabricated smile bore a hole in Margaret's mind. She felt the anger surge through her veins. "I'll get in the car," she said, as her determination reached a new level. "Just don't fucking push me again. No matter what Tony did, I don't deserve to be pushed."

*    *    *

Mary Ellen fell fast asleep next to the fire. Cynthia and Jackie remained awake, in each other's arms. Jackie felt only the unmistakable warmth of holding Cynthia close.

"I hate to get up," he said, "but the fire needs me."

Cynthia allowed him the room to get to his feet.

"Stay there, I'll be right back."

"Let's take a walk." Cynthia said. "If we're going stay out here all night, I need to see what we're up against."

"Good enough," Jackie said. He tossed two pieces of wood into the pit, and Cynthia found the lantern.

They walked hand in hand away from the site. Jackie carried the lantern in his left hand and waited until they were a few hundred feet from Mary Ellen before he lit it. After doing so, he immediately searched for Cynthia's hand once more.

"I love holding your hand," Cynthia said. "It's corny, but people really do need a hand to hold."

Almost as if on cue, Cynthia stumbled forward, and Jackie held her up, guiding her path with the light from the lantern.

"I've always been clumsy," Cynthia said. "I'm not so great at making choices, either."

The noises in the night serenaded them, and yet there was a prevailing stillness in the foreground of Jackie's mind.

"Peter doesn't romance people as much as he plays on their fears," Cynthia said. "I always considered myself a decent person, but he made me lose focus. The thing is, I guess, if a poison snake bites you it's easy to take in the venom. Even with all that, I rationalized it."

"Forget about it."

"I can't," Cynthia said. "He put the money in my hand and the thoughts in my head. I was too weak to fight. I'm sorry, Jackie."

"Don't dwell on it. Peter controlled everyone he ever came in contact with."

"I'm so scared right now," Cynthia said.

"That's because it's pretty scary," Jackie said, with a tension-breaking laugh.

They walked in silence, and although the night air was a bit brisk, Jackie could only think of the stars above him and the peacefulness in his heart.

"So what do you think's going to happen?"

"It's like the calm before the storm, isn't it?" Jackie asked.

"We just going to wait him out?" Cynthia asked. "Mary Ellen might be right. We might be sitting ducks."

"We've got to wait a while," Jackie said. "We'll get him nervous and then go at him. We hold all the cards. We have everything that matters to him. We have his heart and soul right now, and we'll go forward when it feels right."

"He owns the city."

"It seems that way, doesn't it?" Jackie asked. "But he can't beat me down."

Jackie felt a little squeeze on his hand and Cynthia's eyes on him.

"I'll be in trouble for this," Cynthia said. "I helped Peter cover everything up."

"Nothing's going to happen to you," Jackie said.

They were soon surrounded by the sound of chirping crickets and the far-off hoot of an owl. While the night's sounds set a tone of serenity, it was the sound of a nearby stream that captured Jackie's full attention.

"When I was at the orphanage," Jackie said, "I saw a movie about a guy who lived near a stream. He spent, like, half the movie kneeling by the rolling stream picking wild strawberries. I remember there was a church bell tolling in the distance, and, even though I forgot everything else about the movie, I remember the way the guy looked sitting by that stream. I always thought how great it would be to find a place where I felt so comfortable."

"Let's find the stream," Cynthia said.

The stream wasn't moving as fast as Jackie had imagined. In fact, in the precarious light of the midnight sky, the stream didn't appear to move at all. There was a short set of falls that dropped the stream into a waiting pool of calm.

Jackie and Cynthia sat on a fallen tree, five feet from the falls. In the briskness of the night air, Jackie held Cynthia close to him. He felt the movement of her body as she breathed, and he moved his hand just below her right breast to feel the beating of her heart.

"I used to wake up and stare at the ceiling and think about all the other orphans. I'd wonder what we did to deserve it. I'd think a lot about my mom and Alan, but mostly I'd think of my dad. My life would have been so different if he hadn't died. I would've never seen Billy Barth even though, I think, eventually, everyone comes across someone similar to him."

Cynthia's face was inches from his lips. Jackie knew that this was as close as he could come to bearing his soul to another person. "I used to think about the pressure on my Dad and how it killed him. It just rips me apart, because life ain't supposed to be that way. It seems like, when you stack it up, one thing on top of the other, it's pretty easy to make a mess out of it. Yet, somehow, I keep thinking that if you look hard enough, somewhere in your mind, you can find a place like a stream where you feel at peace. If you find peace, you can deal with a lot of things. My dad was always looking. He was a terrific man, but life wouldn't let him find his stream."

"You've probably been quiet all these years so you could think that up," Cynthia said.

Jackie laughed loudly. As strange as it sounded, it was true.

"Yeah, everyone thought I was nutty as a fruitcake, and I was out looking for a stream."

"I love you, you know?" Cynthia said.

Jackie slowly shook his head. "After all this time, you've given me a new, peaceful place. From now on, I'll come back to right now and how warm I feel. I love you, and I hope it's enough. It didn't work for Dad."

The image of his mother flashed in his mind, and Jackie pulled Cynthia tight to his chest. He felt a stray tear work its way down his left cheek. He closed his eyes, allowing the sounds of the night to fill his heart.

\*    \*    \*

Tony raced toward his home. His mind was centered on the idea that he was dragging Margaret into something she had no business battling. The only thing Tony knew for certain was that he'd risked the life of the one person he loved.

Tony ran the stop sign and slowed in front of his house just long enough to notice the battered front door. He punched at the steering wheel.

"I'll kill that fat motherfucker!"

Tony hit the siren, racing away from his house as if in pursuit of a murder suspect. In reality, he was chasing more than that. He was chasing his entire existence.

Tony headed back towards Clinton. He had followed Jackie, Cynthia, and Mary Ellen to the camp, but now he wondered why he hadn't picked up Margaret, first. It was a decision that he hoped didn't turn out to be a fatal one.

*     *     *

Once again, Peter was livid.

"Where the fuck is he?" he asked Margaret for the fifth time.

"I don't know," Margaret said. "He called me and told me to get ready to go. You got there first."

They sat across from one another in the Hanratty construction trailer.

"I'm going tell you a story about your husband," Peter said.

"I'm here," Margaret said. She wasn't in the mood to back down.

"I bought your wedding ring," Peter said. "I bought your house, your furniture, and the fucking toilet paper you wipe your ass with. I bought all those fancy dinners at all those goddamn restaurants. I'm probably more responsible for that baby inside you than he is! I bought your fucking husband!"

"He worked overtime," she muttered, and Peter laughed uproariously.

"Overtime! How much fucking overtime do you think a city cop makes? Come on, you knew it all along. You just didn't want to believe it."

"I didn't know it."

"You know it, now," Peter said. He pulled his huge frame out of the chair. "Your husband's as crooked as my dick."

Margaret's mind did an uncomfortable twist. Even if it were true, she couldn't listen to it anymore. She'd spent too much time watching Tony struggle with his life. She'd endured the sleepless nights and *did* know something was wrong. She just hadn't wanted to believe it. "You won't get him," she said mindlessly.

"I'll get him!" Peter shouted. "I'll get him and squash him like the spineless, fucking jellyfish he is."

Peter's fist met the desk, causing Margaret to flinch in terror. All at once, Peter's face took on a smug look of hospitality.

"I hope your stay with us will be a pleasant one. My men have a tendency to go overboard in their treatment of my guests. Even though you're just a piece of bait to me, please, let me be the first to know if you're uncomfortable in any way." He stepped around Margaret's chair and opened the door of the trailer. "Now, if you'll join me, I'll have my men show you to your room."

*     *     *

Somewhere along the way Margaret's brash attitude gave way to sheer panic. The reality of being sent to a secluded area with Hanratty's disgusting men was enough to make her skin crawl.

The same, greasy-haired, man pushed her into the back of a light blue, Ford Pinto. They slapped a pair of cuffs down on her wrists, locking her arms behind her. The man with the greasy hair leaned to her.

"So pretty and so scared," he whispered. He brought his hand to her forehead and swept his hand across her bangs. He leaned over the front seat and brought his mouth to hers. Margaret was nearly overcome by the scent of nicotine and alcohol on his breath. He placed his lips over her own, and Margaret couldn't control the violent spasm working its way through her body. She retched and gagged and pulled away. The handcuffs tore into her hands, and she tried to focus on her child.

"You fucking bitch!"

He punched Margaret, catching her flush on the chin. She tasted the blood as the tears of pain stung her eyes. She fell back in the seat as the blood filled her mouth.

# CHAPTER FIFTEEN

The driving rain pelted the tent. Jackie stirred from his slumber, slowly opening his eyes. He stayed motionless for a moment, concentrating on the sounds of the howling wind and distant thunder. Cynthia was asleep beside him, and Mary Ellen was curled up in the far corner of the tent.

A slight smile crossed Jackie's lips when he thought of the peculiarity of the situation. The thought passed quickly, and the confidence that they'd break Peter down replaced it. In a maniacal twist of fate, he was being granted the opportunity to fight back. As was true with each morning of his life, Jackie thought of his absent family and quickly blessed himself. This would be the way that he'd atone for some of his pain.

The rain tapered to a light drizzle, and Jackie fought the urge to return to sleep. He quietly got up to check the fire. He thought of warming some water for a cup of coffee and perhaps preparing breakfast before Cynthia and Mary Ellen rose.

Jackie slid through the tent opening. He nearly fell flat on his face upon seeing Tony sitting in front of the fire.

The fire was stacked with wood, and Tony sipped from a cup of coffee. He didn't look up when Jackie emerged and, instead, looked to the roaring fire.

"Morning," he said, almost to himself. He looked like a beaten man. He was still dressed in full uniform but was sporting three days' worth of growth on his face. His tired, waning eyes provided an indication that he was close to defeat.

In spite of his initial shock, Jackie remained silent. He reacted to Tony's presence by acting as if everything was just right. He went to the coffee pot on the makeshift grill on the fire.

"It's real hot," Tony said. "but this ain't a bad set up for a rough camping trip."

"Survival instincts are in my blood," Jackie said.

Tony bowed his head. He held the coffee cup tightly in both hands. "They have my wife." An almost inaudible sob escaped into the air. "If they hurt her, it'll kill me. She's all I got. I don't know what I'd do without her."

Tony was in the midst of a full-fledged crying session. Jackie knew Tony's heart was breaking, but he couldn't summon up any pity.

"You want me to help a man who kicked me in the teeth?"

The words brought another wave of emotion from Tony, and it was quite a few minutes before he gathered himself enough to speak.

"What I did was criminal, intolerable, and unjustifiable, but, please, don't make it unforgivable."

Jackie sipped the coffee. It was way too hot, and he moved away from the fire. He leaned back against the trunk of a tall, maple tree. He prodded Tony, looking for a more detailed explanation.

"I still don't know how it happened," Tony said. "One minute I was watching his every move, and, the next thing I knew, he had me in his back pocket. We had just gotten married. She had all these dreams, and I didn't fight."

Tony picked his head up for a split-second and returned his attention to the ground.

"We wanted a house, a car, and a fucking dog. She wanted to travel, and she kept telling me how great it was going to be that I'd be able to retire early. I kept adding it up, and it wasn't going to work. I was going to bust my hump all my life and then just die."

Tony wiped his brow. He blew on the coffee. "I kept thinking back to William and the miserable way he lived. His wife died, and that was tragic. But, even before, that he just existed. He didn't enjoy life. I know he died a terrible death, but deep-down he only existed to die."

"A lot of people just exist," Jackie said.

"I wanted to be different. I wanted to be the best cop in the world. It just never worked out. No one really cares what kind of job you do, and I couldn't pretend anymore. There wasn't anything I could do to change my world, and Peter offered the only way out. My mind was so out of whack it flat-out whipped what I held dear to my heart."

Jackie thought Tony might cry again, but Tony held it in check. "About four months ago, I confronted Peter. I don't know what I expected to accomplish, and maybe I half-expected he'd make me an offer. Bottom line is, I knew I couldn't keep going like I had been. He's a son of a bitch, Jackie. He did more than snowball me. I knew what he stood for, but he preyed on every shortcoming I had. He recognized the fact we needed a house. He told me, over and over again, that I was responsible for giving Margaret the world. He showed me all the shit he owned and made me want it. He was the goddamn devil to all the decent thoughts in my head, and I bought a fucking cell in hell to be on his side." Tony set the coffee on the ground. "Every day, you've got to get up and fight. There's so many ways to screw it up. The truth is, I'm surprised that more people don't cave in. It's a bitch. Day in and day out you struggle for a pot to piss in."

Tony stopped his thought dead and almost as quickly began again. "He flashed the money, and I saw it as a way out. I don't expect you to understand, but that's what happened. Let me tell you, you can't get away from what's in your heart."

Tony paced the fire. He nervously tossed a piece of wood into the pit. He seemed to be waiting for Jackie to say something, as a man might wait for the jury to deliberate.

Jackie allowed Tony's words to swim back and forth through his mind. What Tony had done was unconscionable. Jackie didn't speak for a full ten minutes. When he finally spoke, he announced the verdict in monotone.

"Let's get your wife back."

*     *     *

"The way I see it," Cynthia said. "We have to split up and still work together. We have the evidence, but Peter has Margaret and the ability to take our lives away. We have to figure the risks and go from there."

Tony circled the fire for what had to be the twentieth time. "Cynthia, you know the man better than all of us."

"I'll tell you one thing," Cynthia said. "If we go to the police, Margaret won't survive."

Jackie looked to Tony for a show of emotion, but Tony seemed resigned to the reality of it all.

"He'll try to get what he wants without giving anything up," Cynthia said. "He wants to teach us a lesson, and, if we go within a mile of him with the evidence, he'll take that back and kill us, too."

"How many people would you say he owns?" Mary Ellen asked. "It can't be that he controls everyone."

"Way too many to count," Cynthia said, and Tony nodded. "He controls the newspaper, the mayor, two or three television stations, and about five thousand working stiffs."

"Not to mention half the police force," Jackie said.

"Yes," Tony said. "Not to mention that."

The proclamation of what they were up against lent a stunned silence to the group.

"We need a plan," Mary Ellen said. "Peter, no doubt, has one."

The group seemed to be waiting for a leader to emerge. It almost seemed as if they were begging Jackie to take the reins. "All right," Jackie said, finally. "We can't afford to be defensive. If we're going to do this, we have to go for the throat. People have been scared of Peter for so long that he won't know how to react."

All eyes were on Jackie as he walked around the fire, following the same path that Tony had worn all morning.

"Two of us should probably head right at him. The other two should take the evidence and look for whomever wants to listen. Tony, you chased him for years, you oughta know his enemies."

Tony nodded once more.

"Who's doing what?" Mary Ellen asked. "I think it's a good idea, but we have to be precise."

"Believe it or not," Jackie said, "The two going straight to Peter are probably in less danger. It's a close call, but, at least, they'll be able to identify the enemy."

"He's in the construction trailer at the JGL construction site," Tony said. "He always hides out there when the heat is on."

"That's good," Jackie said. "Now let me figure out how we want to do this."

"I want to see his face," Tony said.

"No," Jackie said quickly. "You're the only one I've eliminated from going at him. Your pregnant wife is with him, and you won't think clearly."

Tony started to protest, but Jackie's intense stare seemed to trap the words in Tony's mind.

"Besides, you know the streets. You can feel things out."

Tony reluctantly nodded his approval.

"We won't leave there without Margaret," Jackie said. He paused for a moment to collect his thoughts. "In the same respect, I don't think I should be teamed with Cynthia for a lot of the same reasons."

"How can you trust me with him?" she asked.

"Cynthia, if there was even a trace of doubt about Tony, I wouldn't let you cross the street with him. His wife's out there. He's not going to take chances."

Jackie pulled Cynthia to him. "You can take away a man's dignity," he whispered, "but you can't erase feelings in his heart."

Cynthia held tears in her eyes. She looked at Tony. "I made the same mistakes."

"We have to be in complete agreement," Mary Ellen said.

Silence reigned for a moment as each person considered the task.

"Okay, then," Jackie said. "Here's the game plan." As he spoke, the image of his father came to the foreground of his mind.

*　　*　　*

Peter was growing disgusted with the look of frustration in Ben's eyes. There wasn't a person around anymore who could carry an order through to its completion.

"We didn't get so much as a sign of them," Ben said.

"They just disappeared, right?" Peter asked.

"Something like that."

"Can you draw a conclusion from that?" Peter asked.

"They're probably all together," Ben said.

"That's great," Peter said sarcastically as he clapped his hands together. "Now let's try question number two. If they haven't turned up around a police station or newspaper, what does that mean?"

"That they're laying low," Ben said. He rested his head on the inside of his left palm.

"Good! The counselor bitch hasn't called in, either, so she's probably scared, right? And if she's scared, what does that tell you?"

"Nothing," Ben said.

"What did you say?"

"I said it doesn't tell me a goddamn thing," Ben answered.

Peter leaned back in the chair. He felt his jaw tightening, and he ground his teeth so hard he thought he might break them off in his mouth. "It's your ass as well as mine."

"I realize that," Ben said, "but what the fuck am I supposed to do? When we find them, we kill them, right? Then what? Are we going to keep killing people who figure us out? Pretty soon it'll be just me and you here."

Peter fought the explosion. He didn't throw the glass across the room. Ben was trying to state their case as plainly as he saw it. "It's too late to turn back," Peter said. "We can't walk into the police station and confess. We sure the fuck can't cave now."

Ben nodded in agreement.

"I've never steered you wrong before," Peter said. "We still have a couple of pieces of meat we can dangle in front of them. We've already proved that Tony and Cynthia can be bought. The counselor's just looking for a way to save the world from grief and pity, and we can dance around her facade too. She's an intellectual, and we can appeal to her sensibilities."

"What the hell you going to do with Jackie?" Ben asked.

"We don't have a choice there," Peter said. "He's had a death sentence since day one."

Mary Ellen cautiously backed the car out of the wooded area in front of the camp. She watched the rear-view mirror carefully in an effort to keep her path steady and to keep an eye on what was coming at her from behind.

Jackie knew that Mary Ellen was waging a private war over what the group had decided. It seemed as though she still didn't understand Peter's crimes, and Jackie wondered if there was a textbook ever written to prepare Mary Ellen for what might happen in the next few hours.

Mary Ellen backed the car onto the road. The sky was crystal clear, and Jackie flipped down the passenger side visor to fend off the sun.

"Do you know where the JGL site is in West Haven?" Jackie asked.

"I have a general idea," Mary Ellen said. "Why would Peter go there?"

"He's in his own little world out there, and he can bury a body if he has to."

Mary Ellen cringed and turned to face Jackie. "Please don't be glib about this," she said. "That's the kind of talk that made us concerned about you when you were a child."

"That's just my way," Jackie said. "I learned a lot at the orphanage, even if I didn't share it."

Mary Ellen chuckled lightly. "You're a complete enigma," she said. "I spent a lot of sleepless nights imagining what you went through that day in the trailer."

"Sooner or later, you have to remember how to forget."

Mary Ellen concentrated on the winding road as it passed beneath them. Jackie slouched down a bit in the seat to avoid the sunshine.

"If you don't see what's ahead and get bogged down in the past, you're shot," she said.

"And that about sums it up," Jackie said. "This one's for Mom and Dad and Alan." He slid down even further in the seat.

"If I fall asleep," he said, "wake me up when we get close."

"You're going to sleep?" Mary Ellen asked. "You're an hour away from the biggest confrontation of your life, and you're going to sleep?"

"I'm tired," Jackie said.

"You're an enigma," Mary Ellen said. Out of the corner of his eye, Jackie saw the smile flash across Mary Ellen's face.

*     *     *

Tony drove with reckless abandon. He flipped the siren and lights on and watched as traffic parted for him.

"This car's pretty handy when you're in a hurry," Cynthia said.

"We've got a lot to do," Tony said. "We're hurting for time, and we have to nail that bastard."

"How did it all happen for you?" Cynthia asked.

"As they say, every man has his price. I guess mine was pretty low, all things considered. What's really gnawing at me, though, is when you're born, you have the right to choose what sort of life you'll live. Even if you're rich or poor or born in a toilet in the ghetto, you have the chance to do, at least, one decent thing. Excuse my French, but I fucked it up."

"You have a lot of time to make up for it," Cynthia said.

"I hope so," Tony said. A sense of true fear sent gooseflesh racing across his arms. "If anything happens to Margaret, I'll kill myself."

*     *     *

Jackie blinked the sleep away just in time to see the road sign that proclaimed that they were six miles away from West Haven.

"Show time," he mumbled, as he sat up. He opened the glovebox and removed the gun. He held it in his hands for a moment before tucking it behind his back. He pulled his shirt down and positioned the gun a couple of times to hide the bulge.

"We'll play a little psychological game with him. Don't let him see fear on your face. No matter how bad it gets, don't even bat an eyelash."

"I'll handle it," Mary Ellen said.

"You know," Jackie said, "I'm not even scared of him. I lived through a lot of crap. He can't do anything to me."

They pulled into West Haven a few minutes before eleven o'clock.

"The JGL site is actually an industrial complex," Jackie said.

"I got it figured out," Mary Ellen said. "I know right where it is."

*     *     *

205

Tony turned right onto Demunda Avenue. He scanned the houses for a number. "Keep an eye out for twenty-one-forty-five."

"It's on my side," Cynthia said. "What's this cop's name again?"

"Daryl Jeter," Tony said. "He's twenty-two. He reminds me of me when I first started." The statement was almost too painful for Tony to say aloud. "I'm sure he's not on Peter's side. This kid wants to do everything by the book, and he hasn't been around long enough to know the book ain't worth a shit."

"There it is," Cynthia announced. She pointed in the direction of a broken-down duplex surrounded by three huge, elm trees.

"That's his Jeep," Tony said. He pulled in behind the truck. "Come on. Bring a couple of the journals and Peter's notes. Leave the cassette tape and William's notebooks."

Cynthia sifted through the mass of paperwork. She handed the journals to Tony, and they walked up the drive to the door.

Daryl answered the knock quickly. He wore only his uniform pants, and it looked like he just got out of the shower.

"Tony? What's up?" Daryl nodded at Cynthia, and she returned a nervous smile.

"Strictly business," Tony said. "I need you to help me with something." Tony extended the paperwork to Daryl. "This is evidence against Hanratty. It's going to blow the lid off the city."

Daryl skimmed a couple of pages.

"It's all the information we need," Tony said.

"You've gotta be kidding," Daryl said.

"There's a lot of people's lives at stake. You have to do exactly what I tell you."

Daryl nodded, but he appeared more nervous than Tony imagined he'd be.

"Peter's holed up at the JGL site. It's ten-forty now, and I want you at that site no later than twelve-thirty, with no less than five backup cars. I'll be there by then, but Peter'll have his troops there, too. Be extremely cautious."

"I understand, sir," Daryl said.

"Don't bring this stuff with you. The shit's going to really hit the fan and I don't want those papers getting lost."

"Okay," Daryl said.

"No less than five cars and ten men behind you," Tony said. "Don't try to be a hero, Peter's not going to be in much of a mood."

A look of determination swept across Daryl's face, and Tony recognized the look from his early days on the force. "Twelve-thirty sharp," Tony said, and he instinctively looked to his watch.

As they pulled away, Tony again checked for any signs of being followed.

"The next stop's a little more hairy," he said.

"We're going to WGRQ, right?"

"That's right. Give me the tape of Ben and Peter talking about the Patterson murder."

Cynthia held the tape up for inspection. "Let's get them to play a song for us," she said.

"I'm going to get that fat bastard now," Tony said.

\*     \*     \*

Jackie's insides were literally churning. He was on the verge of throwing up, and he flicked a few beads of sweat away from his forehead. "Pull up alongside the trailer."

The anonymous faces of the workers peered into the windows of the car.

"As soon as we get out of the car, we're going to have a couple of guys willing to show us to Peter," Jackie said.

"I'm ready," Mary Ellen said.

"Don't show any fear."

"I won't give them the satisfaction," Mary Ellen said.

Jackie pushed the door open. He had been right. He was instantly greeted by one of Peter's followers. He just hadn't planned on the familiarity of his escort.

"Jackie, hold on," Danny said. The truck driver made his approach with all the nervousness of a man confronting a burglar in his home. Jackie stayed planted in his spot and motioned for Mary Ellen to join him.

"Peter has a freaking all-points bulletin out for you," Danny said. He extended his hand, and Jackie shook it quickly. "I don't have nothing against you, but I have to take you to him."

"I don't have a problem with that," Jackie said. He looked directly into Danny's eyes and offered a sly grin.

"I wouldn't want to be in your shoes," Danny said.

"I'm not sure I want to be in them," Jackie said.

Danny almost seemed to be offering his condolences.

"I have instructions to frisk you."

"I'll save you the trouble," Jackie said. He reached around and removed the gun. He knew he'd eventually have to give it up, but he wanted Peter to believe that he'd come for a fight. Danny nodded at the trailer window.

"He's inside. Jackie, I never meant to lead you into the executioner's den."

"I made my bed," Jackie said.

Without exchanging another word, Danny led them up the trailer steps. Jackie glanced at Mary Ellen's watch. It was three minutes after eleven. They were right on schedule.

\*     \*     \*

Tony and Cynthia entered the waiting room of WGRQ studios a few minutes past eleven. Once again, Tony's police uniform did the talking. The receptionist tapped on the window which housed the studio occupied by morning announcer 'Rockin' Robin Travers.

"'Rockin' Robin is the biggest man in New Haven as far as radio announcers go," Tony said. "He has thousands of listeners who are always ready to take up his cause. The critics hate him, but he's got the voice we're looking for."

"I hate his show," Cynthia said. "He's a raunchy pig."

"If we can get him to play this tape, he'll go down in history."

'Rockin' Robin stood a shade over five-feet-five inches tall. His long, gray hair made him look a bit ridiculous, and the lines on his face showed evidence of a hard life.

"What's up, officer?" Robin asked through his tired eyes. His eyes danced across Cynthia's frame in a matter of seconds.

"I need a favor," Tony said. He extended the cassette tape to Robin. "This is urgent police business. I need this tape played at exactly eleven-thirty."

Robin shook him off. "No can do. I don't play nothing I ain't listened to first."

Tony spun on his heels, displaying a look of true annoyance. "Can you step outside for a second?"

Tony led Robin through the front door. "What's up?" Robin asked as they stepped outside.

"This tape'll put Hanratty in the toilet," Tony said. "I'll give you a hundred bucks to play it."

"Why didn't you say so?" Robin asked. "Keep the hundred. I'd love to nail him. He's a real son-of-a-bitch."

Tony handed the cassette over and slapped Robin lightly on the back.

"Let's go," Tony said to Cynthia.

"What was that all about?"

"Long story," Tony said. "I'll tell you on the way."

They headed to the car, with their plan still firmly intact.

*     *     *

Peter held the telephone to his left ear. His mouth dropped open when Danny led Jackie and Mary Ellen through the door.

Jackie's mind did a flip back in time to the days when he had lived in the trailer home. He blinked the memories away as Danny slid the gun across the desk to Peter.

"Good morning, Jackie, Counselor," Peter said. He let the telephone drop from his hand. "This is a pleasant surprise."

Jackie shot a glance at Mary Ellen. She wasn't showing an ounce of fear.

"I see you're a team now," Peter said. He waved his hands to the chairs directly in front of his desk. Neither Jackie nor Mary Ellen made a move to accept his offer.

"Very well then," Peter said. "Who should I thank for this visit?"

"Don't play games," Jackie said. "Your reign is over. We came to get Margaret."

Peter got to his feet. He picked up the gun and pointed it directly at Mary Ellen.

"Danny, get out of here. Make sure there's no one hanging around outside."

Danny all but ran from the trailer.

Peter held the brown-handled Colt up for inspection. He waved it in front of Jackie's eyes.

"Kind of ironic, isn't it? Do you remember the last time you held a gun in a trailer? It was a pretty bloody event, wasn't it?"

Jackie fought the memories.

"Do you remember who got you out of the orphanage?" Peter asked. "Do you remember who gave your mother a job when she was desperate? Do you remember who gave you a fucking job?"

Jackie stared straight ahead.

"Do you?" Peter screamed. He waved the gun around, and Jackie flashed another quick glance at Mary Ellen. This time, her face was a mask of fear. "How can you just forget what I fucking did for you?"

Jackie realized that Peter was just a slow turn from going around the bend. He was like a beaten fighter trying to clutch the ropes in the last round of a losing battle. Slowly, Jackie walked around the back side of Peter's desk. He stopped just in front of the clock radio at the side window.

"You never made a move in your life that didn't benefit you," Jackie said. He turned the dial on the radio until WGRQ could be heard loud and clear. "Now you're screwed."

The sound of the taped conversation between Ben and Peter came blaring across the radio lines, and Robin Travers's voice was in the background. "This one is for the king of the fat asses. This is a twenty-minute conversation between Peter Hanratty and Ben Potter. If you'll listen closely, you'll understand why Porky Peter will spend the rest of his sorry life in prison."

Robin's voice faded away, and Peter screamed in a powerful voice.

The Colt .45 blast rocked the trailer.

*     *     *

Tony walked across the floor of the front lobby of the *New Haven Register* as if he owned the place. Through the years, he had tried to get an editor to work on a story that would implicate Peter in the drug traffic across Connecticut. Tony hadn't found any takers, but, this time, he believed that the proof was indisputable.

"I have to see Jeff Taylor," Tony said to the receptionist.

"Taylor's at a staff meeting. He'll be tied up all afternoon."

Tony laid the envelope of documents on the desk. "This information is crucial. I don't have time to screen it with him, but be sure he gets it."

The receptionist took it with a look of complete irritation crossing his face. He tossed the envelope onto a pile of papers on his desk.

"If Taylor doesn't get those papers, I'll come back and arrest you for being an asshole."

The kid's eyes lit up, and Tony spun and ran for the front door. He knew his chances of getting spotted in the office were tremendous.

*     *     *

Cynthia checked the mirrors every five seconds. Up to the point of Ben Potter's approach, she hadn't noticed a single movement. The side window shattered, and Ben was in the car, gripping her wrist, in a matter of seconds.

"Listen to me, bitch. I want all the papers. No fucking games, or I'll kill you."

Cynthia tried to turn her wrist free, but pain consumed her every movement.

"Give me the fucking papers."

Cynthia had never seen such anger, and, for a split-second, it froze her mind. "First of all," she said, "take your fucking hands off me."

Ben turned her wrist in another direction, and the pain caused a flash of light across Cynthia's eyes.

"Tony's on his way back," Cynthia said, but she was aware that her threat carried little weight. Ben's biting laugh turned her stomach.

"He won't get out of the building alive," Ben said. "Now give me the fucking papers, or it'll be a double funeral."

The gun was pointed in her face. She saw movement in the parking lot a few hundred feet away but understood that other people wouldn't save her this time.

"Get out of the fucking car, slow!" Ben said. He allowed Cynthia's wrist to fall free, and she opened the door. She couldn't hold back the tears of pain, but she faced the gun with all the courage her body could muster.

Ben ducked down into the police car with the gun held at Cynthia's stomach. Tony darted between two cars a few hundred feet away, and Cynthia's heart did a flip. Just as suddenly, her heart sunk as Tony was tackled from behind by three men.

"Where the fuck are the notebooks?" Ben screamed. He jumped from the car and stood nose-to-nose with Cynthia.

"Jackie has them," Cynthia said.

"You're a lying bitch."

Cynthia saw the butt-end of the gun as it whipped around in Ben's hand. Everything was happening in slow motion. She saw the gun meet the bone of her chin. She fell backwards, and the pain was as real as the taste of blood in her mouth. All at once, her world drifted to black.

*     *     *

The telephone rang for the tenth time, and Peter continued to ignore it. His face was fire-engine red, and Jackie wondered if he were seeing an actual heart attack. The gun remained steady in Peter's beefy hand and focused on a spot in the middle of Jackie's forehead. There were two men working to bind Jackie's hands and legs, and

Mary Ellen sat with her hands folded in her lap. Mercifully, Peter answered the telephone. He glanced up to the hole in the ceiling where the errant bullet had struck.

"What is it?" Peter said. The sound of his heavy breathing seemed to make the trailer windows shake. "Good, bring them to me."

Peter placed the telephone back in the cradle, and his eyes took on a look of hopefulness. "We have your friends. I guess, now, we'll see who's fucked."

The rope cut into Jackie's wrists and legs. He thought of Cynthia, and he automatically shifted to prayer. He watched as the same two men worked to bind and gag Mary Ellen.

*God, if you're out there, I could use a little guidance, now.*

# CHAPTER SEVENTEEN

They were tossed into the trunk of Peter's limousine. Jackie could only think of how strange it was to take such a trip in such a vehicle.

The road was rough under the turning wheels of the limo, and Mary Ellen's sobs were the only sound above the racket of the moving car. Jackie continued to pray silently. The ropes around his ankles and wrists were threatening his circulation, but he knew one thing for certain—in the midst of his fight for life, he was sure that, whether he lived or died, his soul would remain intact.

At the same time, Peter was orchestrating his trip to the outskirts of the JGL property, Ben was fastening the ropes tight around the wrists and ankles of Tony and Cynthia.

\*     \*     \*

Daryl Jeter glanced at his watch. The construction trailer at the JGL property seemed abandoned, and he nervously looked at the time again. *Twelve-twenty-two.* He shook his head in disbelief and watched the dust settle in his rear-view mirror.

"There's no one here," his partner said.

"I don't get it," Daryl said. Four additional police cars moved in behind him.

"You're going to have some explaining to do."

In the distance, Daryl saw a flat-bed truck. He didn't bother to wait for words. He slammed the car in drive and covered the distance.

"Who's this guy?"

"I don't know," Daryl said, "but it looks like he works for Hanratty. Maybe he knows something."

"You'd better hope so. You ain't looking too swift," his partner said.

\*     \*     \*

Danny noticed the police car before they saw him. Slowly, he moved the truck around until he was in view. There was too much at stake to walk away. Being loyal was one thing, but this was freaking murder.

Danny exited the truck and stood in front of the company name lettered in black and gold. He couldn't ignore it, anymore. The police car skidded to a halt a few feet from Danny. He lit a cigarette and waited for the million-dollar question.

"Where's Peter Hanratty?" Daryl shouted.

Danny pointed in the direction of an old, abandoned shack. "You better hurry, he'll kill every freaking one of them."

\*     \*     \*

They were together again. It wasn't exactly how they had planned it, but they were side- by-side in the dirt floor shack. Peter made it crystal clear that they were there to die.

"Flat on your stomachs," Peter said. "Take the gags off them," he said to Ben.

"Why the fuck would you do that?" Ben asked.

Peter waved the Colt .45.

"Just fucking do it. I want to hear them beg to live."

Ben carried out the order as Peter swung the gun around from person to person. He looked mostly interested in their fear, and Jackie refused to show any sign of it. Peter held the gun steady on Cynthia's swollen face.

"My loyal employee. We would've made a great team. You could've had everything, and you fucked it up."

For a moment, fear filled Jackie's heart as Peter steadied the gun at Cynthia's right temple. Slowly, Peter pulled the gun back.

"We have to do this right."

He checked the front window. "Maybe I can go to Hawaii. How does Hawaii sound, Ben? Do you think we could start over there? It'll just be the loyal employees. What do you say?"

"Hawaii sounds fine," Ben said.

Peter paced the floor in front of them. "The papers will say we killed them execution style."

A sob escaped from Margaret's body.

"I want to hear the tears," Peter said.

Peter handed the gun to Ben. "Do me a favor, shoot these fucking people while I tell them why they're dying."

Ben bowed his head, but took the gun. "Just get it over with," he said softly.

Side-by-side, Ben and Peter stood before Tony.

"The great Officer Miller," Peter said. "He spent years accusing me of being the city's most corrupt businessman. When it all came down to it, he was just as corrupt me. Isn't that right, Tony?"

Peter paused as if waiting for an answer. Ben pointed the gun at Tony's right ear.

"Beg for your life," Peter said. "Cry and plead with me. I want your wife to hear what type of man you really are."

"Fuck you," Tony said.

Ben cocked the gun. Peter held Ben's advance back with a wave of the hand.

"You have a pregnant wife," Peter said. "We're going to kill her right after you."

Margaret's shrill scream filled the room.

"This is all about power," Peter said. "Whether you believe it or not, men are made to rule their world. Every man wants power and wealth. Deep-down, we want to hear people scream and cry. I have control over life and death. Beg me for your life, you worthless fuck."

Tony started crying, and the sound was deafening to Jackie's ears.

"That's exactly what I mean. Cry for me, Tony."

Peter seemed genuinely pleased with himself as he pranced around the room. "Shoot that bastard."

The first siren cry sounded through the room. For the first time, Jackie saw the look of true desperation in Peter's eyes.

"Shoot them!" Peter screamed.

Ben was froze in position.

"Kill them!"

"We're done," Ben said. "I'm not doing this."

*     *     *

Jackie knew that it was his time. Through all the years and faced with all the fear in his heart, he realized that his life had come down to this very moment.

"Life's not about power and wealth."

"Shut the fuck up!" Peter bellowed.

"Life's about searching for greatness in your soul."

Ben backed away, holding the gun to the floor. The sounds of the sirens were overwhelming, and Ben's face was lily white.

"Give me the gun!" Peter screamed.

The wall braced Ben against Peter's approach. Jackie's voice rose above it all. "I've seen desperation explode into pain. I've seen people die for believing in the world. The greatest pleasure I'll ever have, Peter, is watching you fall from your tower above me."

Peter lunged at Ben. The gun exploded just as the front door of the shack banged open. The police arrived on the scene just in time to see Peter fall backward onto the dirt floor. The perfectly placed bullet pierced Peter's heart, and Jackie watched the dark blood flow. He closed his eyes tightly, and, once more, his mind shifted to prayer.

# CHAPTER EIGHTEEN

The asphalt beneath the tires made a hollow, whining sound. Jackie shifted in the seat and stole another look at Cynthia. Her head rested against his shoulder, and it was simply amazing that she could sleep so peacefully. Jackie fought the urge to touch the side of her face, and he closed his eyes, letting his thoughts take over.

It was Cynthia's idea to take the bus out of town. Choosing Savannah as their ultimate destination seemed a strange attempt at poetic justice. Of course, deep-down, it really didn't matter where they wound up spending their time together.

*We deserve a chance to make it.*

The road stretched on for miles. They'd been traveling for over three hours, and it seemed as if they had already passed through a thousand small towns. Each flashing yellow light and corner grocery store reminded Jackie that there were so many people who were struggling to be free of something.

*It's a never-ending fight for self-preservation.*

Tony's words rushed back at him. They had parted company in New Haven on the steps of the police station. "I'm eternally sorry for what I've put you through," Tony said. "People make mighty strange decisions when they're faced with an easy way out. I sacrificed my moral code and everything I ever believed in for a chance at money. I honestly deserve the heartache."

"Remember, that the world can be a forgiving place," Jackie told him. He pointed at Margaret's protruding belly. "The most important moment of your life awaits you. Make yourself ready to be a good father."

The city of New Haven was shaken by Peter's sudden collapse. For three solid weeks, Jackie had been pursued by newspaper and television reporters.

*It was the story of the moment, and the moments soon pass.*

Ben was officially charged with the murders of Bennington and Patterson, and the doors of Hanratty's would remain closed for a long time. Tony also faced a court date in his involvement in the case, and, somewhere along the way, Cynthia would be asked to share her story. But, for now, it was Jackie, Cynthia, and a Greyhound bus bound for Georgia.

*　　*　　*

"So are you going to be a short-order cook?" Cynthia whispered.

The bus was completely dark, and most of the other passengers were asleep. Jackie smiled at the thought of his life becoming suddenly simple. "Obviously there aren't too many things I've been able to bank on, but, if you keep moving through the dark, the light will eventually find you."

Cynthia grabbed his hand, pulling it to her bosom. "I just love when you talk like Plato," she said.

"I'm serious," Jackie said. "I know I'll probably drive you crazy philosophizing about everything, but I can't help but consider Mom and Dad. No matter how deep the water seemed to get around them, they always thought they'd find a higher ground."

"We don't have a choice other than to look for it," Cynthia said.

"I guess that's the bottom line," Jackie said. He concentrated on the road under the wheels once more. The night seemed entirely peaceful.

"What more is there?" Cynthia said. She closed her eyes and leaned into Jackie's shoulder once more. "We'll just concentrate on going forward. Remember what Mary Ellen told you when we were leaving, 'Your heart is pure, Jackie, trust it.'"